JUST ONE TASTE

By the Author

An Intimate Deception

Just One Taste

New Horizons Series:

Unknown Horizons

Savage Horizons

False Horizons

Visit us at www.boldstrokesbooks.com

JUST ONE TASTE

by
CJ Birch

2020

JUST ONE TASTE

ISBN 13: 978-1-63555-772-5

This Trade Paperback Original Is Published By
Bold Strokes Books, Inc.
P.O. Box 249
Valley Falls, NY 12185

First Edition: September 2020

Credits
Editor: Shelley Thrasher
Production Design: Stacia Seaman
Cover Design by W. E. Percival

Acknowledgments

A great big thanks to Bold Strokes for all their amazing support, especially Shelley Thrasher, my editor, for keeping me on point.

This is the first book I've written that takes place in my home city, which made researching a lot easier. My Google Maps street view got a bit of a rest. Except for the diner, I've tried to keep to real landmarks if possible. There really is a pink painted building called the Palace Arms (soon to be high-rise condos). Trinity Bellwoods does have white squirrels. I'm not sure if they can be called magical, but this is the only place in the city you can find them. And there really is a skating rink underneath the Gardiner Expressway.

I'd like to thank Geoff Dennis for giving me insight into the mind of a chef. Any mistakes or inconsistencies are my own.

And as always, I'd like to thank my readers for giving these stories life in your imaginations.

For Maire
proof you can find love in the city

CHAPTER ONE

Hayley shoved herself between an obese woman wearing a floral print dress and a businessman in a tight, shiny suit as the doors to the subway slipped shut an inch from her nose. She grinned at her reflection in the scratched Plexiglas. This was now her morning routine.

She'd woken at six in her crowded, tiny bedroom in a house she shared with three other people, waited her turn for the shower, praying there was still hot water left—there wasn't—dressed, and scrambled out of the house in time to walk the two blocks to the subway and catch line one uptown. She'd memorized her route the day before because she didn't want to seem like she didn't know where she was going, like she didn't belong.

Jason, her new roommate, had given her the heads-up about line one. He told her to leave a little extra time in the mornings because it was always crammed to capacity. She'd followed his advice, but this was insane. Hayley was glad she'd decided to get coffee at the end of her commute because it was so packed she couldn't even lift her arm.

The car bumped along the track curving to the right. Hayley slammed into the businessman. He righted her, gave her an indignant glare, and went back to his game of Candy Crush.

"Sorry," she said, admiring his balance. He wasn't even holding on to anything, just riding the car like a surfboard, shifting his weight from left to right, depending on which way the train jerked. In fact, most people were doing the same. With so many people and so few handholds, this was a skill Hayley felt she'd have to learn.

After a minute or two, Hayley discovered she could lean against the door and use it to anchor herself. God, she hoped it didn't open. They were flying through the tunnel now. It would be death for sure.

At the next stop more people squeezed in, pushing Hayley farther into the car, away from the comfort of the door. Now she was stranded in the middle of the aisle. A woman in a purple tank top, with tattoo sleeves of pandas and bamboo, reached up and pulled a handle from the ceiling. Hayley breathed in relief as she grabbed one for herself. At five feet six inchest, Hayley had to stand on her tiptoes to reach. It wasn't comfortable, but it saved her the embarrassment of falling on her ass.

This wasn't Hayley's first time on the subway. She'd been to Toronto lots of times with her family over the years. Her dad was a huge hockey fan, and they'd seen the Leafs play at the ACC a couple of times. She'd been to the ROM on school trips and gone with some friends to Kensington Market to search the vintage shops. And there was the time she came up to visit her sister Hannah at school, and they'd gone to Lee's Palace to see a Talking Heads cover band.

But this was the first time she'd been on the subway by herself at rush hour. Every other time the aisles were clear, and she could usually snag a seat. Rush hour was a whole different beast.

It wasn't that Hayley didn't blend well. As her sister liked to say, Hayley was always too city for Casper Falls, their tiny town two hours north of the city. With her ever-changing colour of hair, which her mom had hoped was a phase she'd outgrow in high school, the string of her white ear buds snaking into her back pocket, and eighties vintage chic, Hayley fit right in with the medley currently crowding her on the subway. But Hayley knew you needed the swagger to go with the look. Everyone around her appeared bored and tired, still waking up. Hayley tried to match that disdain. It was hard. She was frothing over with barely contained excitement. She'd been working her whole life toward this day. It had taken twenty-eight years, but she'd finally managed to escape Casper Falls and the boredom of running her parents' grocery store.

She was now the newest second assistant to the CFO at a tech firm. Not her dream job. Or even a remotely appealing job. She'd be doing grunt work for a man who didn't appear to know that ties weren't designed to be tucked into pants, or that it was polite to look at people when you spoke to them, but it did two important things. It paid her rent and got her out of Casper Falls.

The farther north they went, the emptier the car became, until finally, two stops before hers, she was able to score a seat. Another piece of advice from Jason. Always look before you sit. You never know what could be there. He told her the story of once sitting in gum. Ruined a brand-new pair of jeans. Kalini, another roommate, told her about the time she'd sat in someone's urine. So Hayley made sure to double-check.

Now she could really people-watch. "Electric Barbarella" by the Polka Dot Bikinis came on; eighties cover bands were her favourite. She loved anything eighties, but if it was rehashed in an ironic way by someone who hadn't even been born in the eighties, all the better. She cranked it up and surveyed her fellow commuters.

There was an older gentleman who'd either come off the night shift or had trouble getting up in the mornings. He dozed against the Plexiglas partition, his mouth hanging open, his cheek squished against the glass, a blue satchel on the ground between his dirty work boots.

Farther down the train a child screamed and tossed a bottle out of his stroller. The faint, exasperated voice of his mother drifted down the car. "If you don't want it, just say so." The train screeched into a station, and the bottle rolled toward Hayley, picking up speed as it went.

Hayley reached down and grabbed the bottle before it had a chance to get too far. The doors to the train opened, and the old man jerked awake and stumbled off just as the bell dinged and the doors swished shut again.

Hayley handed the bottle to the mother, who thanked her and moved farther down the train. "And now you won't have any juice until we get to Sharon's. Your bottle's covered in subway floor. Isn't that nice?" The kid blew a raspberry at Hayley as they passed.

Hayley stood ready to exit the train at the next stop. She knew her excitement would fade as the day went on, especially as she got into the busy work of being someone's coffee bitch, but for this moment, for this instant, her world was full of possibilities.

❖

Hayley stared up at the twenty-story building. It was made of glass and metal and reflected the morning sun coming from the east. Caustics danced on the surrounding skyscrapers.

With a strong black coffee in one hand and her satchel in the other, she climbed the two flights of stairs to the lobby still ten minutes early. She'd left herself loads of time to get to work, an embarrassing window of time. She'd rather be an hour early than two minutes late. It sent the wrong impression. And the last thing she wanted to do was give her new employers the wrong idea about her work ethic.

As she rode the empty elevator, she checked herself out in the reflective door. She was wearing black skinny pants, a blue formfitting blazer, and a grey scoop top Kalini had lent her. Her wardrobe consisted mostly of ironic T-shirts and skinny jeans, so if she didn't want to be stuck borrowing her roommate's clothes forever, she'd have to invest in more business attire.

Hayley took a sip of her coffee, the hum of excitement inside helped by the caffeine coursing through her system. She couldn't believe her luck. She'd had four interviews at two different companies over the last month. That was the result of over fifty resumes and how many online applications? Most jobs that paid above minimum wage were hard to get, but jobs that anyone with a brain could do? Even harder. She needed to prove herself invaluable today because this was the kind of company that hired within. If she could move up, then maybe one day she'd get her own assistant.

Right before she'd boarded the Greyhound her mother had handed her an envelope with two hundred dollars in it.

"Don't tell your dad. He'll think I'm being paranoid." She straightened the collar of Hayley's jean jacket. Her mom was always straightening things. She couldn't sit still. Some project, some item always needed fixing or cleaning. She seemed afraid if she stopped moving it would feel too good and she'd never get up again. Hayley leaned out of reach, hiding the move by stashing the envelope in her carry-on. You'd think she was eighteen leaving home for the first time instead of the twenty-eight-year-old, absolute, one-hundred-percent-independent adult that she was.

"Save it for emergencies." Her mom raised her hands, stopping any protests. "Not plural. Sorry. I didn't mean it like that. I know you'll do great." She sighed, the sound heavy in the morning air. "You've always been so good at taking care of yourself." She gave Hayley a

huge hug before turning back toward the car. Her dad kissed her on top of her head, and she waved and then turned, never looking back. She couldn't wait to get the hell out of Casper Falls.

The doors opened on the fifth floor to rows of open-concept desks and what should've been a bustling hive of activity. It was empty and silent. No one was at their desks, and the clunk of the elevator doors shutting echoed in the huge room.

Panic filled Hayley. Had she gotten the day wrong? Was it Sunday? She pulled her phone out of her back pocket and checked the date. The reminder of her first day of work was still up on her home screen, glaring at her with four exclamation marks.

"What the...?"

Hayley had been here only once before, the last interview before she was hired. On that day there'd been a hum of almost chaotic productivity, every desk filled with people hard at work.

She walked down the hall toward Jeff's office. "Hello?" she called.

A confused voice responded from an office off to her right.

Hayley popped her head in to see a young man in his late twenties, balding, sitting at a desk covered in file boxes and stacked folders.

Hayley waved from the doorway. "Hi. I'm Hayley Cavello. I'm supposed to start today?"

He blew out an exasperated breath and stood. He was wearing worn jeans and a Pac-Man T-shirt. Hayley approved. "Shit." He came around the desk, and Hayley held out her hand to shake his. He looked down at hers, hesitating, then grabbed it limply and pumped it once before dropping it.

Hayley was starting to freak out. "What's going on? Where is everyone?"

"Shit," he said again. Hayley expected him to say more, but he didn't. Instead a pained expression crossed his face.

"Are you one of the managers? Are you—"

"The company went out of business over the weekend."

Hayley's mouth opened, closed, opened again. "What?"

"God, Jeff's such an asshole. There was an email, but I guess because you're new, you didn't have one set up yet. The company went under."

She'd seen this movie before. Michael J. Fox spent a lot of time in his boxers and got a private jet and Helen Slater at the end. She doubted her story would end with her in a limo making out with Helen Slater.

"Jeff should have emailed you." He shrugged, his way of apologizing. As if a shrug of the shoulders was enough to say, *That's life, it sucks, but what're you going to do?*

Hayley was asking herself the same thing. What the hell was she supposed to do now? The guy in the Pac-Man shirt turned back to his desk and began packing up his files again.

"That's it?" Hayley asked. "The company went out of business so we're all out of a job?"

He shrugged, not even bothering to look up at Hayley. Again with the shrugs. What was wrong with people?

Hayley turned and left, picking up her pace as she neared the end of the hall. She slammed her fist into the elevator button and waited. She was about to take a sip of her coffee, but the idea of putting anything in her stomach nauseated her. The elevator dinged and the doors opened. She dropped the coffee into the trash on her way into the elevator.

"Fuck," she said as the doors closed. *Now what?*

Chapter Two

"What do you mean you're quitting?" Lauren stared in shock at Pete, her most reliable line cook.

He scrubbed the back of his neck, shamefaced. "I'm sorry, Lauren. I got accepted into that woodworking program I told you about. With the way the classes are set up, I won't be able to do both." He looked down at his baggy jeans, chewing the inside of his cheek. "Maybe I can do part-time?"

She shook her head but didn't say anything. Instead she stared out at the diner and the oddball patrons left after the breakfast rush.

What was she going to do without Pete? He'd been here eight years, not quite as long as her. She did quick math in her head—over fourteen years. And now she was manager and Pete was still just a line cook. Okay, he had a point. Line cook at a diner was a dead-end job if you had higher ambitions. She couldn't even remember the last time Greta had given him a raise. Aaron hadn't approved any raises last year, which meant he hadn't had a pay increase since before Greta died, which was over two years ago.

Greta's Diner wasn't a big place—a line of five booths on one side and the counter seats on the other. It's what Greta used to call a classic fifties diner. After she'd died, her son Aaron had taken ownership, but that's about all he did. Everything—that didn't include raises—fell to Lauren.

The place had an eclectic feel to it that fit in with the neighbourhood. What had once been a run-down part of the city with short-stay hotels and low-income housing had begun the slow crawl toward gentrification about ten years ago. It still had some distance to go. The Palace Arms a few blocks away still rented rooms by the hour, and the park across the street hosted a variety of characters—cyclists, drug addicts, the homeless, can ladies as well as families, dog owners, and the regular mishmash of eccentrics that made the city interesting.

Lauren loved every bit of it.

The diner itself was fifties kitsch. The booth's cushions were all red vinyl and the countertops faded Formica. A row of matching red stools swept the length of the counter, faded and ripped in places and, except for the one at the end, which screeched like fingers on a chalkboard when it swivelled, were still comfortable.

Picture frames covered every inch of wall space. Old Coke and Pepsi ads mixed in with archival images of the city before cars, during streetcar and subway construction, when the city was young and optimistic. Lauren loved comparing the old intersections to what the city looked like now. Some buildings had stayed as regal as ever, and glass monstrosities had replaced others. She preferred the old historical buildings.

Lauren reached over and straightened a metal ad for Heinz celery sauce. "When do classes start?" she asked. Maybe they could find a replacement before he left, although that would be damn hard. Sure, Ramiro, their head cook, was great, but he couldn't work all the time. If she could clone Ramiro, her life would be perfect. Maybe not perfect, but easier. Instead she had Theo, who only worked part-time and was slow as cottage traffic in June, and Ezra had a bit of an attitude she could do without. Pete had been her go-to guy, her old reliable, her friend.

Pete blinked his long lashes as he peered up at her, clearly miserable he'd caused Lauren stress. After eight years of working together, he knew her moods better than his. Not that she was great at hiding her feelings. Lauren was one of those people who wore their moods like a costume, slipping in and out as easily as a quick-change artist. "I start on Tuesday."

Lauren huffed and blew her black bangs off her forehead. That gave them a week. Rats. It would be tough but not impossible.

"This Tuesday." Pete stuffed his hands deep into his pockets, edging his pants down to show the top of his smiley-face boxers.

Lauren took a deep breath. "Tomorrow's Tuesday."

Pete almost dived for cover. This was bad. "I didn't want to see you mad. And it kept getting closer and closer, and I was like, 'Pete, you need to tell her. You need to tell her.' But..." He shook his head. "That look." He pointed at her face. "I didn't want to see that look. It gives me nightmares."

Lauren turned away, staring at the specials board. She couldn't deal with this. Not today. Of all days, not today. Pete's callused hand wrapped around her arm. She blinked a couple of times to make sure he couldn't see the wetness pooling in her eyes. This was no time to cry. She needed to pull it together, especially before the lunch rush.

"Couldn't you miss the first few classes?" she asked, turning back to him. "Until we find someone?"

He gave her a withering look. "After the money I spent on this course? Are you kidding me? I love you like a sister, but you know how expensive this shit is. I'm sorry I didn't tell you sooner, but you've got Ezra and Theo. Ezra's a good cook." They both shared a look that said, *even if he is an ass sometimes.* "You'll find a replacement in no time. Everyone's looking for work."

He was right. She could probably walk out onto Queen Street and shout they were hiring, and she'd have several people leaping over the counter into the kitchen. Finding someone wasn't the problem. Replacing Pete was the problem. And by the look of contrition on his face, he knew it. Maybe she could ask Ramiro to pick up an extra shift or two until they at least hired another body.

Cooking greasy diner food wasn't hard. They served mostly burgers and breakfast foods. It was the speed and getting to know the orders. Greta had been a huge fan of fifties diners, the lingo in particular. Therefore, everything was routed to the kitchen in almost gibberish. For instance, chicks on a raft was eggs on toast, a blondie with sand was coffee with milk, and burn the British was a toasted English muffin. If you didn't know what people were ordering, it slowed everything down. And Lauren prided her staff on serving the fastest breakfast in the west end.

"Miss?"

Lauren gazed up to see an older woman with tight, curly white hair waving a five in her direction. She swiped her hands down her crisp turquoise uniform, ridding herself of Pete's betrayal, and stepped back into her role as server. "I'll be right with you. You had the eggs Florentine with a tea, correct?" The woman nodded. Pete followed Lauren over to the register as she punched in the order.

"At least wish me luck, huh?"

She turned and smiled. She didn't have to force being happy for Pete. She genuinely wanted him to succeed. She was just sorry to be losing him here.

He squeezed her arm. "Maybe you should think about joining me. Not with woodworking. But maybe you should consider going back to school. Finishing your degree."

After Pete left and the lunch rush ended, Lauren sat at the end of the counter with a cup of coffee and her thoughts. She'd never imagined going back to school. Once she'd made up her mind to quit and Greta had taken her into her warm embrace, she'd closed that chapter of her life. But what if it wasn't closed for good? Look at Pete. He was five years older than her. In a year he'd be forty, and if he could jump off the scary deep end of life, what was stopping her?

❖

Lauren dropped onto her battered and sun-bleached chaise. She shifted her ass so it wouldn't stick out the bottom where two straps were missing. She'd found it on the corner of Massey and Adelaide shoved between a recycling and compost bin. With a lot of Javex and scrubbing, it'd turned out perfect for her rooftop refuge.

She pressed the cool beer to her forehead and closed her eyes. What a nightmare day. She'd been on her feet since five a.m. It was after nine in the evening now. Luna had called in "sick," so Lauren had worked her shift, turning Lauren's double into a triple. Aaron was going to flip. He hated paying overtime, but she didn't have anyone else to call in. Vic had taken the long weekend off to spend with her kids before school started, and Lucy had worked a double yesterday.

With school starting up again she'd be able to hire a few more part-time people, but until then she was short. And so it fell to her.

Lauren took a long sip of her beer and leaned back, pillowing her head with her arm.

September had descended on the city with another heat wave. It was still a balmy twenty-five degrees at this late hour. The sky was an azure blue tinted orange from the west, with just the hint of wispy clouds. The way the orange and blue blended reminded Lauren of a painting she'd done in school. She preferred abstract because then, as the viewer, you could choose what the painting meant to you instead of what the artist wanted you to think it meant.

And that thought reminded her of Pete and the worst part of her day. On the one hand she was over-the-moon happy for Pete. He'd been talking about going back to school as far back as she could remember. And with his talent, he didn't belong in a diner kitchen. Pete built furniture—artsy, abstract furniture. The kind that usually cost a gazillion dollars on Queen West, but that he gave to his friends and family for free.

She had one of his nightstands next to her bed. He'd carved it out of a trunk he'd found on his uncle's property. The sides were shellacked bark, but the drawers and cubby hole were hollowed out from the wood. On the bottom the hint of the roots was visible. It was beautiful, artsy, and brilliant.

He'd wanted to go back to school to get formal training in woodworking for a long time. She wanted this for him. She did. But she also wanted things to stay the same. More than a competent cook, Pete made the diner fun. She noticed the difference when he was on the grill versus Ezra or even Theo. What was she going to do without him?

Lauren sat up and walked to the edge of the roof. She'd changed out of her uniform into a loose tank top and cutoffs. Her bare feet soaked up the heat of the tar covering the flat roof. This was her favourite place to sit and people-watch.

Lauren lived above the diner. She'd taken the two-bedroom apartment over from Greta when she'd moved into a home a year before she passed away. From here she could see into the park and all along Queen Street. Usually on summer nights like this one, street performers outside the iron gates of Trinity played or juggled or banged on overturned plastic tubs. Lauren preferred the drummers. It took imagination to make music from everyday objects. It was surprising and authentic.

She placed her beer on the cement ledge, the condensation pool marking its territory. The notes of a lone banjo player drifted up from the street. She leaned over, watching as people passed on their way home or out with friends, taking advantage of the last few weeks of pleasant weather before winter.

It was the same comforting view she watched every night, but for some reason tonight it didn't calm her. After Pete's announcement everything felt unsettled.

Lauren turned toward the rustling noise behind her. A family of raccoons scooted along the edge of her roof, brazen as could be. She watched as the parents helped the babies bumble their way onto the fire escape and out of sight.

The one thing that kept playing back in her head, the thing she'd tried to keep from swamping the rest of her day, wasn't a simple *what if.* Lauren had made peace with her life long ago. If Pete thought she needed a degree to be happy, he didn't know her that well. More than anything, that made her sad. If she'd finished school, she'd have a meaningless business degree, because she had no interest in business whatsoever. It had been her mother's dream, not hers. She liked her life at the diner. It was a reliable income, a predictable routine, and, most importantly, safe.

The sun dipped behind the buildings and out of sight. As dusk fell, Lauren tilted her head back and finished the last dregs of her beer and went inside. Tomorrow was another double shift.

❖

The morning sun spilled through the front window, casting a shadow of the diner's logo on the floor. This was Lauren's favourite time—an hour before the morning rush, when the day was still fresh and new and not enough people had come through to taint it with their stupidity.

Only the diehards were in this early—a few regulars and a tourist couple from somewhere a few time zones to the east. They were the only animated thing in the place, planning their day over an open attraction map in one of the booths. They smiled at Lauren as she refilled their coffees.

"Do you guys want to order anything to eat?" she asked, still holding the coffeepot.

The husband, who was wearing a large sweater despite the

humidity of the morning, blinked at her through thick glasses. He peered down at the menu to the right of the map and placed his finger on one of the items. "Please, what is this?" From the accent, Lauren pegged them as German.

Lauren leaned forward. "Greta's Benny. It's eggs Benedict, but instead of pea-meal bacon, it's tomato and cucumber on a crumpet instead of an English muffin and homemade hollandaise sauce." Ramiro's hollandaise sauce was so good, Lauren had dreams of bathing in it. "That's one of our most popular breakfasts. I highly recommend it."

The man looked at his wife. Was he asking permission? Then he glanced back up at Lauren and nodded. "I will have this, and my wife will have the poached eggs on toast."

Lauren smiled, but the couple had already ducked back to their map. "Two chicks on a raft and Greta's benny," she called into the air.

"Two chicks and a benny coming up" came Ramiro's bass from the kitchen.

Usually Pete opened with Lauren, but Ramiro had taken over a few of his shifts until they found someone. Lauren sighed as she replaced the coffeepot on its warming element. She watched Ramiro dance around the kitchen, his giant frame lumbering from flipping to stacking and stirring. He hummed along to the music playing from the battered radio duct-taped to the wall in back. With his black, curly hair squished beneath his beanie, he paraded around the kitchen. He caught her watching and winked, a dimple forming in his left cheek as he smiled.

It was hard to stay sad around Ramiro. If he wasn't laughing or grinning, he was humming or dancing. She'd never seen Ramiro in a bad mood. Ever. If anything went wrong, he'd just shrug and move on. More than once she'd wished she could be like that. Someone didn't show up for their shift, shrug it off. One of her customers skipped out on the bill, shrug it off. Someone quit, shrug it off.

When she'd told Ramiro about Pete, he'd grinned, slapped her on the back, and said, "Good for him." When Lauren didn't smile with him, he'd added, "Not to worry, sweetums. We'll find someone else, and who knows. Maybe you'll like them better than Pete."

She'd forced a smile for Ramiro's sake but didn't agree. Pete was Pete. She'd never had to talk him into a shift or deal with a tantrum when a customer sent something back. She'd never had to ask him to turn the radio down or watch his language. She'd never had to ask him to empty the dishwasher if Murphy hadn't shown up, or to wear his hairnet or beanie a million times. Pete never argued with her; he made her job easy. He showed up, joked around, kept his head down, and got to work. He was unobtrusive and awesome, and now she'd have to break in a whole new person.

Ramiro dinged the bell next to her head, and Lauren shook herself. "Benny and two chicks." He placed the plates on the sill. She might be upset about Pete, but wallowing wasn't going to solve the problem or make her life any easier.

CHAPTER THREE

By the end of September, Hayley was getting desperate. She'd had to give notice with Jason and Kalini. No way could she afford October's rent. She'd sent out what felt like a million resumes and heard nothing back. She'd applied everywhere she thought her skills would translate and even pushed it beyond those limits. But most offices didn't want to hire a woman with blue hair. She'd thought about dying it but didn't want to give them the satisfaction. It was discrimination. Kalini had mentioned on more than one occasion that pride might feel good in the moment but didn't put food on the table. She'd heard a similar argument from her mom most of her life. But she didn't have to admit they were right. Her options were getting low. Her optimism had lasted until the last box was taped shut.

She sat on her bed, which would become Philipe's bed tomorrow, watching the rain fall. The weather had finally turned, and a cold front had moved in. Perfect time to be homeless.

A soft knock on the doorjamb pulled her attention. Kalini stood there, her expression mournful. "Let's get out of here. Go for coffee. I know a place that has the most amazing almond croissants."

"It's raining."

Kalini shrugged. "And? That's what umbrellas are for." She held out her hand, wiggling her fingers. "The croissants alone are worth it. My treat."

Hayley nodded. She needed to suck it up, or she'd bring everyone down.

Grnds wasn't much bigger than Hayley's soon-to-be-former room.

They'd snagged a table by the window where they could watch people rush from the streetcar to the nearest overhang in the pouring rain.

Kalini was right. This was the best almond croissant she'd ever had. Not too much icing sugar on top, and just the right mix of sweet-almond and buttery-croissant goodness. She licked a little icing sugar off her thumb, which lifted her mood a tiny bit.

"As I see it," Kalini said, her mouth hovering above her overpriced cortado. "You've got three options. One," she held up her index finger, her dark-red nail polish pristine. "You can give up and go home."

Hayley was shaking her head before Kalini had even finished her sentence. "Not an option. I've been here a month. I can't crawl back to Casper Falls without anything to show for it."

Kalini took a sip, nodding. "Fair enough. Two. You can couch-surf until you find something of your own." She held up her hand to stop Hayley from speaking. "I'd say our couch is your couch, and if it was only Jo and I, that would be fine, but Jason would kill me. He already thinks it's too cramped."

Hayley turned away. She'd been saving that hope. But Kalini was right. It would be weird and awkward. Kalini and her fiancée Josephine lived in the attic bedroom of their house, while Jason and Hayley had the other two bedrooms on the main floor. With only one bathroom, the house felt overcrowded, especially since Jo was an artist and worked from home. More than a few times, Hayley had come home from job-searching to find the living room or dining room overtaken with canvases.

Unfortunately, she didn't know anyone here. She'd been so busy looking for a job and not spending her dwindling money that she hadn't had the chance. God. This month had looked so different in her imagination. The weeks leading up to moving were full of scenarios, none of which included this one.

"What's option three?" she asked.

"Get a temporary room at a youth hostel—there's a decent one on Spadina—and find any job, doesn't matter how awful, until you get back on your feet."

Hayley stared down at the foam in her vanilla latte. If that's what sucking it up entailed, she could do that. "That's probably my best option, huh?"

Kalini reached across the table and squeezed Hayley's arm. She was a very touchy-feely person, always connecting in some way. The gesture reminded Hayley a little of her mom. "So what skills do you have? What did you do back home? Besides manage an entire grocery store?"

"It's not as impressive as it sounds. It's my parents' store and not like the megastores here. It really is just a mom-and-pop type place."

"Still, that takes a lot of organization, which is why I can see you being good at executive assistant, even if those assholes in HR can't."

"Well, I can type?"

Kalini gave her a withering look. "Honey, everyone can type. I'm talking about blue-collar shit. You're going to have to make up a new resume and cut out all the crap about running a grocery store."

"I've worked at that store my entire life."

"Yes, but you have something far more valuable than most people—common sense. Just lie—"

"I don't want to lie."

Kalini's smile said, *Oh, sweetie. I have so much to teach you.* "Believe me. You want to lie. Everyone lies on their fall-back resume."

"Fall-back resume?"

"Yes, see, you always make two resumes. Your real one, which you want to keep as honest as possible, because, hello? Skills. And your fall-back one, for in-the-meantime jobs. For instance, I used to work at this boutique store in Yorkville, and I'd padded my resume with a ton of retail experience, none of which I'd actually done. I mean, how hard is it to sell watches to rich assholes? But while I was working there, I was still applying for teaching jobs. And because I had shift work, it was easy to pick up teaching jobs on the side before I found an in. That's what you've got to do." Kalini wiped her mouth with her napkin, even though there wasn't anything there to wipe away. "What about cooking?"

"Cooking?"

"You're a great cook. I've never seen someone enter a kitchen with nothing in it and produce one of the best meals I've ever had."

"Huh." Hayley crumpled her napkin. Across the street a woman in an oversized blue raincoat pushed a shopping cart overflowing with cans and bottles. The wind kept whipping at the tarp covering the top. As she turned into the gates of the park, her cart caught on a bump and overturned, spilling cans and bottles everywhere.

Hayley sipped her latte, watching the poor woman scramble to pick everything up before the wind caught them and took them away.

A woman with a red umbrella stopped to help. She was in a skirt and ankle boots. All Hayley could see as she bent to pick up a can was long, tanned legs poking from beneath her umbrella, which she'd turned to the side to reveal its heart shape. It was encouraging to see that some people in the city had compassion. So far that hadn't been Hayley's experience. It wasn't that they didn't care. It was more that they didn't want to show the weakness of caring, in case it was rejected. One thing for certain, very few people put themselves out there, too afraid they'd look foolish. Every single person she'd encountered so far appeared more worried about their reputation than giving a shit.

Hayley sat mesmerized for a few moments before drawing her attention back to Kalini, who was caught up in giving advice. One thing was for sure—people weren't afraid of giving advice.

❖

Lauren swept into Greta's with a gush of wind and rain, her uniform soaked from helping a woman pick up a cart full of empties. Living above the diner had its perks, especially in winter. She usually dashed down the alley in nothing more than a sweater. Today, when she saw the woman struggling, she'd crossed the street.

Lauren hated how indifferent this city was. She'd lived here her whole life, and the only time people came together was during a crisis. Her dad was always saying meanness was a disease that could only be cured with an act of kindness. So if she wanted people to be nicer, it started with her.

Vic sat at one of the booths doing a crossword puzzle. She raked her fingers through spiky red hair, tugging the ends as she contemplated the clues. The beats of Daft Punk filtered from the kitchen. She shook her umbrella and hung it on a hook near the door, nodding to one of the regulars at the end of the bar on her way to the back.

Ezra was showing their newest hire around the kitchen. Lauren grabbed a towel from a stack near the freezer and wiped her uniform down, contemplating going back upstairs and changing before her shift. Ezra caught her eye above the head of the new line cook, whose name she could never remember. His eyebrows rose high into his forehead, a classic sign he was unhappy in his current task. Last night she'd listened to him complain about how stupid this new guy was.

As always, Ezra was dressed as if he were about to hit the clubs. His tight black V-neck conformed to his torso, sculpting his muscles like shrink wrap. His black jeans were clean and tight, proving Ezra didn't have an ounce of fat on his body, and the black beanie he wore covered his ears and neatly trimmed blond hair.

The man standing next to him was a lesson in contrasts. He'd shoved his shaggy brown hair into a hairnet, but most of the back had fallen out. His baggy jeans hung low, with grass stains on the knees. He was the third line cook they'd gone through after Pete quit. He was hired last week, and this was only the second time he'd been able to work.

Ezra was explaining the different stations as he retied his crisp white apron. "Orders come in here. When it's dead like now, the servers will just shout their orders, but when it gets busy, we ask that they write them down and attach them to the carousel." His eyes widened at Lauren as he said this. She had a bad habit of forgetting to write hers down.

The new cook bobbed his head, obviously processing, then looked up at the carousel. "So…the orders come in here? And then what happens?" Ezra pursed his lips. He'd told Lauren he suspected the new guy was on drugs or medication, because it took forever to get a sentence out of him. He paused every few words.

"We prepare the orders," said Ezra, grabbing a rag and wiping down an already pristine counter. "That's—that's your whole job. Line cook. We just spent twenty minutes going over that part."

More head-bobbing. "Right…okay."

Ten minutes later, Ezra slid into a booth across from Lauren, who was refilling napkin dispensers. "He needs to go, Lauren. The guy is seriously deficient in the brains department. I just spent the last five minutes explaining what a spatula was."

"What's his name again?"

"Does it matter? He's dead weight. Anyone working with him will spend most of their time practicing fire prevention."

Lauren pointed a finger to the back. "And you left him alone in there?"

Ezra waved her off. "I've got him counting plates." Lauren raised her eyebrows. "It's keeping him busy until you can go back there and fire his ass. I'd rather work the dinner shift on my own than have him in there with me."

Lauren groaned. As she saw it, she had two choices. She could trust Ezra and fire this new guy, which would put Ezra in a good mood, and that always made working with him easier. It meant they'd be rushed all night and might suffer some tips because of it. And she'd have to start looking for yet another line cook.

Or she could keep this new guy on, which would piss Ezra off, and they'd probably be just as rushed if Ezra was right. And that's what it came down to. Did she trust Ezra's opinion?

Lauren tightened her ponytail and squared her shoulders. She hated firing people. "Call Theo. See if he can come in," she said. It was a long shot. Theo rarely agreed to work when called last-minute, but it was better to ask than assume. A bit more wisdom from her dad there.

Ezra clapped once. "Awesome. Thank you."

That night, her last night with a roof over her head, Hayley pulled out her laptop to create her fallback résumé. She hadn't had a lot of experience looking for jobs. She'd spent most of her life working at her parents' grocery store. It wasn't very big, not like the super chains outside of Casper Falls, but it was big enough for the essentials like produce and eggs and milk. They had a bakery section with fresh bread delivered every morning. It was boring as hell and the best incentive to get out on her own.

Now, after less than a month here, she'd already failed. She hadn't told her parents what had happened. She couldn't face her mom's fake cheer or her dad's disapproving silence. And she didn't want them to worry. She'd phoned her sister Hannah instead, who was always one to wash the glitter off the second she got home.

"You should tell them." Hannah's voice was firm. Someone screamed in the background. It sounded like two kids fighting over a toy.

"Where are you?"

"At the clinic. I hate keeping secrets for you. I suck at it."

"Why are you at the clinic? Is something wrong?"

"Derek and I are getting an ultrasound. Well," she paused, probably looking over at Derek as she said this. "I'm getting the ultrasound, and Derek is here to make sure I don't ask what the sex is." Hannah was just over four months pregnant with their first baby, and Hayley had almost decided not to come here until after the baby was born. But she knew if she hadn't left, then she never would have. Yet after what had happened with Violet, she'd needed to get away.

"Oh my God. I can't believe I'm missing this. You'll have to send me all the pictures."

"You could just come home, and then you wouldn't miss any of it."

Hayley pulled the covers over her head and sank lower on the bed. "I can't, Han. I need to do this, even if it sucks and I have to get a crappy job again. I can't come home a failure."

More screaming. "I know. I do. I get it. You've always needed to find a bigger pond. And I want you to. But I keep thinking you'll get your fill and move back home."

Home. It might be home to Hannah, because she had a great life there. She was a dental hygienist with a husband, a house, and two dogs. And now she was expecting a baby. She might be older than Hayley by three years, but she'd always known what she wanted. Hayley envied her that. At twenty-eight, Hayley still had no idea what she wanted to do with her life, only that she didn't want to live it out in Casper Falls as the gay younger sister of one of the most popular graduates of Casper Falls Secondary School.

As shitty as her first month had been, it was also the most exciting of her life. Everything here was amazing—the noise, the controlled chaos, the extravagance of choice. She lived within walking distance of three pizza places, a sushi place—which was questionable—a Mexican restaurant, two Indian restaurants, and the best shawarma place she'd ever eaten at. There were bars and clubs and cafes and bookstores, old game shops. She'd almost bought a retro Super Nintendo until she realized their TV wouldn't connect to it. And by tomorrow she wouldn't own a TV, so it was for the best.

"I think I'm hooked, Han."

She spent the rest of the grey afternoon building a new resume topped with bullshit. She'd print some off tomorrow. Kalini had mentioned that if she was applying for restaurant or retail jobs, it was best to show up in person with a real live copy of your resume. At least this way she'd get to see a lot more of the city. If she'd been working this whole time, she'd have a very narrow view of the neighbourhoods. It wasn't much of a silver lining, but she'd take it.

CHAPTER FOUR

Lauren taped the *LINE COOK WANTED* sign back up in the front window. It had so much previous tape on it, she was starting to wonder if the sign was bad luck. The soft humming coming from the kitchen made her smile. When she'd told Ramiro about the new cook, he'd shrugged and said they'd find someone better this week. She hoped that was true, for going through the hiring process was painful.

The rain and drizzle from yesterday had given up, and the sky warmed with the approaching sun. The bell above the door chimed, and Luna, their youngest server, strolled in, stuffing the last of a breakfast wrap in her mouth. Lauren noticed the logo on the front of the dark-brown paper.

"Where did you get that?"

Luna tucked the paper in her bag and shrugged. "Down the street somewhere."

"Grnds?"

Luna slipped her jacket off and hung it on her hook in the back. She pulled her long platinum hair into a top bun and switched into her running shoes. "Can't remember." Luna was a terrible liar, not because she was into honesty, but because she usually didn't care enough to try to be convincing.

"Ramiro, did you hear that? Grnds is selling breakfast wraps. They've expanded into actual food."

Ramiro stopped humming for a second. "They any good?"

Luna shrugged. "It's all the same thing, isn't it?" She pulled out a piece of gum and stuck it into her mouth.

"No gum-chewing in the front," said Lauren as Luna passed by and smiled in her overly-sweet-it-must-be-fake way.

"I don't want to smell like egg. I'll get rid of it before anyone sees."

Lauren rolled her eyes and said in a voice only for Ramiro, "She drives me nuts."

Luna folded an apron around her waist and stuffed her order pad into the front pocket. She'd worked here for just over a year now, but to Lauren it felt like a million. Luna came in on time, mostly, and did a good job, but something wasn't quite genuine about her.

"Waffles," Luna shouted through the order window. "Hold the fruit. And a cluck-and-grunt flop 'em with whiskey down."

Ramiro set to work pulling the waffle batter out of the fridge and pouring it into the waffle iron. "What are you really worried about? Most cafés have breakfast items."

"Sure, bagels and those horrible breakfast sandwiches at Starbucks, but nothing actually good."

Ramiro slapped four pieces of bacon on the griddle and grabbed two pieces of rye toast and placed them in the toaster. "They may take some of our to-go business, but we could get one of those fancy espresso machines so we can pull some of their hipster business our way."

"Aaron will never go for that."

"Not to worry, sweetums." He gave her a side hug, making sure to keep his clean hands free of her uniform. "We've been here forty years. We're a staple in this neighbourhood. People love us." He waved a spatula at her. "Plus our food is better than Hipster Dan's over there."

"Don't call me sweetums," she said as she shoved him playfully toward the griddle.

It wasn't so much that she was worried Grnds would take some of their business; they'd already done that. Greta's had been steadily losing customers to them since they opened two years ago, but not enough to do any real damage. She was worried about Aaron. He was already paranoid about how much money they were pulling in and was going to go ballistic when he found out about this.

Lauren tightened her apron and headed to the front. The place was picking up for the morning rush. In the next two hours the seats at the front counter had a line—always a good sign. As soon as one customer got up to leave, another would sit down. And the booths were always full. There were only the five of them, and Luna was good at turnover. Lauren had to give her that. She might not like her attitude sometimes, but Luna was a great server.

As breakfast died down and they finally had a moment to breathe, Lauren could almost believe Ramiro. They'd be fine.

❖

"Sorry. We're not hiring at the moment." It was the same thing Hayley had heard from over a dozen places that morning. She gave them her fake smile and walked out. She'd been looking for hostess jobs, since they didn't involve math skills or anything more than being able to take reservations and deal with seating people. She suspected her blue hair was yet again the culprit. Yet again she nixed the idea of dying it to conform to others' expectations. She'd come to the city partially because she'd expected people would just accept her as is. This was who she was, and she didn't feel like she had to change in order to fit in.

She had to broaden her search. Most of the places were hiring line cooks more than servers or hostesses. Maybe she could get hired as a cook somewhere. She'd never worked a grill, but how hard could it be? She was a fast learner. She'd spent her whole life watching her mom and grandma in the kitchen and knew a lot more about cooking and baking than she did about managing someone else's schedule. And as Kalini said, everyone lied on their resumes. The trick to keeping the job was backing up those lies with competence, which Hayley knew she had. She could wing it for a week while she picked up the specifics of the job—no problem.

She stopped in at Grnds to grab a table to fix her resume. By the time she was done with this process she'd probably have five different ones, depending on what she was looking for. The place was cramped, and the only spot was at one of the window stools. Didn't people work in this city? Maybe not. Maybe everyone was like her, in constant search mode. It still didn't explain how they paid for things.

She decided to save money by getting a plain coffee and the cheapest thing on the food menu, a piece of day-old banana bread. This would be her breakfast and lunch, so she took small bites to ration it.

Once she'd added a few items of relevant work experience to her resume, she saved it to her USB drive and headed over to the Sanderson library to print off ten copies.

Hayley wanted to find a place in walking distance of her new digs so she didn't have to take transit anywhere. It would save her six bucks a day, and keeping her spending down right now was everything. The place she'd found to stay wasn't great. In fact, it was downright horrible.

The Palace Arms, a short-stay hotel, rented rooms by the hour. The neon hourly rate sign had drawn her attention in the first place, although the building itself was hard to miss. The brick was painted a light pink, and it had turrets, like a castle. At one point in history it had probably been upscale, but unfortunately for Hayley, that was probably a century or two before she was born.

Her room smelled like mildew and stale beer. The paint was stained with nicotine, and the window didn't have curtains, which meant the streetlight outside illuminated the room all night, but it was dry and cheap, two things Hayley desperately needed at that moment. She kept telling herself that as soon as she found a job, she could start saving up to find some place better, although at this point, almost anything was better.

With her fresh resumes still warm from the printer, Hayley headed into the autumn afternoon.

❖

Lucy stuck her head into the kitchen. "Aaron's here."

"Rats." Lauren flicked her finger into the bathroom sink. Blood flecks splattered the white porcelain. "Why does he always show up during a rush?" She wrapped some toilet paper around the cut on her finger, and it quickly turned red. "Stupid one-ply." She grabbed the roll and wrapped it several times around her finger. When it looked like a giant moth cocoon, she popped open the first-aid kit and searched for a Band-Aid. They desperately needed a resupply. The only Band-Aids she could find were Star Wars. No doubt Theo had been the last to make a supply run. She discarded the mass of one-ply into the trash and wrapped the scowling face of Chewbacca around her index finger.

Aaron was sitting at a stool at the end of the bar, taking up valuable real estate. He was dressed in a dark-grey suit that cost more than Lauren's entire wardrobe, dumping sugar into a coffee. A silver tie was thrown over one shoulder to keep it from dipping into his mug.

Lauren had known Aaron since he was in his late teens, and besides the clothes, not much had changed. He'd always had an air about him that he was better than others. What made it worse was that he tried to fit in, make it appear like he belonged in a diner wearing a two-thousand-dollar suit.

When he spotted Lauren he turned toward her, creating a screech so loud the entire diner stopped for a second.

Lauren pointed at the stool. "You've been promising me for months you'd have that fixed. I had a kid in here yesterday who sat there for an hour twisting back and forth. At least five people left because of it."

"Why didn't you ask him to stop?"

"Since you're here, can I get you breakfast?"

He poured a few tablespoons of milk into his coffee. "I already ate." He pointed to the sign in the window as he took a sip of his coffee. "I thought you'd already replaced Pete."

"The last guy didn't work out."

"What happened to your finger?"

Lauren looked down at the Chewbacca Band-Aid. "That stupid register keeps jamming. We need a new one."

"How come the last guy didn't work out? What was wrong with him?"

And that's how it went with Aaron. He asked rapid-fire questions, rarely waiting for an answer or even expecting one. Lauren felt it was his way of proving he knew what was going on here, even though he stopped by only once a month, if that.

"I'm handling the hiring. I've got a bunch of interviews lined up today." She always made a point of seeming on top of things where Aaron was concerned, even lying if she had to. Otherwise he'd step in and make a mess of things. For the most part Aaron could forget he owned a diner. If you'd met him at a dinner party, you'd never know that his mother had left him this tiny place tucked beneath Trinity Bellwoods. But it was the times he did remember that worried Lauren. It meant he'd try to take charge and micromanage, and if there was one thing that Lauren avoided at all costs, it was Aaron micromanaging her diner.

The last time he'd stepped in to take charge, they'd ended up with two dozen boxes of frozen, chocolate-flavoured bratwurst. They were still in the freezer, currently holding up part of the shelf.

"Okay, but if you don't find someone by today, I have a guy who'd be perfect for the job. I'll call you tomorrow."

Lauren gave a tight-lipped smile. "Don't worry, Aaron. I've got it handled."

Aaron stood, pulling his tie from his shoulder and smoothing it against his light-grey shirt. "Well, it can't hurt to have a backup plan, can it?" He stooped to pick up his briefcase. "Oh, I stopped by to let you know I have a man coming in to inspect the place this week. His name is Civan Keyzer." Aaron turned and left, leaving Lauren stunned and speechless.

Lucy sidled up to Lauren with a pot of coffee in her hand. "Did he just say he was sending an inspector?"

Lauren nodded, still too shocked to form actual words.

"You know the only time someone hires an inspector is when they're getting ready to sell." Lucy clucked her tongue as she refilled a cup. She moved slowly down the line, refilling as she went.

Lauren took a deep breath, pulled back her shoulders, and delved back into the chaos, hoping the noise and bustle of work would keep her mind off what Lucy had just said. It was ambitious, even if it didn't work.

Even if Aaron was planning to sell, it was unlikely the building would be torn down to make condos, like so many other places in the city. The entire block was attached, so everyone would have to sell, and that would never happen. But whoever bought the place would probably gut it. This neighbourhood didn't want tiny little diners like this anymore. It was filling up with places like Grnds, or boutiques selling clothing made from paper, or vape stores. Aaron kept this place because it ran itself. At least to him it probably felt that way. As a lawyer he didn't need the money. But what if he had decided to sell? He'd make a fortune. The building alone had to be worth a couple of million or ten.

CHAPTER FIVE

Lauren took a bite of her Jack Benny and wiped some of the gooey cheese from the side of her mouth. This was the first chance she'd had all day to get off her feet and eat something. Her stomach had been growling at her for the last hour.

Lucy slid into the booth across from her with her ever-present Pepsi with a straw, no ice. Lauren figured she downed five or six full glasses a day. How Lucy didn't have an ulcer Lauren had no idea. She wasn't anyone to judge. A grilled cheese sandwich with bacon for breakfast wasn't even close to healthy. She'd have to remember to have a salad for dinner, or get Ramiro to add a tomato to a burger.

"It's not the same without Pete," Lucy said in her soft Jamaican accent.

"He's been gone a month." Lauren took another bite of her sandwich. She didn't want to admit that Lucy was right.

"And this place hasn't been the same since he left. Even Ramiro isn't humming or dancing as much. I think he misses him too."

Lauren had noticed, but she'd tried to ignore the pall that had fallen over the diner. Pete was so happy right now. Every time she'd texted him, he'd been excited about everything. She didn't want to ruin that for him by lamenting about how much they missed him around here.

"It's weird," Lauren said, "how one person can change the whole dynamic of a place, isn't it? Like a linchpin. And I never would've thought it'd be Pete."

Lucy had worked at the diner almost as long as Lauren. She'd started only a year or so later. If Lauren was going to guess at a linchpin, it would've been Lucy. She was like the mother of the place, especially after Greta died. Lucy was a caregiver, which meant she was in your business whether you wanted her there or not. She was constantly trying to set Lauren up, and she'd always scolded Pete for wearing fall jackets in winter and reminded Ramiro of everyone's birthday. After ten years working together, he still couldn't remember Pete's was on the twenty-second of June or that Lauren's was on March twentieth. She had a presence that said everything was going to be okay.

Lucy took a sip of her Pepsi and said, "I always assumed it was you."

"Me?"

"You've been here the longest of everyone, now that Greta's gone. After she died I kinda felt like you took her place. You watch over everything."

Lauren couldn't be more surprised if Lucy'd climbed on top of the table and done the cancan. "I…"

"I think someone just took a bite."

"Hmm?"

Lucy nodded toward the front window. On the other side stood a young woman with the richest dark-blue hair Lauren had ever seen. It must take skill to get it that colour. Also, she had the palest skin ever. The combination was startling. The woman was staring at the help-wanted sign like she'd found a water fountain in the desert.

The door chime rang as she entered, surveying the place as if judging whether it was a cool enough place to work. She bent to look at a picture in the front of Queen Street from the 1870s, when horses were still pulling the streetcars. Lauren tracked her gaze as it moved from the archive pictures to the old ads to Ramiro cooking in the kitchen and finally landed on Lauren and Lucy in the last booth.

She did a half wave, which was both awkward and adorable. "Hi. I saw the sign outside." She chucked her thumb toward the front door. "Is the manager around?"

"You're looking at her." Lucy pointed toward Lauren.

The woman held her hand out and smiled. "Oh. Hi. I'm Hayley." She fished out a resume from a leather satchel that looked like it had spent the better part of a decade wedged under heavy boxes.

Up close her eyes were pale blue, but when she turned her head and the light hit them, they were almost azure, like the shallow waters off the coast of St. Maarten.

"Do you have experience working in a kitchen?" Lauren scanned her resume.

"In high school I worked in a kitchen, prep-work mostly."

Lauren nodded without looking up at her, still studying her credentials. "Do you have time to fill out an application?"

Lucy got up, taking her Pepsi with her, and came back a few seconds later with a sheet of paper littered with questions and a pen. She handed both to Hayley.

"Fill this out, and then I'll introduce you to Ramiro, our cook. He'll have some questions for you." Lauren spent the next ten minutes tending to customers, but every minute or so her gaze would wander over to Hayley in her booth. She was wearing tight black jeans and a worn form-fitting leather jacket. As she filled out the form, she unzipped her jacket, revealing a T-shirt with a small bomb with legs and eyes.

"Something bothering you?" asked Lucy.

Lauren shook her head. "Is that what you'd wear to a job interview?"

Lucy put a hand on her hip. "To a diner? To apply for a job cooking burgers?"

Lauren didn't answer. Instead she busied herself by restocking the back counter with clean mugs.

❖

Hayley couldn't believe her luck. She was standing in a kitchen listening to the cook, Ramiro, detail what the job was. She might actually walk away with a job today. Forget the fact that she'd never actually cooked for anyone but her family before, but how hard could flipping burgers be?

The guy had some serious girth. His arms were bigger than her thighs. He kind of reminded her of that God in that Disney movie, minus the hair and the tattoos. At five-six, Hayley wasn't necessarily short, but she had to crank her neck to stare up at Ramiro.

Ramiro peered down at her resume. "Says here you worked in a restaurant in high school. What kinds of things did they have you doing?"

Hayley used the same lie she had with Lauren. "Prep work mostly." When Ramiro's face fell, she decided to embellish, sell herself a little. "But I can do burgers and pancakes, and I'm a quick study. Anything I don't know I can pick up fast."

Ramiro fished in a bin under the centre island and produced an onion, set it in front of her, and nudged a knife her way. "Cut this for me."

Hayley held up her hands. "Should I wash first?"

Ramiro shook his head. "No need."

Hayley grabbed the onion and sliced it in half through the onion root, like her mom had shown her. Then she flipped one half on its edge and made four slices horizontally and then five vertically, creating a grid. She then turned it ninety degrees and sliced along the onion, creating perfect cubes. She did the same to the other side and set the knife down. The whole thing had taken about a minute.

Ramiro pursed his lips. "Decent technique, but you'll have to be a lot faster than that to keep up with the rush."

Hayley shrugged. "I'll get faster. It's been a while."

"Okay, Pollyanna. How can you tell if a burger's done?"

"By the feel?"

Ramiro rolled his eyes. "That's guesswork. Whoever told you that didn't know shit. Now what I do." Ramiro took a patty from the fridge, pressed an indent in the middle of the patty with his thumb, and placed it on the grill. He adjusted the heat to high and grabbed a spatula from the counter. "I listen for the sizzle." He bent down, putting his ear to the grill. "Hear that?"

Hayley stared. Was this guy for real?

"When it gets really loud, I flip it and wait for the sizzle to get loud on this side." Ramiro took a bun from a bag beside the grill and placed it on the top part of the grill to toast. He flipped his burger. When the buns were toasted, he buttered them and placed them on a plate with lettuce, tomato, and two pickle slices. He knelt down to the grill again. "Hear that? All done." With a flourish he flipped the burger onto the bun and shut it. "And that's how you grill a burger."

"By sound?" Hayley asked, skeptical. The grin on Ramiro's face told her he was trying to pull one over on her. "That seems about as arbitrary as using the feel method."

"You don't like my method?"

"It's bullshit."

Ramiro roared with laughter. The sound that bubbled out of his chest, enchanting and contagious, made him less intimidating.

He crumpled her resume and application up and tossed it in the garbage. "Tell you what, Pollyanna. I don't believe for a second that you've ever worked in a kitchen, but I'm going to give you a shot. Be here tomorrow at five a.m., and we'll try you out."

Hayley glanced at the garbage. "You just threw my application in the trash bin."

"Yep. I have a feeling your references are either your boyfriend or your roommates or a combination of."

"But you're giving me a job?"

"I'm giving you a chance, which may turn into a job or a life experience you can share during future dinner parties. The great part is, you get to choose which one you get."

It took a minute for Hayley to work through what that meant. He was giving her a job on a probationary term. When that realization clicked into place, she launched herself at him. "Thank you, thank you, thank you." She pulled back but didn't have any other words, so she hugged him again. Ramiro stood there, seeming unsure what to do, with a smirk on his face.

"Okay, Pollyanna. We get the picture. You're excited." He held up his index finger. "Just don't let Lauren know you don't have any kitchen experience. She'll freak."

Hayley nodded. "I won't. Thank you. See you at five a.m." She bounded out of the kitchen and diner before Ramiro could say anything else.

❖

"So you hired her?" Lauren rested her arms on the window between the kitchen and front counter, watching Ramiro slap three burger patties on the griddle. He twisted and laid out three plates with their garnishes. Watching him work was like watching a choreographed dance—hypnotic and soothing.

"*We* hired her. She's going to do great."

"How can you tell already?"

"She didn't baulk at the five a.m. start time. Didn't even faze her. That tells me two things. She really wants this job, which means she'll work hard to keep it, and two, I won't have to listen to Ezra bitch about the early shift cutting into his womaning." Ramiro turned three burgers in rapid succession without looking at them. "Why? You have a problem with hiring her? I thought you said Aaron was on your case about filling the position."

"No. It's fine." She waved him off. "I can handle Aaron. Chances are he'll forget he was even here."

"Okay, because the way you say 'it's fine' doesn't sound like you think it's fine. We agreed I get final say for kitchen staff."

Lauren bit her lip. She wasn't even sure what it was about Hayley that made her so uneasy. "I know. And you do. I guess she just didn't seem to fit in. That's all." She looked back at the booth Hayley had been sitting in earlier. That wasn't it either. And uneasy was the wrong word for how she felt. It was more a sense of something she couldn't even name, a sense of change coming. And if there was one thing Lauren didn't need right now, it was change.

Ramiro pointed his spatula at Lauren. "Trust me. I can tell when someone's going to fit in."

"Like the last guy?"

Ramiro flipped the burgers onto buns, added the tops, and set the plates on the counter in front of Lauren. "That was a favour for my girlfriend. I told you he was only going to be temporary until we found someone better." His grin stretched his cheeks. "And we just did." He shooed her away. "Go serve stuff."

Lauren grabbed the plates and delivered them to the three men at booth one. She spent the rest of the day with half her mind on the diner and the other on impossibly azure eyes.

CHAPTER SIX

At four forty-five the next morning, Hayley stood outside the diner waiting for someone to open up. She was an equal mixture of nervousness and excitement. She loved a good challenge, and that's what this would be because she was going in blind. She had no fucking idea what she was doing. But she'd found a job. To celebrate, last night she'd splurged and bought a bag of Doritos from the street meat vendor down the way.

Was it a bad sign when the street vendors knew your order by heart? It probably wasn't the healthiest of meals. With her first paycheque she'd make sure to buy some vegetables. Who knew what kind of meat they were using to make those sausages? When you drowned them in ketchup and sauerkraut, they tasted good enough though. Also, getting a job on her second day meant she didn't have to spend today looking for one. Job-hunting sucked donkey balls.

"You're early."

Hayley jumped a foot. Her hand went to her heart. "Jesus Christ. You scared the shit out of me."

"Sorry." Lauren offered a smile and brushed past her to unlock the door. She smelled like vanilla, honey, and coffee.

"You came out of nowhere."

"I live above the diner." She pointed up.

Hayley stepped back and took a look at the windows up there, which had a little ledge under each one. "Cool. Best. Commute. Ever."

Lauren ushered Hayley in ahead of her. "But I get called in more often since I'm so close."

"And I guess, as the manager, you kind of have to set an example."

Lauren paused, and her polite smile faded a bit. "Yeah." Then she shrugged and the polite smile was back in place. "But it's why I get paid the big bucks."

Hayley doubted she got paid very much. She hadn't enquired what they were going to pay her because at this point she didn't care, but it couldn't be much.

"Feel free to make yourself something for breakfast. I'm not sure if Ramiro went over any of the perks, but you get meals for free when you're working."

"For free?" The force with which Hayley spoke made Lauren take a step back.

"I'm guessing Ramiro didn't go over much with you."

To be honest Hayley had skipped out before he'd had a chance. "I get to eat for free?"

Lauren laughed. She'd never seen anyone so excited about free food. "Yes, within reason. But from the looks of you, I doubt you'd be able to put away much."

"This has officially become the best job ever. Can I make you anything?"

"No thanks. I don't eat breakfast."

"I don't usually, but I'm starving." Hayley took a seat at the front counter and decided to wait a bit. It felt weird entering the kitchen without Ramiro there. "Do you know when Ramiro's coming in? He said to meet him here at five, that he'd go over everything with me."

Lauren hung her cardigan up in the back and came out, turning on the coffeemaker, the stereo, and the lights all in three quick, practiced motions. "Unfortunately, Ramiro broke his ankle playing basketball last night. So for the first little while, you're going to be on your own until I can get Ezra or Theo to come in. Is that going to be a problem?"

Panic. Extreme panic was the only thing that went through Hayley's mind at that moment. "By myself?"

"We're not that busy now. We don't pick up until about seven thirty. That should give you time to at least have a poke around in the kitchen and get the lay of the land. By then someone will be in to review the menu with you. The only hard part is picking up the lingo."

"The lingo?"

Lauren smirked. "Greta had a thing about fifties diners, so

everything has a name. Like bossy in a bowl is beef stew, and frog sticks is French fries, or two dots and a dash is two eggs and a strip of bacon." At the look of horror on Hayley's face she added, "Ramiro didn't mention anything about that, did he?"

Hayley shook her head. No, he certainly hadn't. And now she was being thrown into the meat grinder. She'd be lucky to make it to lunch still employed. A cold, dead terror settled in the pit of her stomach, replacing the emptiness that had been there a minute before. How was she going to figure out how to cook if she also had to figure out what the hell they were ordering?

Lauren placed a steady hand on Hayley's wrist. "You need some coffee. Everything's better after coffee."

All Hayley could do was nod. Coffee was a good idea. Coffee would help. She needed to focus on one thing at a time.

Lauren squeezed her arm and turned to fetch some mugs. "How do you take it?"

"Just black is fine." She watched Lauren work, her movements efficient. They spoke of years of doing the same thing. She didn't look much older than Hayley, maybe early thirties. Her black hair was pulled back into a ponytail, small wisps that were too short to fit curled into the collar of her uniform.

"Here you go." Hayley dropped her gaze to the darkness in her cup. It matched her mood at that moment. Her excitement had given over to the nervousness she'd felt earlier. She watched Lauren load hers up with two creamers.

"How long have you worked here?" Hayley asked.

Lauren threw her head back, looking up at the ceiling. "Geez… Fourteen years?" Then she frowned into her coffee. "God, I'm old."

They sat that way for the next few minutes, sipping their coffees and watching the city wake up. The only street traffic at this time were the streetcar and delivery trucks. It was bliss.

"This is my favourite time of day." Lauren inhaled the steam from her coffee deeply before taking a sip. "Right before we open, when it's just minimal staff, before the deliveries and the first rush of the day." She rested her elbows on the counter. "Kind of like the calm before the storm."

Hayley nodded. "I used to work in a grocery store, and my

favourite was inventory day. Every once in a while, when we were closed for a holiday or something, a couple of us would come in and count everything. I always liked it better without customers."

Lauren laughed, deep and throaty. "The world would be a better place without them. But…" She raised her arms to indicate the diner. "My life revolves around making them happy. So for a few short minutes every day I get to pretend they don't exist."

"Mmm." Hayley sipped her coffee. It was good. She usually didn't like brewed coffee, but this had a nutty aftertaste that was rich and smooth. "This is really good."

"Thanks. Greta passed on the secret of how to make brewed coffee taste like coffee instead of burnt battery acid. So what did you do at this grocery store?"

"Everything. You name a position, I've done it. I guess except janitor, but I can clean up an olive-oil spill better than anyone."

Lauren's phone buzzed. She pulled it out of her pocket and checked an incoming text. "Okay. Ezra said he'll be here in an hour, which is a record for him. That man takes longer to get ready than a prom queen." She dropped her phone back into her pocket and watched Hayley with a strange mix of scepticism and compassion. "You're nervous."

Hayley nodded. "Wouldn't you be? I always get nervous my first day of any job." And while that was true, Hayley hoped Lauren never learned the real reason her nerves were a bundle of hot wires. She had no fucking clue what she was doing.

"I'm sorry Ramiro isn't here to show you around, but you'll do fine. Ramiro wouldn't have hired you if he didn't have faith that you could do the job."

Hayley stared into deep-brown eyes, and all she saw was kindness. But that kindness and compassion might not last once Lauren realized Hayley had lied on her resume.

Lauren looked up at the clock above the door, breaking the moment. "We've got a few minutes before the first delivery arrives. We get our doughnuts and pastries in first and then our breads. Make sure you use up the day-olds first, unless they feel really stale."

Hayley finished her coffee and stood. "Can I take your mug to the kitchen?" she asked.

Lauren drained hers and passed it over. "Just place them in the sink closest to the dishwasher. We have someone come in around eight to do the dishes."

Hayley nodded. She felt like she was heading toward the firing squad.

❖

Alone in the kitchen Hayley set to work figuring out where everything was. Lauren had given her a list of the menu and the corresponding lingo next to it. She reviewed it quickly and then stuck it to the board near the griddle.

Then she decided the next best thing was to cook herself breakfast. Even if she was no longer hungry, she would be later, and it was the fastest way to get familiar with the kitchen.

Hayley wasn't a bad cook. With both her parents working the hours of small-business owners her whole life, she'd become self-sufficient. By the time she was ten she could make homemade lasagna. Hayley knew she could do the work, but that wasn't the issue. She was worried about the amount of people she'd have to cook for.

She pulled a bowl of eggs from the fridge, grabbed a loaf of bread from the bread bin, and turned toward the griddle. It had four knobs, but none of them looked like an on switch.

"Shit." She knelt and took a look underneath, hoping for something familiar. Her mom had one of those small griddles that you plugged into the wall, but Hayley had never used a commercial griddle before. She looked out the window. Lauren was busy setting out napkin dispensers in the booths. If she asked how to turn it on, assuming Lauren knew, she'd be found out for sure.

Maybe she could call her dad. But he'd still be asleep right now. She pulled out her phone to check the time and realized she had all the answers sitting in her hand. "Duh. Google." She found the answer on reddit within a few seconds. She needed to turn on the pilot valve for each burner with a flat-head screwdriver. As if proving she was on the right track, a greasy screwdriver sat in a red-plastic cup duct-taped to the wall next to the phone.

Once she had the griddle turned on and heating, she set about collecting the rest of her ingredients. She'd make egg in the hole, something her mom used to cook for her when she was feeling sick. That's what she needed—a little comfort food. And she better make it good because who knew when she was going to eat again. There was a very real chance she wouldn't have a job by the end of the day.

The trick to good egg in the hole was mixing garlic into the butter you used for the toast. She also liked to use a bit of dill on the egg. She found garlic in a bowl on the spice shelf, grabbed some fresh dill from the fridge, and set to work mincing the garlic and folding it into some soft butter. She buttered two pieces of bread and cut two holes out of the middle.

Next she spread a little butter on the griddle and slapped on both pieces of bread, swirling them around to soak up the melted butter. She cracked two eggs in the centre of each piece and picked some fresh sprigs of dill, sprinkling them on the yellow yolk.

The front door chimed, and a skinny man with the curliest long hair Hayley had ever seen walked through the door carrying three boxes of pastries. "I've still got three pies in the van." He set the boxes down on the counter next to the register. "Tessa wanted to know if you'll try her new cherry pie tomorrow. She's also got a banana and chocolate pie with graham crust." He leaned toward Lauren, who was sorting through the boxes. "It is to fucking die for, Lauren. To die for."

Lauren's eyes sparked and she grinned. "With that kind of recommendation, Kaleed, I'll try both."

Kaleed's nose went in the air. "What is that awesome smell?"

"That's our new line cook's breakfast, I'd guess."

"Whatever she's making smells fucking fantastic."

"I'll let her know. Thanks, Kaleed."

Lauren poked her head into the kitchen. "What're you making?"

"Egg in the hole. You want one?"

Lauren walked over to the griddle just as Hayley flipped first one, then the other. "No thanks. I really can't take food in the morning. But it smells great."

"Thanks." Hayley flipped her breakfast onto a plate.

"Forks are in the front. You can eat it at the counter."

As soon as Hayley sat down, the door chimed again, and in walked a sculpted blond man. That was the only way to describe him. He looked like he'd been chiselled out of stone. He was gorgeous, and by the way he sauntered in, he knew it.

Lauren looked up from a crossword puzzle she'd been working on. "Hey, Ezra. Thanks for coming in." She pointed her pen Hayley's way. "This is Hayley, our new line cook. Hayley, this is Ezra. He's going to show you around today."

Hayley waved her fork at him, swallowed her food, and said, "Hi." She'd never been so happy to see anyone.

He gave a quick salute in their direction. "You ruin my kitchen yet?"

"I tried, but it's harder than it looks," said Hayley and cut into her second egg in the hole.

Ezra took a minute, watching her eat. Hayley assumed he'd decided it was a valid answer because he took a seat next to her, extending his hand. "Nice to meet you."

Hayley wiped hers on a napkin before shaking his. "You too."

Lauren set a mug of coffee down in front of him. "You've got half the time to prep, so I suggest you take that to go."

"As long as she's better than the last guy, we've got nothing to worry about." He picked up his coffee and headed toward the kitchen. "You coming?" he asked Hayley.

She grabbed her plate and followed him back.

"Where's your hairnet?"

Hayley groaned as she placed her dishes in the sink near the dishwasher. This was going to be a long day.

Chapter Seven

Hayley collapsed on her bed face-first and stayed that way for several minutes. It was a little after five p.m. She'd been on her feet for over twelve hours. The nicest thing she could say about the day is that she'd survived.

Ezra probably thought she was a simpleton. She hadn't remembered a single order because most of it sounded like gibberish. Even with the items on a list next to the griddle, she kept having to ask Ezra what the hell the servers were yelling at her. And it only got worse when they started writing it down. Each server had their own shorthand for taking orders, and she couldn't read anyone's writing. Lauren had continued to shout her orders through the window. Each time, Ezra grumbled under his breath, getting moodier as the day wore on.

She'd burned three orders, had three returned, and almost set the place on fire once. When Ezra told her to show up at five the next morning, she couldn't be more surprised. As the day went on, Hayley had this growing sense of dread that one more mistake would be the one that got her fired.

But she hadn't. Hayley turned over and stared at her ceiling. Below, she could hear someone's TV blasting *Jeopardy*. The guy was yelling the answers at the top of his lungs, every one of them wrong. Each time they were wrong, he'd shout at Alex Trebek to get a fucking clue.

Today her room smelled like burnt rubber, like someone had left something on the radiator and it had melted. She should feel disheartened and sad, but a big grin spread across her face. She'd found a place to live close to work that was cheap. And even though she had to share a washroom with four strange men and listen to all their strange habits, she had her own space. She'd found a job and made it through the first day, and the best part? She got a percentage of the tips and ate for free while working. That would keep her going until she got paid in two weeks. If she saved everything, she might have enough to pay her rent at the end of the week. Next week would be harder, but she could worry about that when it got here. Ed, the manager, had told her he didn't extend credit, but she had a feeling she could sweet-talk him into an extension.

But more surprising was the fact that when she wasn't terrified of screwing up someone's order or getting fired, she'd enjoyed herself. The only other thing in her life she'd enjoyed as much was baking with her nana when she was little.

She was surviving on her own. And that was more important than her sense of accomplishment or a full stomach.

After showering the grease off, Hayley snuggled in with a bag of liquorice—a splurge from the 7-Eleven down the street for getting (and keeping) the job—and a book.

She already missed her evenings with Jo and Kalini. They'd had an easy-going system that had slowly become a routine. Most nights they'd find themselves in front of some bad reality show, a plate of whatever Hayley had made everyone for dinner in hand and a good amount of sarcasm to share.

It would take her a while to find a new routine. And it wasn't like she'd never see them again. Once she started making more money, she could afford to build a social life. That thought made up for the fact that she'd felt like a bit of a recluse since she moved to the city.

She cracked the book open and slipped her bookmark farther back to mark how much she'd allow herself to read that night. She popped a piece of liquorice into her mouth and settled in for the evening.

❖

Lauren watched the iced coffee ebb and flow with each movement of the subway car. Someone had spilled their drink, and it had taken up residence in the indentation of one of the blue priority seats. The ice danced back and forth, oblivious to the fact that it was no longer needed.

She watched a man in windbreaker pants and a red pleather jacket hold an entire conversation with his Pomeranian. Every few words the dog would lick his face and nip at his beard.

She watched a lone grape roll its way from one side of the car, hit the edge, then roll the other way. Several people had almost stepped on it as they entered the train, but it had swerved out of the way at the last second every time.

Lauren loved the people-watching the subway provided. It was almost better than her rooftop oasis, but not quite. The subway was sometimes crowded or too hot, or someone she didn't want to talk to would sit next to her and start up a conversation. She preferred zoning out with her music, keeping to herself, and observing. It was where she did her best thinking.

Today she found herself thinking of their new hire. Ezra had complained that first day, but he always complained about new hires. She hadn't burned down the place. That's what he'd said, which was high praise from Ezra.

Lauren took this route every Monday to visit her dad, who'd moved to the east end. They'd looked for a one-bedroom closer to Lauren after her mom died, but the west end was more expensive. At the time Lauren was less concerned about the travel time because the east end had more green space. But her father hadn't left his apartment in over a year, unless it was to visit the doctor's. This was starting to worry Lauren. It wasn't so bad when he still worked, but now that he was retired, he had no excuse to leave. It hadn't happened all at once either. When he retired, he still had his poker nights, but then his friend Bill had a stroke, and then Jim and his wife moved to Florida. After that the poker nights fell apart, as did Friday nights at the Firkin for darts and a couple of beers. It wasn't good for him to lose his social life like that.

Lauren wondered if she should stop bringing him groceries every week. That would force him to get out. But he would probably order in delivery every night. She'd find more pizza or Chinese containers in the fridge than she already did. She preferred to give him the option of having something to eat that wasn't full of empty calories, even if he didn't always make the right decision.

The truth was, and she would never admit this to anyone, she was getting tired of giving up her one day off to make the trip over to see her dad. She loved visiting with him, but over the past year it had become a chore, something she had to do instead of wanted to. If she didn't show up to look after him, he'd just let his place and his health fall to waste. Her mom would never forgive her if she let that happen.

She unlocked the door and pushed inside. Several days' worth of mail were sitting under the mail slot. She stooped to pick up the bundle and went into the kitchen.

"Hey, Dad."

"Can you grab me a Coke?" he asked from his chair in the family room.

She placed the grocery bag on the counter and began unpacking the premade meals she'd cooked last night and this morning. "I didn't buy you any Coke. You should be drinking water or milk."

"Milk's for babies. There's a can in the fridge."

She opened the fridge and found two cans of Coke next to a pizza box sitting on several Pyrex containers from last week. She pulled out one and opened it. The broccoli and fish she'd made him last weekend was wilted and slimy.

"Dad." She stormed into the living room. Her dad was in his chair, a P.D. James soft-cover over the arm and an empty can of Coke on the side table. *Hollywood Squares* was playing softly on the TV for background noise. "Why do I even bother making you this food if you're just going to let it go bad? This stuff isn't cheap, you know."

"I don't know, honey, but I've told you about a million times I don't need a nursemaid." He was wearing a dark-blue sweater that did a good job of hiding his belly. Every time she saw him, she'd swear he was getting bigger. It didn't matter how many calorie-conscious meals she brought over for him; he still found a way to stuff his face with junk. His hair, what was left of it, needed a cut. The white strands curled at the ends, obscuring the top of his sweater collar. His skin, which had once been a rich, deep brown, had faded to a pasty white, with sunspots sprinkling the tops of his hands and forearms.

"I'm not trying to be your nursemaid. I'm trying to make sure you're following doctor's orders. Dr. Chun said you need to eat healthy if you want to stay ahead of your diabetes."

He shrugged. They'd had this argument every Monday since he was diagnosed with type 2 diabetes a year ago. He picked up the book on the arm of his chair and held the cover out to her. "Have you read this one? It's about—"

"Dad, you know I hate those kinds of books," she called from the kitchen without looking at what he was showing her. She didn't need to. He only ever read mysteries or thrillers. As far back as she could remember, he'd always had at least two on the go at any given time. She'd asked him once why he always read two at the same time, and he'd said it was because he liked to have options, in case he wasn't in the mood for one.

"These ones aren't graphic. They don't have any blood or guts in them."

"I like happy books." She placed a plate with baked chicken and steamed broccoli on the table next to him with a glass of cold milk.

His nostrils flared. "I'm not eating that. I thought I asked you to bring me a Coke."

Lauren threw her hands up in the air. "Gah."

❖

On her way home, Lauren decided to take the Dundas streetcar so she could cut through the park. The sky was overcast, but the air had a warm breeze to it. People were out enjoying what was probably the last good day of the season.

It was still so close to summer that none of the leaves had turned yet. The city seemed to be in limbo, not quite autumn but also not summer anymore.

Lauren took the path that led past the off-leash dog park. It was packed with dogs and owners making the most of the weather. A lot of barking was going on at the far side, and when she looked, caught in the middle of several dogs trying to grab at a ball held way over their heads, was a blue-haired girl. Lauren stopped so fast, the couple behind her almost ran her over with their stroller. Lauren stepped off the path to watch. She had no doubt it was Hayley. There was no missing that hair or what Lauren had come to think of as Hayley's signature leather jacket.

Lauren continued down the path, which curved with the dog park, never taking her eyes off Hayley. She was mesmerizing. Her head was thrown back, and she was laughing so loudly that the sound carried over to where Lauren was standing. She'd throw the ball and watch as the dogs raced and scrambled over the grass, all eager to be the one to get it, and then they'd all rush back so fast Hayley would almost get knocked over by their exuberance. She'd pull the ball from some dog's drooling mouth and hold it up and laugh as they tried to jump up her to get it.

Hayley's hair was down, the blue locks blowing in the breeze, and she looked so carefree and happy, the sight sent a shock wave through Lauren. She couldn't remember the last time she'd been that happy herself, if ever. An emotion tugged at her, and she couldn't place it. It wasn't jealousy or nostalgia or regret for not being the type of person who could show that much emotion in public. But in a way she did feel all those things, just not with any malice. No, what she was feeling was different, almost a physical sensation deep in her stomach, something close to longing, but Lauren couldn't tell what exactly she was longing for. The idea of letting a bunch of filthy dogs paw at her was unappealing in the extreme.

Hayley hadn't worked at the diner for more than a few days, but Lauren already sensed she did everything big. She talked big, gesturing wildly with her arms, and she laughed big. Sometimes Lauren could swear she heard her laughter all the way in her apartment above the diner. Even her smile filled her entire face. She made rooms feel small and ideas seem massive, and in that package, Lauren found something very enticing. She just hadn't figured out what yet.

Several large barks drew Lauren's focus back to the dog park. She'd been standing there for ten minutes watching Hayley. It was only when Hayley turned and their eyes met across the park that Lauren realized it was a bit creepy to be watching one of her employees. She did a pathetic wave and continued on her way to the diner, only to stop again when she heard her name being called.

"Lauren, hey." Hayley was out of breath by the time she caught up.

"Aren't you forgetting something?" Lauren looked around but couldn't see a dog following her anywhere.

The lines in Hayley's face dropped. "Was I supposed to be working right now?"

Lauren pointed back to the dog park. "Your dog."

Hayley smiled one of her full-face smiles and laughed. "Oh, God. I couldn't afford a dog even if I had the time to look after one." She pointed back at the park. "This is the free version of owning a dog. All the fun of playing with them and none of the downsides." She bit her lip in contemplation mode. "Although snuggles at night would be nice. I wonder if you can rent dogs for an evening?"

"Snuggles are one of the best reasons for owning a pet." At least that's what Lauren imagined. She'd never had a pet that was actually good at snuggling, mostly because she'd only ever owned cats.

"True. So what are you up to on your day off?"

Lauren scrunched up her face, embarrassed by her lameness. "Visiting my dad. He doesn't get out much since he retired, so I like to take him groceries and precooked meals. Healthy stuff, or else he'll order junk." Since when had she become an over-sharer?

"That's sweet."

"It's lame. You probably got up to all kinds of exciting things on your day off."

Hayley smirked. "How did you know it was my day off?"

"I make the schedule."

Hayley's cheeks pinked. "Right. Being my boss and all." She dug her boots into the dirt at the side of the path. "Well, I should probably get going. I'll see you tomorrow." She waved and was off before Lauren could say anything else.

As she watched Hayley saunter down the path like she had nowhere important to be, it hit Lauren what she'd been feeling. Anticipation. And it was such a strange, complex thing to be feeling for her line cook.

Chapter Eight

So, are you having a boy or a girl?" Hayley had her phone propped on her windowsill, so she had her hands free. She'd begun FaceTiming her sister lately, and it felt good to see a friendly face.

Hannah frowned through the phone. "I told you, Hale. Derek doesn't want to know, and that means I can't."

"Please. I'm sure you peeked." Hayley was sitting cross-legged on her bed counting out the money she had left. It came to a little more than eighty dollars.

"Have you ever seen one of those things? The technicians need a degree to tell if it has a penis or not. There's no way I could tell from just a quick look."

"So you're really going to leave it until it pops out?"

A short pause on the other side of the phone. Hayley knew this suspense was killing her sister. She was a planner. From an early age she would organize her toys, using every sort of method—her dolls arranged by size, books alphabetical, CDs by artist and year. She'd even organized her clothes by type and use. The idea of decorating a nursery without knowing the baby's sex would slowly drive her crazy. Hayley was kind of glad she wouldn't be around for that.

"Yes. Derek wants to be surprised."

"But you hate surprises, Han. You're really going to spend the next six months calling the baby 'it'? What about names?"

"Stop. We made this decision, together, and I can live with that. We'll decorate the room in neutral colours. You know I hate blue and pink anyway. And we'll pick a boy name and a girl name, or something gender neutral."

"Okay." Hayley stuffed her money into an envelope and slipped it under her mattress. She'd go to the bank tomorrow after work and deposit it. She didn't feel comfortable having it sitting in her room. Ed had warned her to always leave her door locked, like, no shit, but that didn't mean someone couldn't pick the lock.

"What do Mom and Dad think about this?"

Hannah's voice grew very quiet and tight. "For Christ's sake."

"Okay, sorry. Geez. Subject change."

"How's the new job going?"

"I have to wear a hairnet. But I like the people and the work."

"How's your boss?"

"To be honest, I'm not really sure who my boss is. Right now, everyone's my boss. Lauren's the manager of the whole place. Then there's the head cook, Ramiro. He's in charge of the kitchen and the cooks. But he broke an ankle the other day, and I haven't seen him since he hired me. So I have this guy named Ezra bossing me around until Ramiro gets better."

"Have you told Mom and Dad yet?"

"No, and I'm not going to. I'm still applying for real jobs. Something will come up soon, and then I won't have to worry them."

"Just promise me you're being careful."

"I promise. You have nothing to worry about."

She hadn't told Hannah about getting kicked out of her place. Losing her job was bad enough. She didn't want to stress her out more, especially with a baby on the way. Hannah hadn't said anything, but Hayley could tell when her sister was stressed, and this baby, especially with how Derek was, would worry her because she couldn't control this situation. Derek, being Derek, would go overboard trying to do things for her, to make her comfortable, keep her from overworking, and that would make her nuts. Hayley liked Derek, he was a great guy, but he had a lot to learn about her sister. Sometimes she wondered how he could be so clueless. They'd dated for three years before they got married, which had been two years ago. And in all that time he hadn't figured out he'd married a control freak.

Lauren reminded her a little of her sister. In the short time she'd known her, she seemed to need to have things just so. She'd watched Lauren that first day from the kitchen. Every time customers left, she'd rearrange the salt and pepper shakers so they lined up with each placement. She was the only server to do that. Lucy just shoved everything up the counter so it wasn't in their way.

Even the way she looked, with her ironed uniform and neat hair and trimmed nails, told Hayley she took a certain pride in looking put together. Hannah was the same way. She'd never show up in public with chipped nail polish or wrinkled clothes. Growing up, Hayley had loved finding the perfect way to push Hannah's buttons. She found she had the same urge with Lauren, just to see how she'd react. Lauren made her want to cut through that perfection to find the messy interior.

❖

Ramiro hobbled into the kitchen with two crutches squeezed under his armpits, Lauren trailing behind him. "I told you not to come in today. Theo and Ezra have the kitchen under control."

"I wanted to see how Pollyanna was doing."

"Pollyanna?" asked Lauren.

"The newbie. Hayley."

Lauren rolled her eyes. For as long as she could remember, Ramiro gave people nicknames, but only people he liked. So if Ramiro had already given Hayley a nickname after knowing her for only a few minutes, it meant she'd passed some unknown test. His approval eased Lauren's mind a bit, as she was still unsure about Hayley. She was probably being paranoid. Aaron had called earlier yesterday to check up on the cook situation, and she'd been happy to tell him that they'd hired someone.

Ezra hadn't asked to be reassigned after their shift together, which was his highest compliment.

"She's not in until this afternoon." Lauren was following Ramiro around clucking at him, afraid he might topple over any second.

He leaned his crutches in the corner next to the fridge. "Well, I can relieve someone and work the evening shift with her." He had a plastic walking cast wrapped around a plaster cast. Lauren wasn't sure if he'd bribed someone to give him the walking cast. Didn't you get one of those only after you'd had the plaster one taken off?

Ramiro looked down at his cast and back up at Lauren. "Relax, sweetums. I just have to wear the plaster cast for a week, and then I'm in this plastic thing. If I wasn't so indestructible it could've been a lot worse."

She hooked the cloth she was carrying in her palm and placed her fists on her hips. "Indestructible?"

"If you were indestructible you wouldn't be walking around with a limp, old man," said Ezra from his station in front of the griddle.

Ramiro waved him off. "It's a temporary setback. How'd Pollyanna do?"

Ezra shrugged as he flipped a pancake. "She didn't annoy the shit out of me. But she's totally gre—" He stopped when he saw Ramiro run his thumb across his neck from behind Lauren. "We need to get rid of this fu—" He saw the look of death on Lauren's face and switched words. "Frigging lingo. It messes everyone up. It's probably what messed Hayley up the most."

"This is still Greta's diner, and as long as it is, the lingo stays. It's part of the charm."

Theo blew a raspberry. "Not my word choice." He exchanged a look with Ezra as he slipped by to grab a container of prepped cucumbers for the lunch rush.

Ramiro rubbed his head as he passed and limped over to Ezra. "That's the nicest thing I've ever heard you say about anyone, ever. You got a crush on her or something?"

Ezra laughed. "Yeah, right. She's not my type."

"Oh yeah? When Theo started working here, you told me a one-armed orangutan on ecstasy could do a better job than him."

"It's true." Theo laughed. "Although I think the city would frown on me using my feet to flip burgers."

"All I said was that she didn't suck. Besides, I'm not her type, anyway. I've got the manly bits where she prefers the lady bits." He demonstrated with his hands.

"Okay," said Lauren, covering her eyes with one hand. "I think that's incredibly inappropriate talk about an employee who's not here to join that conversation."

"You're probably just jealous she didn't spend her whole shift checking out your pecs." Ramiro flicked one of Ezra's pecs playfully.

"I'm okay letting the weird ones pass me by."

"Weird?" asked Theo, the only one who hadn't met her yet.

"Yeah." Ezra plated his pancakes and set them on the ledge and rang the bell. "She's...I don't know, she's weird looking."

"She's not weird looking," said Lauren.

"She's got Smurf hair."

"Lots of people have blue hair. Doesn't make them weird looking," she said.

"Doesn't matter what she looks like, as long as she can do the job," said Ramiro.

"Besides, I think we should be more worried about the breakfast sandwiches Hipster Dan is making." Theo pulled a bowl of tomatoes out of the fridge and scooted around Ramiro and Lauren to place it next to his station on the griddle.

"Sandwiches? I thought they were making wraps."

"They've got a bunch of stuff now. Luna gave me a bite of hers this morning."

Lauren smacked Theo with her cloth. "Why are you encouraging her?"

Theo ducked out of the way. "I wanted to see what we're up against."

"And?" she asked.

"I think we need to start making more to-go items."

"That good?"

"I noticed we've lost a few regulars this week. It's too early to say. Maybe it's just an off week..."

"But maybe not," Lauren said. "Poop."

Ramiro chucked a slice of cucumber at her. "Swear like an adult, wom—"

"Hey." She held up a finger at him. "I can swear any way I like. Go home and let these guys work. Rest up. I don't need you tripping over something and breaking your other ankle."

Ramiro blew a raspberry at her too. "Stop clucking at me. I'm fine. Maybe I'll go over and check out Hipster Dan's stuff."

"Don't you dare. It's bad enough that Luna's giving him her money."

"Lauren," Vic called from the front. "You're needed."

"Okay." She pointed a finger at Ramiro. "Go home. Hayley will be fine with Theo this evening. I don't want you worrying about her."

"Lauren, I told you I couldn't work a double shift today."

"Lauren," Vic called again.

"Coming." She threw the cloth into the laundry bin and went out in front to help Vic with the customers. "This isn't finished."

❖

Lauren flipped the open sign on the door and rolled her shoulders a few times. She'd worked a double today, and it felt like each hour had placed a ten-pound weight on her shoulders. She'd finally ordered Ramiro home, convinced him that Hayley could close up without his help.

The first strains of "Echo Beach" drifted in through the kitchen, followed by Hayley's soft humming. By the time the chorus had started, the volume was at double. When Lauren stuck her head into the kitchen, Hayley was scrubbing the griddle with the scraper, bobbing her head to the music, her blue hair piled in a high messy bun on top of her head. She'd thrown her apron on the counter behind her, and underneath was a yellow T-shirt with the words *it's on like* written above an eight-bit Donkey Kong.

Ezra was right. Hayley was kind of weird. She reminded Lauren of a perpetual teenager, those people who refused to grow up and take on adult responsibilities. Lauren had been dealing with the type most of her life, because at some point they all thought it would be cool to work in a retro diner.

"I'm going to run back to my apartment to grab a sweater. Are you okay by yourself for a while?"

Hayley nodded without looking up or stopping her bobbing head. "Ramiro gave me a list of what needs to get done. If I have questions about a task, I'll just leave it until you get back. That cool?"

"I won't be gone long."

On her way up to her apartment she tried to figure out what it was about Hayley. She'd only known her for a few days. She was polite, a good worker, and she was always on time, eager to do things the right way. But she'd thought about Hayley more than any other employee she'd had. Ever. And that was unsettling. She didn't have any reason to be putting this much thought into her.

By the time she made it back to the diner, the music was cranked full blast, and Hayley was fist-pumping to "Love Will Tear Us Apart," singing at the top of her lungs. She wanted to cross the kitchen and turn down the music, but then the bridge started, and Hayley began drumming on the counter to the beat. The sight actually froze her on the spot. She didn't want to make any movement that would stop what was going on in front of her. She'd never seen anyone lose themselves so fully in a song. And then Hayley turned around, and the spell was broken. She lunged for the volume nob and yanked it to a reasonable level.

"Don't let me stop you." Lauren took a step into the kitchen. "What are you listening to?"

"Joy Division." Hayley followed that admission with a look that said, *duh.* "Don't you like eighties music?"

"I like it fine. Were you even alive in the eighties?"

"I missed it by this much." She held her thumb and forefinger a millimetre apart, a lopsided grin on her face. "But that doesn't mean I can't enjoy it anyway. My sister says I was born in the wrong generation. I grew up obsessed with retro game systems."

"I can tell." Lauren pointed at her T-shirt.

And then Hayley blushed. It started at the base of her neck and swept across her face. It was the most adorable thing Lauren had ever seen. And that's when it hit her, what she found unsettling about Hayley. She didn't take anything seriously. She let everything wash off her back like it was no big deal. It was the same attitude Ramiro had, which was probably why he'd hired her in the first place.

Lauren turned away from Hayley, disappointed not in Hayley but herself. When had she become her mother?

Growing up, Lauren hadn't noticed how much of her life her mother had controlled. It wasn't until after she died and when Lauren's dreams were cast adrift that she'd realized they were her mom's dreams. Her whole life she'd been living her mom's life; she'd just never known it until that guidance was gone.

Every activity and class she'd ever taken was because it's what her mom wanted, although at the time Lauren had thought it was her idea. Even though she hated ballet, she'd spent six years doing it until finally her ballet instructor had pulled her mother aside and told her Lauren had no talent and that no amount of practice would help. The truth was, she could see what Lauren couldn't, that she didn't have the drive to be talented.

Lauren had applied to the university her mom wanted her to for the courses her mom wanted her to take. Lauren wouldn't have known what to do with a business degree if she'd gotten one.

When Lauren was eleven, she'd asked to take a baking class. Her best friend's mom used to decorate these elaborate cakes, and Lauren and Tracy would sit at the breakfast bar watching Mrs. Gardner sculpt amazing fantasy worlds out of nothing more than melted marshmallows and icing sugar. It was a revelation to watch her work, and Lauren wanted to be able to create something out of nothing.

Her mother had told her baking was for the Dark Ages. No self-respecting woman should spend her time in the kitchen baking. She could see her mother's expression perfectly—lips poised in a straight line, her red lipstick perfectly applied as she uttered the word frivolous.

Lauren still loved creating beautifully intricate cakes; she'd had to teach herself over the years. It had gotten easier with YouTube and the endless treasure trove of tutorials. But she didn't really broadcast her interest, because somehow she felt like she was betraying her mother's wishes. Without even knowing it, she'd internalized her mother's issues and made them her own.

CHAPTER NINE

Hayley tightened her arms around her chest. As cool as her leather jacket was, it had no warmth at all. The zipper had split last year, and she had no idea if it could be replaced or how much that would cost. Besides, it was vintage, and you didn't mess with vintage.

She hadn't thought to bring her winter jacket, which was sitting in a closet back home. She'd ask Kalini if it was okay if her parents sent her stuff there. They still thought she was living with her and Jason, and she didn't want them to know otherwise. Not until she got a better place.

The leaves were just starting to turn those brilliant shades of fall. She took a deep breath. This was her favourite time of year—after the heat waves but before the snow fell. You could be comfortable during the day, although at night it was chilly. Tomorrow she'd bring an extra sweater to layer up until she got a warmer jacket.

As she rounded the corner, she spotted a cop car parked up on the curb in front of the Palace Arms. Hayley skirted around it. Nobody was inside, but the lights were still twirling, sending red and blue blotches dancing on the pink building. As sad as it was to say, seeing a cruiser parked next to the building was a regular occurrence. After the third day in a row coming home and seeing the red and blues, she'd lost all her anxiety.

The F-word floated down from upstairs as Hayley opened the door. That would be Dunne. She could tell his gravelly voice anywhere. A few years ago he'd gotten punched in the throat by one of the other guests and hadn't talked normally since. He was her closest neighbour, and as far as she could tell, he was a giant teddy bear. A barely functioning alcoholic, but always a friendly drunk.

Right now he was yelling at someone for going through someone's personal stuff. He stopped speaking as someone talking much lower responded to him. She climbed the last flight to see a group of people standing outside her door.

She stopped.

A tall female officer, Ed, and Dunne were standing in a semicircle around her open door. Light was streaming out, and both Dunne and the lady cop were speaking to someone inside. Her heart started pounding. Why were the cops in her room? Had someone called them saying she had drugs? She didn't, but what if someone had left some behind?

Dunne saw her first, and he looked so relieved she thought he might faint. He was in his nighttime uniform of a dingy-brown terrycloth housecoat and Mr. Rogers-type house slippers. His hands were jammed into his pockets, stretching the fabric at his shoulders, revealing a tear in the seam.

"Oh, thank fuck. Hayley, get over here. They're messing with your stuff." He rubbed the top of his head. He was bald except for a ring of curly salt-and-pepper hair around the nape of his neck.

"What's going on?"

The female cop stepped farther into the hall. "Are you the occupant of this room?" she asked.

Hayley nodded. She peered in to see a male officer on his hands and knees with half his arm down the air vent. "What's going on?" Hayley almost didn't want to ask. This all looked so bad.

The policewoman guided Hayley to the right, positioning herself so Hayley had her back to her room. "I'm Officer Ragasa. We were called in on a noise complaint an hour ago. You're Hayley Cavello?"

Hayley turned to look back in her room. Her mattress was overturned and slashed up, and most of the fabric had been torn off, exposing the springs underneath.

"Don't worry about that right now."

How could she not worry about that? Her money had been under that mattress. What had they done with her money?

Dunne walked up beside her and took a flask out of his housecoat pocket. He unscrewed the top and offered Hayley a sip. She shook her head. Dunne shrugged and took a nip.

"Sir?" the officer Ragasa asked. "Can you please put the alcohol away?"

"Why? This is my place of residence. I've retired for the evening. Or I would've." He waved in the vague direction of Hayley's room. "If that shithead hadn't ruined my peaceful evening."

"What's going on, Dunne? What happened to my room?"

"Alan happened to your room."

"The guy below me?"

Dunne nodded. "He came home mad about something and kept banging on people's doors. Your door must have popped open. I found him in there going nuts with your stuff."

"Where's he now?"

"He took off when Ed called the cops. Who knows where he is now? Probably coming down from his high."

"Got it," the cop yelled from inside Hayley's room. He came into the hall holding a serrated hunting knife.

"That's not mine," said Hayley. The thing looked like it could kill just by being near it.

"It's Alan's," said Dunne. "I saw him drop it down there before he took off. He was screaming something about blue mice in the vents."

Hayley took a step toward her room, then stopped and looked back at Ragasa. "Can I go in?"

Ragasa motioned her forward. "Please. Take a look around and see if anything's missing."

The only thing Hayley cared about was her money. She stepped inside and froze. The place had been torn apart. Not that there was a lot of furniture—just a bed, her dresser, and a chair she'd used as a holding place for worn clothes. All the drawers in her dresser had been pulled and thrown upside down on the floor, scattering her clothes. The chair wasn't even in the room anymore, and her mattress was on its side ripped to shreds.

The first thing she did was kneel under the bed and check for her money. She'd kept it in an envelope between the mattress and box spring. Not the best place for it, but she'd meant to put it in the bank. She'd just never gotten around to it. She'd almost had enough for rent this week. Two more days of tips and she would've been fine for another week.

She reached her hand underneath the bed and felt around. There was no envelope. Only dust.

The next thing she checked was her laptop bag. Her computer was still there, zipped tight.

"Is anything missing?"

Hayley turned. Ragasa was blocking the doorway while the other cop spoke with Ed.

"Yes. I had a hundred and thirty dollars in an envelope."

The woman pursed her lips and made a note in her pad. Hayley was thankful she refrained from telling her it was a stupid place to keep her money. "Anything else missing?"

"Not that I can tell right now."

"Okay. We'll most likely pick up Alan sometime within the next twenty-four hours. He still has a room in the building, and it's likely he'll come back." She held up her hand to stop Hayley from speaking. "However, it's unlikely we'll recover your money. I don't want to get your hopes up, but he's probably spent it. And if we do find money, it will be a long time before you'll be able to claim it."

"But why?"

"It'll be very hard to prove that's your money. Alan could say it's his, and since no one saw him take it, it's your word against his."

"And you'll take his word over mine?" Hayley was on the verge of tears. All of this was so unfair.

Ragasa's shoulders dropped and she entered the room. "I know it's frustrating. Can I offer some advice?"

"Don't keep my money under a dusty mattress in a shitty hotel?"

Ragasa sighed and offered a sad smile. "Also? Find a better place to stay soon."

"It was this or the streets."

Ragasa bit her lip. Hayley got the impression Ragasa saw too much of this in her job. What a shitty job to have to deal with the worst in people all day. She handed Hayley a business card with her name, badge, and phone number on it. "If you notice anything else is missing, give me a call. I'll touch base in a few days to update you on what's happening. But..."

"But I'm basically up Schitt's Creek, right?"

"'Fraid so."

"Great." Hayley stared at the remains of her room. She tried so hard not to, but all she could think about was how things couldn't get any worse. She didn't want to make it a coherent thought because that's when things would get so much worse.

❖

"Come on, Ed. Please."

Ed was in his signature Hawaiian shirt, a coffee in one hand and a cigarette in the other. She'd found him out back hiding the next morning, no doubt trying to avoid this very conversation.

"I have people I have to answer to. This isn't just me sitting behind a desk making my own decisions."

"I was robbed. Alan has your rent."

"No, nope." He stabbed his cigarette in Hayley's direction. "It's not my rent until you give it to me. Right now, it's Alan's money, and as long as he pays his money at the end of the week, I don't care where it comes from."

"Are you serious? How can you be such a jerk to my face? You know he stole it from me."

Ed shook his head back and forth several times. "I told you this was not a place for girls."

"I am not a girl. I am a woman. Do people continuously go around calling you a boy?" Hayley was starting to build up steam. She pulled herself up to her full five feet six inches and jabbed a finger right in the centre of one of Ed's pineapples. "No. You get to be a man. All guys get to be men. Why can't I have the same fucking courtesy? I am a fucking woman."

Ed held a hand up in surrender. "Okay, okay. Jesus Christ. I'll float you a week." He dropped his cigarette at his feet and stubbed it out with his toe. "But you owe three hundred at the end of next week."

"Thanks," Hayley mumbled as she stalked off toward the diner.

"Goddamned feminists," Ed cursed quietly, but Hayley still heard. She decided she didn't have it in her for round two.

❖

Hayley was in a foul mood the rest of the day. She'd just found out she wasn't going to get paid until the end of the month because she'd started after the last pay period, which meant she wouldn't have the three hundred dollars to give Ed next week. She still had another week after that, and who knew how big her paycheque would actually be?

Ramiro pulled his jacket off its hook. "Shrug it off, Pollyanna. Tomorrow will be better."

"That's what they say."

"And 'they' is usually right."

She hadn't told anyone at work about getting robbed last night. She didn't want them knowing she lived at the Palace Arms. It was bad enough that she was on the verge of being kicked out of the low-rent hotel in the first place, but to prove everyone who'd said she didn't belong there right? Well, that was too much.

"If you ever need to talk about anything, you can tell us. We're like a family here. We take care of our own."

Hayley nodded. She was tempted to say something. Ramiro and everyone at the diner had been nothing but welcoming, which she appreciated because she'd needed that more than even she knew. But this situation felt too personal a thing to share with someone she'd known only a little over a week.

Ramiro shrugged into his jacket, grabbed his crutches, and shoved off from the counter. "Well, I'm off. I'll see you tomorrow."

"See you."

"Bye, sweetums."

"Don't call me that."

Hayley smiled. She loved listening to Lauren and Ramiro banter. They were like an old married couple, and she found that thought comforting for some reason. Imagining that they were the mom and pop of the diner, and the rest of them were the kids, really did make it feel like a family.

Hayley went back to closing up for the day. She scrapped the griddle, turned it off, and began wiping down the counters. A loud crash from below stopped her.

"What the hell was that?" Hayley grabbed the broom leaning against the sink and stepped out into the dining area.

Lauren placed the debit receipts on the counter, her eyes wide. Another crash. They both stood there for a moment, and then Lauren exhaled in disgust. "Damn…damn, damn." She collected the receipts and placed them in a bag, along with the cash and credit receipts.

"What's going on?" Hayley asked as Lauren stood and grabbed the broom from her. She followed Lauren down into the basement on stairs that reminded Hayley of every horror film she'd ever been forced to watch. They were warped from decades of use and announced each foot with a loud groan.

"The window in the basement doesn't latch properly. I've been asking Aaron for months to get someone in to check it out, but he keeps putting me off because the windows are so small not many people could squeeze through them."

Hayley followed close behind Lauren, her apprehension mounting with each step. Lauren, for her part, had taken on a kind of badassery that was sort of hot. Okay, more than a little hot. It almost made up for the fact that a homicidal clown with a fetish for diner food was going to murder them.

"But, unfortunately," Lauren said as they reached the bottom of the stairs, "sometimes the racoons find a way in." Lauren flicked on the light. Several sets of eyes froze. A family of four—a mom, dad, and two babies—had cracked open a bag of potatoes and were feasting on them raw. In the process they'd managed to knock over a tower of boxes containing napkins, paper take-out containers, and a box of mugs, which had shattered on the cement floor.

Lauren smacked the broom on the ground and then waved it toward them. One of the racoons, presumably the mother, hissed at her.

"Block the stairs so they can't get up into the restaurant." Lauren walked over to the window and propped it open with a paint stir-stick. "I'm going to try to shoo them back out the window." She took up the broom again, wielding it like a hockey stick.

"Don't racoons have rabies?"

Lauren shrugged like this was the least of their problems. "Some. Just don't let them bite you." Lauren took a step forward, and the mama racoon hissed again.

"No big deal." But Hayley felt like it was a very big deal. She grabbed a toilet-bowl brush—the only thing she could find—and took up position blocking the stairs. Lauren worked her way toward the furry, hissing bandits. She'd tied her hair up in a messy bun earlier, and Hayley thought she looked like those women warriors from myths who strode into battle without fear of the consequences. Okay, maybe that was going a bit far. No one here was going to die, unless they got rabies, and even then, Hayley wasn't sure if you could die from rabies. But Lauren was doing all sorts of things for Hayley right now.

Hayley mentally slapped herself. Lauren was her boss. Lauren was straight. And Hayley didn't lust after straight women. She'd been down that road, and it was littered with broken hearts, booby traps, and land mines.

Hayley inched back, ready to act as the cheerleading section when needed. And she hoped that's all she'd be needed for. Unfortunately, the racoons had different ideas. One of the babies fell off the boxes and panicked, running toward Hayley. She shrieked in a way she was sure would've gotten her kicked out of the strong-ass-women club and threw the toilet brush at it. The racoon, which couldn't have been bigger than a teapot, squealed and ran in the opposite direction back toward its family.

Lauren pushed the broom toward it to corral it into the corner, where she was trying to coax them up a pipe next to the basement window.

"Should we call animal control?" Hayley's sole experience with racoons was when her dad had accidentally hit one while driving home from one of her school plays late at night. It had been a quick thud, but the next day she'd seen the crumpled remains on the side of the road. It looked like someone had dropped their teddy bear and forgotten it.

Lauren slammed the door to the storage closet shut to keep them from escaping into the enclosed space. "It would take forever for them to get here. This is easier."

"I take it this isn't your first experience with racoons."

Lauren laughed. "I grew up here. You name it, I've dealt with it. They're intelligent, tenacious, and a pain in the butt."

Evidently deciding they'd had enough, one of the parents lifted the closest baby onto her back and began to scale the pipe. Seeing this move, the other adult racoon followed suit, and soon the basement was quiet. A mess, but quiet.

"Well, fuck. That was new." Hayley bent to pick up the toilet brush and place it back in the washroom.

Lauren only nodded, busy assessing the damage. She looked lost and tired and completely drained.

"Since you already have a broom, I'll go get the dustpan."

Lauren waved her off. "It's okay. You don't have to stay and help clean up. I'll take care of this."

"By yourself? That's hardly fair."

"Seeing as how Aaron would kill me if I let you go into overtime...I don't have much choice."

"Are you saying I'm off the clock?" Hayley grabbed the broom from Lauren.

Lauren checked her watch. "Your shift ended about five minutes ago."

"And I'm sure yours ended around the same time." Hayley knew Lauren had been there since the morning shift, and she doubted Aaron okayed her overtime. Even if she was paid more, it still wasn't fair to make her clean up the mess by herself. "Seeing as how I've got nothing else to do tonight, why don't you just say, 'Thank you, Hayley. I would love the help.'"

Lauren's smile was tired but brilliant all the same. "Thank you, Hayley. I would love the help."

Chapter Ten

H e hates me."

Theo gave an exaggerated eye roll. "Ezra hates everybody."

"But he hates me more."

This was only Hayley's second time working with Theo, but you'd never know it. The two had bonded over Donkey Kong and Super Nintendo's Super Buster Bros ten minutes into working together, and it was as if they'd known each other for years.

"I spilled hollandaise sauce on his shirt." Hayley was getting much better in the kitchen; she'd almost mastered the entire menu, although the close quarters were still a challenge. Yesterday she'd turned when she should've pivoted, and Ezra's shirt was one of the casualties of that mistake.

"Ouch. He'll hate you for life now."

She punched him playfully on the arm.

"No. I'm serious. You're in his shit books for good now." He laughed and dodged her next swipe. Theo laughed a lot. Like Ramiro, he had this easy-going nature about him. He didn't sweat the small stuff, as Hayley's dad liked to say. Besides Ezra, most of the kitchen staff had an easy-going nature, and she had a feeling Ramiro liked to hire with that quality in mind. It's probably why he decided to take a chance on her. Hayley's optimism had helped her out more times than she could remember.

They worked side by side happily. Theo was the best because he gave her the most to do. Ramiro wasn't bad, but he tended to hover and teach too much. She preferred Theo's method. He let her screw up first and then let her figure out how to fix it. That method was slower, but she learned more.

Hayley watched as Theo dropped two waffles out of the waffle maker by turning the handle quickly and tapping the top with a spatula. One day Hayley wished she could be so smooth. "So how long have you worked here?"

Theo shrugged. "Dunno. Since high school. My sister used to be a server here and helped get me the job. But then she went on to university, and I stuck around here instead." He smirked, a mischievous twinkle in his eyes. "School and I don't mix."

A kid squealed from up front, followed by a loud crash.

Lauren stepped into the kitchen and grabbed a broom. Hayley's eyes lingered a little too long on Lauren's back as she rushed back out. She'd had a dream about Lauren last night. The naughty kind. Ever since their encounter with the raccoons the other evening, Lauren had been in her thoughts a little too often.

"So what's the deal with Lauren?" Hayley asked as she plated a chicken burger. Her patty missed the bun and flipped onto the counter.

"Oh, so are we going to do the girlfriend thing now?" Theo fixed his beanie and arranged his facial features in a vaguely feminine way, fluttering his eyelashes, puckering his lips, and feathering nonexistent hair. "Okay. I'm ready. Go."

Hayley raised her eyebrows in question.

"You've got a thing for Lauren. Dish."

Hayley's face pinked. "I don't have a thing for her. I was just wondering what her deal was. That's all."

"Give it up, girlfriend. She's straight." He paused and looked up at the ceiling. "At least I think she is. She's never dated anyone as far as I know. But Lily's always trying to set her up with men. So ditch any ideas you have of swooping in and wooing her."

Hayley placed the tongs she'd been using to add sauerkraut to a plate of bratwurst on the counter and turned to face Theo fully. "First of all, I don't have a thing for Lauren. That's like shitting where you eat. And second," she waved a finger at him to emphasize her point, "I've learned the no-straight-girls lesson the hard way, and that's like going into a burning casino to gamble with paper money."

Luna slammed her hand on the windowsill. "Where's my German farmer out to sea?"

Theo reached around Hayley and glided the plate of bratwurst toward Luna. "Here you go, bossy."

"It's getting busy, so you're going to have to start picking it up." She grabbed the plate and twirled away.

When Theo turned back to Hayley, she was grinning at him. "What?" he asked.

"You two are screwing."

"Ugh. First of all, we're not. And second, screwing is such a filthy term. You need to come up with something better."

"Like fucking? Doesn't matter what term I use, you two are doing it."

Theo slapped his hand to his chest. "A gentleman—"

"Which you are not."

"Never tells."

"Mmm-hmm." Hayley wasn't convinced. She stepped over to the fryer and loaded a batch of fries into the basket, smiling the entire time. She even started humming the tune to *The Love Boat*, which seemed to aggravate Theo.

He caved in less than thirty seconds. "Okay. We hooked up once. After last year's staff Christmas party. It was a one-time thing, so believe me when I say sleeping with people you work with is not a good idea."

Hayley set the timer for the fries. "Duh. But from the looks of things, you enjoyed it and want to hit that again."

It was Theo's turn to smack Hayley in the arm. "What are you? A locker-room jock?"

Hayley laughed loudly. "Are you one of those guys who uses the term 'make love'? Please tell me you're not."

Theo sighed, plating a burger with a side salad and placed it on the sill. "I know she seems—"

"Like a stuck-up bitch?"

"Hey. I wasn't going to say that."

"You didn't, but I did."

"She's just shy."

"Oh, don't give me that bullshit. She thinks she's better than everyone. I see nothing but heartache in your future, my man."

Theo plopped two patties on the griddle. "Funny. I see the same outlook in your future."

Hayley rolled her eyes. "Whatever."

But now that she was aware of her crush, everything about Lauren was enhanced. The subtle florals of her shampoo filled her senses when she walked past her to start her shift. The way she flicked her bangs to the side as she took a customer's order. How she bit down on her lip when she was thinking about something. During lulls, Lauren would sit at the back booth and do the crossword in the *Globe*, twirling the pencil between her thumb and forefinger and biting down on her lip. Hayley would watch from the kitchen, mesmerized.

She was aware it would never lead anywhere. She needed this job, and besides, Lauren was most likely straight, and she didn't want to be that girl. She'd decided it was a harmless crush, but in the meantime, there was no harm in admiring from afar.

❖

"Lauren," Vic called. "You've got a gentleman caller." She wiped her hands on a cloth and pointed to the stiff in a suit standing at the register in front of her.

Lauren dropped off the plates she was carrying to the couple in the middle booth and headed to the register. A heavy weight settled in the base of her stomach as she neared. One glance at him, and she knew he was the inspector Aaron had sent over. He had a look about him, barely over the age of thirty and already bone weary. Everything about him was generic, from the black tie to the cheap black suit and white-collared shirt, even the clipboard tucked under his arm.

He stuck his hand out for Lauren. "Civan Keyzer. You must be…" He checked the paper on his clipboard. "Lauren Hames."

He pumped her hand a few times, then let his fingers slip out. His hands were sweaty. "That's me." She pulled him farther into the diner, out of the way of traffic. "Aaron said you wanted to inspect the building. What is it that you need from me?"

He looked around, almost nervous at being in such a busy place. He brushed at his upper lip. "For the diner, almost nothing. I prefer to look around on my own. However," he wiped his palm on the front of his tie, smoothing it down the front of his shirt, "for the apartment above, I would need access to that. It's my understanding that you live there?"

"My apartment? Why do you need to see my place?" Aaron hadn't said anything about letting a stranger poke around her things.

"It's part of the building. I need to inspect the entire thing if I'm going to create a report."

Lauren bit the inside of her cheek. Aaron owned the building, which made him her landlord. She couldn't refuse. He had a right to inspect the place, and he'd given her fair warning that the man was coming. "All right. Can you do the diner first? We're finishing up the lunch rush, and I'm needed down here for a bit longer."

He looked around, observing the busy tables and general hubbub. "I was hoping to do your apartment first. It'll be much easier when less people are around."

Lauren huffed. Vic could probably handle the place for a few minutes. She waved at Vic to get her attention. "I gotta step out. He needs to take a look at my apartment."

Vic raised her eyebrows. "Whatever they're calling it these days, honey, it's none of my business."

"Oh, get your mind out of the gutter. I'll be back soon."

"I've had men take less time."

Lauren's cheeks flamed red. Vic always managed to embarrass her somehow. Didn't matter how long they'd known each other, Vic always found a way.

From top to bottom the entire inspection had taken a little over an hour. When he was at the door about to leave, Lauren asked, "Is Aaron planning on selling the building?"

Civan clicked his pen and placed it in the top of his clipboard. "I have no idea."

"But that's usually why people get inspections done."

"Yes, that is one reason, but people also have their places inspected before doing renovations. Aaron didn't confide his reason for the inspection. Sorry," he added before letting the door close.

Damn. The idea of Aaron wanting to renovate this place was about as likely as the Leafs winning the cup this year.

❖

Hayley's rent was due tomorrow. Three hundred dollars. And she didn't have it. She wasn't even close. The most she'd been able to save in the last few days was sixty-five dollars, and that was only because she hadn't bought anything since last week and they'd had a really great tipping day yesterday.

She ate at the diner only when she worked, which meant on her day off she had nothing unless she smuggled out some day-olds and cheese. Part of her was so stressed and worried that she would be on the street in a couple of days, and another part was wondering why she was putting up with this. She had an easy solution. She could go back to Casper Falls. But the idea of failing before she'd even started was scarier than living on the street.

She had one last option. Asking for an advance on her first paycheque. She hated even the idea. Her mom used to complain about that at the store. It sent such a horrible impression, but she had no choice.

"Lauren?" Hayley approached Lauren, who was sitting in the last booth working a crossword puzzle. She was back on morning shift, and it was their first lull of the day. Lauren bit the inside of her cheek as she gazed up at Hayley, who wasn't sure if the butterflies in her stomach were from the way Lauren's eyes looked in this light, like chocolate-coloured glass, or from what she was about to ask.

"You know video games, right? Luigi archrival? Seven letters, second letter A."

Hayley dropped into the booth across from her. "Please tell me you're kidding."

"I never played video games when I was a kid."

Hayley slapped her hand to her chest. "What kind of childhood did you have? Were you locked in a closet?" She paused, horrified with what she'd just said. "You weren't, right? Please tell me you weren't." This was not a good start to asking for money from your boss.

Lauren laughed. "No. And I had a perfectly normal childhood without video games."

"Debatable." Hayley flipped the crossword around and held out her hand for the pencil. "May I?" When Lauren nodded and handed her the pencil, she filled the word "Waluigi" in the boxes.

Lauren peered over at the answer. "Yeah. I'd never have gotten that. I've never heard of Waluigi."

"He's Wario's doubles partner in *Mario Tennis*."

"That sounds like important information to know." Lauren smirked and slid the puzzle back in front of her.

"It sure is. Your puzzle would've gone unfinished without it." She had just a hint of flirtation in her voice. She placed Lauren's pencil in front of her and rolled it toward her.

"True." Lauren pushed her crossword puzzle aside. "So, did you just come over here to save my puzzle, or do you have an ulterior motive?"

Hayley drummed a beat on the tabletop, building up her nerve to get out what she wanted to ask. She'd rehearsed it a couple times in the kitchen, but now that she was sitting in front of Lauren, she was finding it hard. "So here's the thing. I was wondering if it were possible to get an advance on my first paycheque." She looked up with hope. "It's not something I normally would ask for. It's just that my rent for this week got...I had some bad luck this week. That's all."

Lauren placed her hand on the table between them. "I'm sorry you're having bad luck this week. And if it were up to me, I would. But Aaron handles the cheques for payroll, and he's really strict about advances. I'm sorry."

Hayley nodded quickly and stood looking away. Her eyes prickled with tears, and she didn't want Lauren to see her tear up. "Okay. I understand. Thanks." As she walked away she could've sworn she heard Lauren groan, but she didn't turn around. Instead she made a beeline for the kitchen.

She was working with Ezra today. He was wearing a dark-blue shirt that was so tight Hayley wondered if he had his clothes tailored.

Later, as Hayley was finishing her shift, Lauren tapped her on the arm and pulled her aside. "How much do you need for rent? Maybe I could loan you some money."

Hayley backed away. "No thanks. I'll be fine." She'd rather be homeless than take a loan from her boss. It was different when it was an advance. That was something she was earning. But she'd never feel she'd earned a handout.

"No, really. If I can help, I'd like to."

Hayley grabbed her bag. "I'll manage." She slipped past Lauren. She couldn't get out of there fast enough.

CHAPTER ELEVEN

Dunne caught Hayley as she was coming around the corner. He was in his going-to-grab-a-pack-of-cigarettes uniform, ratty old jeans, a grey cardigan with holes in the elbows, and a ripped leather jacket.

"Ed's looking for you."

"Shit."

"You short?"

She nodded. She was more than short. She'd managed to make another sixteen bucks in tips today, but that wasn't going to help.

"Can I spot you some? How much are you short?"

Hayley looked up at the kind, unfocused eyes staring back at her. This was the second offer she'd had today, but for some reason it meant more coming from Dunne. She knew he didn't have any to spare. "That's really amazing of you, but I couldn't take money from you."

"Sure, you can. What else are you going to do? Sleep in the park?"

She patted his arm. "I owe him three hundred bucks, and I don't even have a third of that. I'll avoid him tonight and then think of something tomorrow."

"Yeah. He's removed your stuff from your room and locked you out. I put it in my room, but unless you pay him what you owe, he won't let you sleep in your room tonight."

Hayley groaned. She hadn't counted on Ed being such a hard-ass. What a naive thing to think. He dealt with people way more cunning and devious than her every day. She couldn't sleep in the park. It was too cold for that, and a shelter was out of the question. Maybe she could call Kalini and ask to sleep on the couch? The only other people she knew were at the diner, and she didn't know any of them well enough to ask them to couch-surf.

Dunne tugged on her arm. "Have you eaten? I know a great little diner around the corner. They have the best bratwurst in this part of the city. My treat."

"Greta's?"

"That's the place."

"That's where I work. No offence, but I don't feel like hanging out there after I've already been there since five a.m."

"That's where you work?"

Hayley let her hands fall to her sides. "For now."

"Okay. I have an idea where we still get to eat but don't have to sit in the diner to do it."

Hayley followed Dunne down the street. He had her wait at the entrance to the park while he grabbed takeout from Greta's. Hayley stood under the giant archway that led to the park. Two large iron gates were pulled open and fastened to two poles sticking out of the ground. The light was just beginning to fade. She watched as Dunne dodged a streetcar and met her under the arch holding a large white take-out bag.

"Come on. I know the perfect spot to eat these." He led her through the gates and down the path.

Trinity was one of the bigger parks in the city. It had tennis courts, baseball diamonds, and a large off-leash dog park at the bottom of the ravine. On Saturdays in the warmer months, there was a farmer's market on the north side, rain or shine, and so many trees it was almost like entering a tiny forest.

Dunne led her to a picnic table overlooking the dog park and climbed up so he was sitting on the table with his feet on the bench. He set down the bag and patted a spot next to him. Hayley climbed up and sat with the bag between them.

From this vantage point they could see the entire north side of the park. It was beautiful this time of year, most of the trees yellow and red, with only a few having lost their leaves.

Two dogs were chasing each other around the dog park, their owners off to the side chatting. It was peaceful, the perfect spot to take a break from the city.

Dunne pulled out the takeout and opened the container: three large bratwurst covered in sauerkraut gleamed in the light overhead. Dunne cut one of the bratwurst in half and stuffed the other into his mouth. The juice spilled out, sliding down his chin. "I just fucking love these things. They're one of the best things about living at the Palace." He scooped up some sauerkraut and shoved it into his still-half-full mouth.

Hayley picked up one of the forks and stabbed a bratwurst. She'd had three of these already today, but it didn't matter. They were so good she could probably live on them.

Dunne pulled a flask from his pocket and took a swig. He offered some to Hayley, but she shook her head.

They ate in silence, watching night descend on the park. By the time they'd crumpled their napkins and shoved them in the bag, the lampposts that dotted the path had come on. A twilight mist had invaded the park, making the lights glow like amber fairy lights.

"Has anyone told you about the white squirrels yet?"

"White squirrels?"

"Yeah. This is the only place in the city they live."

"You're messing with me."

Dunne hopped down from the bench and tossed their garbage in the bin. "Ask anyone. Or better yet, google it."

"Have you ever seen one?"

"Only once. A long time ago."

"Go on. This sounds like there's a story behind it."

Dunne motioned for her to follow him. "I ever tell you about Jill?"

Hayley followed, shaking her head.

"Jill was my wife."

Hayley couldn't picture Dunne married, but then she knew only this version of him. According to Ed, he'd had a whole life before becoming an alcoholic and landing himself at the Palace Arms.

"We met on a beautiful fall day back in the early nineties. I'd just graduated and was at the first adult job I'd ever had. I used to live up on Wallace and would take a shortcut through the park on my way home from work. On this day I was walking through the park, and I looked over, and there it was, a white squirrel sitting on the back of a bench eating a granola bar from a woman's hand." He took a swig from his flask. "Fuck, Hayley. This woman was gorgeous. No." He waved his hands in the air. "Gorgeous doesn't even do her justice. She was a goddess. Her silky red hair was loose around her shoulders, the wind blowing it. Her green eyes were like emeralds, and her smile…" He held his hand to his heart, a sad, misty smile on his face. "God. Her smile was enough to melt your bones. I walked up to her to ask about the squirrel, and she told me they liked the trail-mix granola bars the best. And that was it. I was smitten."

"That was Jill?"

"Yep. We got married a year later. I've never seen another white squirrel since."

They walked in silence for a few minutes, looping around the park, taking the south path back. Hayley was afraid to ask what happened. Obviously they weren't together anymore.

"It's okay. You can ask."

Hayley kicked a branch out of the way. "What happened?"

"She got ovarian cancer. It was quick, so I know she didn't suffer." He took another sip from his flask and offered some to Hayley, who again declined. "It was about ten years ago now. But nothing's been the same since."

Hayley didn't know what to say, so instead she took a sip from his flask when he offered it again. This seemed to make him happy.

She still had her doubts. It wasn't that the possibility of albino squirrels was fantastical. It was that this was the only place they lived in the city. The city had tons of parks, and this wasn't even the biggest one, although she hadn't been to any of the others. Hayley's world had sucked her into this small neighbourhood, which tended to happen in the city. People rarely ventured out of their worlds. They became too safe and comfortable, and this area was definitely becoming comforting to Hayley.

She followed Dunne through the park. "Thanks for dinner."

"It was my pleasure. I'd like to think I'd introduced you to one of the finer things in this city, but seeing as how you work there, I kinda failed."

"Well, the companionship was very welcome." They came to the edge of the park. The night was one of the milder ones they'd experienced, but still too cold to sleep outside.

As if reading her mind Dunne asked, "Have you thought about where you're going to sleep tonight?"

She shook her head. He said it so normally, like asking where you wanted to go for drinks. He'd probably spent a good chunk of his life in this situation himself. Dunne had shared a few things about himself. A work accident several years earlier had put him on disability, which didn't amount to much. Money was always tight, and he was one bad decision away from being on the street himself.

Across from them the diner glowed in the night. It was getting close to closing. Luna and Theo were working. Maybe she could talk Theo into letting her spend the night in the diner. He might let her. Or he might ask her a million questions she didn't want to answer. Was there a way she could stay there without anyone knowing?

There was the basement window that didn't latch properly. If she could sneak in before the alarm was set, she could hide out in the supply closet and wait until everyone left. The alarm system was simple, no motion sensors or anything, so if she was already inside once they locked up, she'd be good until morning.

Hayley looked up at Dunne with a wicked smile. "Yeah. I think I just might have found a place. Can I grab some of my stuff from your room?"

He looked reluctant. "Sure. You're not actually going to sleep in the park, are you?"

"No. Don't worry. I'll be perfectly safe." She didn't want to tell him in case he tried to talk her out of it.

Thirty minutes later she was peering down at the basement window. Hayley didn't have to worry about making too much noise. Theo would be in the kitchen with music blaring and wouldn't hear a five-piece band if it were playing in the basement.

The window, located down a side alley where the garbage cans were kept, looked smaller from the outside. If she couldn't squeeze through, she was out of options. The bell from the front door of the diner dinged. It was the same alley Luna used for smoke breaks. Hayley pushed all her nerves deep. This was the perfect time to sneak in, while she knew Luna was occupied out here. If Luna spotted her, would she know what Hayley was up to? Probably. Luna wasn't dumb. Even Ezra begrudgingly agreed she was one of their best servers. She never forgot orders or missed substitutions.

Before Luna could turn the corner, Hayley opened the window and lowered her backpack in, then turned and fed her feet through the opening. On her stomach she pushed herself backward through the window. Before she could drop out of sight her shirt got caught on a sharp edge of brick. At the front of the alley Luna stopped to light a cigarette. Hayley yanked her shirt as hard as she could, tearing the fabric as she dropped to the basement floor, landing with a loud thud on her ass.

The tear had completely destroyed her Bob-omb T-shirt, one of her favourites. "Ugh. That sucked." She opened the top of her backpack and pulled out a sweater.

Now that she was in the basement, she wasn't exactly sure what to do next. When Theo and Luna were done, they'd lock up and set the alarm, and because she was already inside, she didn't have to worry about it because there were no motion sensors. But she should get out of sight before they left.

The basement was dark and dank. She pulled out her phone and turned on her flashlight. There was a washroom and a storage closet, and that was all. She wasn't sure what was in the storage closet because it was always locked. She couldn't risk hiding in the bathroom in case one of them came down to use it or clean it, although the latter was unlikely.

The only place left for Hayley to hide was in the small space between the back wall and the stairs. If she moved a couple of boxes aside, she could squeeze in beside them. As it turned out, it was perfect. From her vantage point she could see the hall and the bathroom but wasn't visible. Now she just had to wait. Hayley checked her phone—nine twenty-five. It didn't usually take more than forty-five minutes to close up.

She settled her things around her and laid her head back against the wall. Dunne had lent her a small blanket and an old backpack to keep her stuff in. It was better than lugging a giant suitcase around. When she came into some money, she'd have to take him out to dinner to pay him back for all this.

Hayley let the music upstairs wash over her and snuggled into her sweater, glad she'd thought to grab an extra one when she was selecting what to bring with her.

What felt like seconds later, Hayley jerked forward. Everything was dark and quiet. She must have fallen asleep. She pulled herself up and grabbed her backpack, listening for any sounds from upstairs. Nothing. The place was closed for the night.

When she reached the top of the stairs, she pushed open the door.

The place looked different at night. For some reason it reminded her of Christmas and sneaking down to have a peek at the tree. The clock above the counter read ten fifteen. They'd been gone for a while. She was reasonably confident that no one would be coming in until early the next morning, but she selected the back booth just in case.

Hayley pulled the blanket out of her bag and wrapped it around herself like a cocoon. She used the backpack as a pillow and settled in with the help of Gary Numan drifting through her headphones.

The sounds of the city floated into the diner, lulling her further— the clank of the streetcar going past, a fire truck and ambulance several streets away. Someone across the street yelled something and smashed a glass. These should be scary sounds, so foreign from her upbringing in Casper Falls. But they didn't scare her. In the short time she'd been in the city, they had become familiar, and it had become her home. She couldn't imagine moving back to Casper Falls now. Besides, the only thing there was the reminder of a horrible breakup. Okay, and her future niece or nephew, but that's what the Greyhound was for. She hated that she would be missing this big moment for Hannah, but for once in her life she needed to be selfish.

Hayley had always done exactly what her family wanted. And while they may have loved living in a small town, knowing the same people their whole lives, Hayley was bored. You could hear the same stories about the same old people only so many times.

When she'd told her parents she was leaving, they'd been upset. Not angry, just sad. That's what she loved about her family. They'd support her, she knew they would, but they would miss her, and that felt good.

Sleeping on a diner bench wasn't a warm bed in Casper Falls. She should be depressed right now. She was homeless and broke, but she wasn't depressed. All she could think of at that moment were the good things. She had a dry place tonight that wasn't the park or a doorway. She had a job, so this homelessness was only temporary, and she had people like Dunne in her life who were looking out for her. This situation sucked donkey balls, but at least it would pass.

Everything in her life had led her to believe that if you worked hard enough at something and trusted in yourself, things would smooth out. And they were. Sort of. She might not be where she wanted to be at this exact moment, but sometimes you had to slow down and enjoy the journey. It was like Ferris Bueller said, "Life moves pretty fast. If you don't stop to look around once in a while, you could miss it."

Well, that's all this was, an excuse to stop and have a look around. And when it was over, she'd appreciate her success all the more because she'd worked her ass off to get there. She remembered the first time she'd passed Super Mario 3—back before you could save games. She'd put her sweat, tears, and frustration into that game. It took her three months, but when she'd finally done it, the high lasted for days. This wasn't exactly comparable, but she knew if she just persevered, she'd be all the prouder when she made it. Besides, her life could be so much worse. She could be stuck in Casper Falls dealing with the fallout of her breakup with Violet.

Chapter Twelve

Lauren was five minutes late for her shift. She was never late for her shift. Living above work made that easy. Currently, Lauren's head was stuck under the sink dismantling the drain of her garburator. She'd thought she was disposing some eggshells, but when she'd flipped the switch, she'd heard a loud crack, followed by a grinding noise that had probably shaved years off her garburator.

"I shouldn't have started this before my shift," she said, her voice muffled by the cabinetry. Her phone was balanced on her knee playing a how-to-take-apart-your-garburator-if-you-accidentally-grind-something-you-shouldn't video. The man was saying you should never reach into a garbage disposal, because even if it wasn't sharp enough to rip your fingers off, it would still hurt.

"Gee, thanks for that bit of useful advice." She scrubbed forward with her finger until he got to the part about removing the unit from the sink. He demonstrated placing an Allen key in the hole at the base and turning it to loosen the unit. She did the same with hers. When she had it loose enough to stick her hand in, she reached up and pulled out a mangled ball with crumpled bells inside. As soon as it was free, a heavy ball of fluff and hair landed on her stomach.

"Ooof. God, you're heavy. One of these days I'm going to stop feeding you." The cat stared, his yellow-green eyes unrepentant. "How did this get in here? Huh, Jerkface?" She held the ball up a few inches from his nose, and in answer, he swatted at it. She huffed, shoving him off her lap to get changed for work. She was still in sweats from her morning off. She'd been experimenting with cake pops all morning. Halloween was coming up, and she was playing with making them look like ghosts. So far, her attempts had been passible, but not where she wanted them to be.

She rushed into her bedroom half out of her T-shirt and kicking off her pants and grabbed a fresh uniform out of the closet. Only after trying to zip it up did she realize she wasn't wearing a bra. Jerkface sauntered into the room and claimed his place at the head of the bed on the pillow next to hers. His hair took a few more seconds to settle around him.

"It's because of you I'm late."

Jerkface stretched a paw out and proceeded to lift his leg and groom his nether region. Lauren turned away in disgust. Sometimes she felt like she'd been had. She'd found him as a kitten between compost bins behind the diner and couldn't resist. His adorable little eyes had stared up at her with all the sweetness the little fur ball could muster, and she was a goner. That sweetness had lasted until the door had shut behind him. Then, as if he knew it was too late for Lauren to do anything, he claimed his domain with all the hauteur of a king claiming his throne. Hence the name Jerkface.

He was a menace to anything on a flat surface. He would go out of his way to knock things off shelves, especially if they had liquid in them or were made of glass. She'd had to install a child lock on her toilet because he somehow figured out how to open it and would drop random things he collected around the apartment into the basin. She was convinced he was sent to test her patience.

But in the end, he was right. She couldn't give him up. She was a glutton for that one percent of love and affection he gave her. At night when she'd had a bad day, she swore he could sense it because he would nestle into her stomach and purr up a storm.

She rooted through her drawers for a clean bra, shoved her arms through it, and ran into the bathroom still zipping up the back of her uniform. She opted for the fastest hairstyle she knew how to perform, which was taking a hair elastic and pulling her hair back into a ponytail a few times until she got a messy bun. It was less neat than she liked, but she didn't have time to comb her hair.

By the time she made it through the door, she was ten minutes late. Vic rushed past her as she entered. "I have to go. Jack didn't pick up Megan, and she's been sitting around waiting for someone to get her."

Lauren stepped into the kitchen to hang her jacket on her hook.

Ramiro was showing Hayley his fridge, something he took great pride in. Every new line cook and server got Ramiro's *mise-en-place* speech.

"If everything has its place, it makes everything run fast and smooth because you always know where to find something if you run out or if you're cleaning up after." They both had their heads stuck in the giant fridge at the back.

Hayley was wearing grey skinny jeans that hugged her ass like they were tailored for her. As soon as Lauren realized what she'd been doing—checking out Hayley's ass—she pulled her eyes up. Too late. Ramiro smirked and pointed at her as if to say, *I saw that.*

Lauren ignored him as she grabbed an apron and tied it around her waist, heading for the front.

❖

By seven o'clock the place was pretty dead, which was unusual for this time of day. Lauren sent Luna home early and tried not to worry it was a trend. It could be the cold weather. Today the air had that hint of snow on the wind. Part of her was thrilled. She loved Christmas, but the end of October was way too early for it to snow, not that it hadn't before. It just shouldn't. She had definite ideas about when snow was allowed to show itself and when it should stay the hell away. The week before Christmas was acceptable, but the week before Halloween was not.

Lauren stepped into the kitchen to tell Hayley she could head home for the evening but stopped when she saw what they were doing. Ramiro was sitting on a box full of tomato sauce with his cast propped up on Hayley's knee. She had a Sharpie in hand drawing an intricate design. Her whole face had transformed with intense concentration. Her lips were pursed, revealing two dimples, one on either side of her face. And every so often her nostrils would flare. She was so absorbed she obviously didn't notice Lauren approach.

"Pollyanna's tagging my cast." He chucked a thumb toward Hayley with a face that said, *Get a load of her.*

"Okay. I give. Why Pollyanna?"

Ramiro stared at Lauren like she'd worn the day's special instead of her uniform. "Hayley Mills? You never watched *Pollyanna* when you were a kid?"

Lauren shook her head.

"I worry about what kind of childhood you had."

"What about the *The Parent Trap*?" asked Hayley.

Lauren stepped closer and peered down at Ramiro's cast. What had looked like a geometric design turned out to be a giant dragon cooking a little mushroom guy in a frying pan. "The one with Lindsay Lohan?"

Hayley frowned. "No. The original, with Hayley Mills."

"My family wasn't big on movies when I was a kid." Lauren pointed to the drawing. "That's really good. Are you an artist?"

"Thanks. It's Bowser cooking Toad on the grill." She grinned. "I'm pretty good at copying stuff. Nothing serious."

"When you're done, you can head home."

"Home?" Hayley looked like she'd just found out eggs were the by-product of a hen's menstrual cycle.

"We're dead out there. No need for both of you to stick around."

Hayley nodded and returned to her drawing, but she seemed a lot less enthusiastic than Lauren would expect. Maybe it had something to do with money. Getting let go early would mean less hours and less money. Maybe she should've let Ramiro go early.

The bell rang, and she turned toward the front. It was too late now to change her mind. She'd give Hayley an extra shift next week to make up for it. Ezra never minded giving up a shift. He made money as a part-time DJ for his brother's wedding-entertainment company.

Later, after Hayley had left, she went back to grab some scraps for Jerkface. "Can you make me up a doggie bag for Jerkface?" He went crazy for their haddock from the fish and chips (minus the deep-fried coating). They didn't sell a lot of it, and the helpings were pretty big, so there was usually some left over from the day.

Ramiro pointed to the fridge. "I've already made a bag up. Is it really a doggie bag if it's for a cat?"

Lauren opened the fridge and noticed the bag. He'd drawn a cat with whiskers on it. "A catty bag just doesn't have the same ring to it."

"True. And speaking of segues, what's up with you and Hayley?"

Lauren turned around, almost dropping the bag of fish. "Me and Hayley?"

"Don't give me that face. You were checking her out."

"I was not."

He folded his arms across his chest and leaned against the island in the middle of the kitchen. "Yuhuh."

"I'm her boss." It was the first thing that popped into her mind to say. Not, I don't date women, or I'm not interested in women, even though those things were also true. Weren't they?

Ramiro simply smirked and went back to wiping down the griddle.

Lauren shook her head and left the kitchen. Even if she were into Hayley, which she wasn't, dating was so far off her radar at the moment. And she didn't date people she worked with. She didn't date women.

Ramiro stuck his head through the window between the kitchen and the front. "Admit it, though. You think she's hot."

"Hot? Not the word I'd use."

"Granted she's not conventionally good looking, but even you have to admit she's cute."

Lauren began pulling the condiments from the booths, getting ready to close for the evening. "Why do you care so much what I think of her?"

"When was the last time you even dated? I'm just worried you're too focused on work and your dad. It doesn't have to be Hayley, but maybe you should let Lucy hook you up with someone."

"The last time Lucy hooked me up with someone, I was so bored I finally understood the phrase 'chew your own leg off.'"

"It couldn't have been that bad."

Lauren placed a tray of salt and pepper shakers on the counter in front of her. "He spent most of the night talking about his hobbies, one of which included extreme ironing."

"What—"

"Apparently you iron things in extreme places like on a raft in the middle of a river or while rock climbing."

He mimed plugging in something. "How—"

"I don't know. I didn't let it get that far. It would've given the false impression I was interested."

"So you gave up?" Ramiro hobbled out into the front and took a seat on one of the stools. "You're not still—"

"No," she said loudly, waving him off. "I'm not hung up on Ben. I'm just..." She shrugged and took a seat on the stool across from him. She played with one of the napkins, looking for a way to put into words what she felt. It had been years since her divorce from Ben. The heartbreak—his—had been too much for her to take, so she'd decided not to date until she was sure what she wanted.

"I'm tired of going through the motions." She gazed back up at him. "I'm waiting for the jolt, the one that says this is the one we've picked out for you."

Ramiro turned on his stool, spinning back and forth. "You believe in that shit?"

She leaned over and punched him lightly on the arm. "Yes." She laughed. "I do. And so do most people. They're just afraid to admit it, especially in this city. It doesn't mean I think it'll last forever, but there's someone out there for me."

"And if it never happens? You're just going to live alone for the rest of your life?"

"I'm not alone. I have Jerkface."

❖

It was well after ten by the time Lauren made it upstairs to her apartment. She'd scrubbed the bathroom extra hard since she knew Luna hadn't the night before. As soon as she opened the door, Jerkface's accusing eyes were staring up at her. "Rats. Sorry, Jerkface. I forgot your scraps. Tomorrow, I promise."

He turned, strutting away, and flicked his tail at her, usually a sign she'd committed a cardinal sin. Lauren groaned. She had two choices. She could either spend the night with a pissed-off cat, who, on a good day, was temperamental, or go back down to the diner and get his scraps. He jumped up on the counter and hissed at her.

"You know what, mister. I'm not going to let you bully me into giving you your way. You're just going to have to be happy with tuna from a can tonight. Deal with it." She discarded her jacket and flicked off her Merrells. The kitchen was still a mess from her earlier project. She spent the next twenty minutes cleaning up and opening a can of tuna for Jerkface. He sniffed at it, then swatted it way.

She shrugged and went into her bedroom to change into sweats. At least three episodes of *The Great British Bake Off* were waiting for her on her PVR, as was a glass of pinot.

Wine in hand, her feet up on the coffee table, she clicked on the TV, and Jerkface jumped up on the console. He paced from one end of the TV to the other, blocking her view. When Lauren tried to remove him, he hissed again and swatted at her.

"You are evil. I don't know why I put up with you." But that was a lie. She couldn't throw him out. No one else would want him. He was too much of a jerk. "Fine. You win. I'll go get your stupid scraps."

She jammed her feet back into her Merrells and threw on a jacket. She pulled the keys for the diner from her pocket and slammed the door behind her. He was getting more impossible to live with. At least she didn't have to go far.

The night air bit at Lauren's face as she descended the stairs at the back of the building. She wrapped her jacket tighter. A mama raccoon and three babies darted across the alley in front of her. Like Jerkface, she hissed at them. The bane of her existence. Two years ago they'd somehow found a way into the narrow space between the walls from the roof and used some of the wiring for nests. Aaron had been furious at the cost of the repairs, like it had been Lauren's fault the building was slowly falling apart. It was over a hundred and fifty years old now. Maybe that's why Aaron had wanted it inspected, because he was assessing repairs. Maybe the Leafs would win the playoffs this year.

She unlocked the door and disabled the alarm before it started squawking at her. She knew her way around this place so well she didn't even bother turning on the lights, plus, the lights from the streetlamps were enough to give her a hint of where everything was.

On her way out of the kitchen, she stopped cold. Out of the corner of her eye, she'd seen something move, and when she slowly turned her head to the end booth, she noticed a sizeable lump on the bench.

Lauren searched for something to use as a weapon, but all she could find was a roll of Saran Wrap from under the counter. She raised it like a bat ready to swing and approached the lump.

She almost dropped the roll when she saw the blue hair peeking out from under the blanket. It was Hayley. What the hell was she doing sleeping in the diner? And how the hell had she gotten in?

Chapter Thirteen

Hayley jerked awake and screamed. Startled, Lauren screamed too. "What are you doing in here?" Lauren dropped the Saran Wrap to her side. "How did you even get in?"

Hayley sat up, pulling the blanket with her. "I'm sorry. I didn't want to sleep in the park."

Lauren remembered her asking for an advance a couple of days ago. "Why would sleeping in the park even be an option? Where were you staying?"

Hayley scrambled off the bench. "At the Palace Arms."

"That place is a crack den."

"It is not." Hayley snatched her backpack from the booth and began stuffing her blanket and other belongings in it. "I'll admit it's not ideal, but it was all I could afford. I just moved here, and I don't know a lot of people." Her eyes filled with tears.

For the moment Lauren wasn't concerned with why it should bother her that Hayley had been staying in that hellhole. All that mattered now was making sure she had somewhere to go tonight, and then they could figure things out tomorrow. "You can't sleep here."

"I know. Don't worry. I'm going." A tear spilled down her face, and she swiped it away.

Lauren grabbed Hayley's arm, stopping her from rushing out. "I'm not kicking you out on the street. I'd be the biggest jerk in the world if I did that."

Hayley stopped and looked around, obviously confused. "You're not?"

"I have a spare room upstairs you can use until we find you somewhere more suitable."

Without any warning Hayley burst into tears and threw her arms around Lauren's neck. A thank-you might have been thrown in there, but Lauren couldn't be sure because her world had suddenly gone white. It had been a long time since she'd hugged anyone, like really hugged them. Hayley was warm and soft, and she smelled like Dove soap and baked bread, two of Lauren's favourite scents.

She rubbed Hayley's back in slow, comforting strokes, feeling the impressions of her spine through her sweater. They stood like that for several minutes, pressed together, until Hayley pulled away before it got awkward.

"I'm sorry," Hayley said. "God, this is embarrassing. It's just been a really hard few months. My first week in the city I got laid off from the job I had lined up, and then I couldn't find another one. And things just sort of snowballed from there. And then my rent got stolen…." She wiped her eyes with the back of her sleeve and took an unsteady breath.

Lauren reached over and removed a few napkins from the dispenser on the counter and handed them to Hayley. "Here. Geez. You sure are one for keeping things close to your chest."

Hayley shrugged and blew her nose. "I didn't want to bring everyone down. I mean, it didn't seem so bad at first, but everything kept getting slightly worse, until all of a sudden I was homeless and sleeping in a booth at work." She laughed, the sound slow at first, and then it bubbled up until it echoed through the empty diner. "Sorry," she said when she could breathe. "I also laugh at inappropriate times."

Lauren picked up Hayley's backpack. "Come on. I was just about to watch *The Great British Bake Off* with a glass of wine."

"Both of those things sound amazing."

Lauren slung Hayley's backpack over one shoulder and grabbed Jerkface's scraps off the counter, where she'd left them. A part of her wondered if she should be worried about letting an almost-stranger into her home. After all, what did she really know about Hayley? But that part was swallowed up by the majority of her, which believed this was not only the right thing to do, but also something she had to do for so many reasons she couldn't name.

❖

Hayley opened her eyes to find two yellow-greenish slits staring at her from across her pillow and a furry paw resting on her lip. The sun cut a sharp line across its fur. Shocked, Hayley didn't move. Lauren had mentioned she had a cat the night before, but said cat had streaked for Lauren's bedroom the moment Hayley had appeared.

Lauren had offered her a glass of wine, but she'd been so exhausted, and the thought of a real bed after sleeping on that bench was too tempting. She'd passed on both the wine and the indulgent TV.

Hayley hated cats.

They were assholes who didn't give a shit about anyone but themselves. They didn't play fetch or come when you called, and when you made it home from a long day, they didn't rush you at the door. If they deigned to appear at all, it was because they were hungry or thirsty. She'd had several exes who would argue all those points, but she'd never met a cat who wasn't evil through and through.

But how to extract herself from this situation without getting swatted? Hayley blinked a few times, and the cat refused to budge. Hayley inched backward. The paw stayed on her lip, and almost in slow motion, the claws extended. She ducked, but not fast enough to stop her lip from getting caught. The sharp claw ripped through her bottom one.

"Shit." Hayley scrambled off the bed and out of the room faster than she could remember ever moving.

Lauren was in the kitchen making coffee and wearing a very thin, very short, black robe, revealing long, muscular legs. Her dark hair was piled on top of her head, and even though she didn't wear a lot of makeup, seeing her like this made her look even more pale.

Hayley averted her eyes from the welcoming sight. More than ever she had to tamp down this crush. Lauren was her boss and apparently her new temporary roommate.

"I met your cat."

Lauren turned to Hayley, who was still in the ratty sweats she'd been wearing last night. The cougar that adorned the bottom half had faded, and the C and P from Casper Falls had been torn off at one point, so it looked like it said AS ER FALLS COUGARS along the neckline.

"Oh no," Lauren said as she noticed Hayley's lip. "That's Jerkface." She grabbed a few sheets of Kleenex and handed them to Hayley.

"Jerkface?" Hayley dabbed at her lip. "Then you're aware of its—"

"Poor behaviour and manners in general? Yes, my cat is a jerk, but I can't give him up." She shrugged as if it were obvious why. "I'm sorry he attacked you."

"It wasn't so much an attack but the creepiest way to wake up. Ever."

Lauren stepped close and peered at her lip. "He doesn't have rabies, if that makes you feel better."

At that moment, Jerkface appeared, stalking out of the bedroom and meowing loudly. He hopped onto the counter and swished his tail at Lauren's toast. She shoved him off the counter. "Go. You crazy cat." She turned to Hayley. "He likes to mark his territory with hair. Be forewarned you will be covered in copious amounts of hair before you leave. You'll see one of those sticky clothes brushes by the door. Feel free to use it. Coffee?" She pulled down a mug from the cupboard and handed it to Hayley. She had to get on tiptoe to reach the shelf, and Hayley couldn't help herself. She watched as the robe rose to reveal the back of Lauren's thighs. She inwardly groaned at the image vying for attention and physically turned to view the apartment.

It was fairly large. It encompassed the footprint of the diner. She hadn't seen the size of Lauren's bedroom, but the spare was big enough for a desk, a double bed, and a corner stacked with boxes. The kitchen was small but made up for it with a large living room and dining area next to the kitchen.

The place had a rain-forest feel. Plants were everywhere—on shelves, in the windows, hanging from the ceiling. The artwork on the walls was contemporary though. A lot of black-and-whites of places around the city. The kitchen was outdated but in a way that was very retro and coming back into fashion.

Lauren took her toast to the table off the kitchen, and Hayley joined her with a full cup of coffee.

Lauren crossed her legs and picked a couple of hairs out of her toast before taking a bite. "One thing's been bugging me since last night. How did you get into the diner? I had the alarm set."

Hayley sipped her coffee. Should she lie? She didn't see much point. It wasn't like she was some mastermind criminal. "I never left. There's a place behind the stairs that's a good spot to hide. After my shift I went down to the basement when no one was looking and never came out."

Lauren paused. "How many nights have you been sleeping there?"

"Last night would've been my second. I got locked out of my room and was kind of desperate."

"I wish you'd come to me."

Jerkface jumped onto the table and waved his bushy tail in Hayley's face. When he moved on to Lauren, she had several more hairs in her coffee.

"I take care of myself."

Lauren was silent, staring at her over her coffee.

"I really appreciate you letting me stay here last night. I'll try to be out of here as soon as possible."

Lauren set her coffee on the table and pushed her toast away. She'd obviously given up on picking the hair out. "Look, rent is expensive, and finding a decent apartment is hard. Don't feel like you have to settle on something just to get out of here. This apartment has housed many people who've needed help. When I came to work at the diner, Greta helped me out by letting me stay with her. I didn't have anywhere else to go. And I'd like to pass that forward."

Hayley swallowed what she was about to say. She usually rejected any help. She didn't like feeling obligated to anyone, and this was really huge. This wasn't someone lending her money or letting her go ahead of them in line. This was coexisting with a virtual stranger. "You're going to let me stay with you? But you don't even know me."

"I know enough."

Hayley raised a brow as she took a sip of her coffee. "Like what?"

"You love old video games, you're obsessed with the eighties—"

"I'm not obsessed."

"From where I'm sitting it looks like a bit of an obsession."

Hayley would've liked to argue that fact a little more, but she was actually enjoying the teasing. Where she was from, you teased only people you were fond of. It also showed that perhaps Lauren had noticed her as much as she'd noticed Lauren. "Go on," Hayley said, cradling her mug between both hands.

"You respect people's time, you don't always think before you act, and everyone at the diner likes you. I can't think of a better recommendation than that."

Hayley was left speechless. She wanted to say yes because why wouldn't she? A room above where she worked with a beautiful woman. However, that was the hitch in the plan. She had a crush on that beautiful woman, and this situation could end up being torturous for her.

"Just say yes. I mean, where else are you going to go?" Lauren sipped her coffee, holding the cup with both hands. The sight was so inviting Hayley was finding it hard to argue all the reasons why this was a bad idea. But she had only one reason to say no, and she couldn't tell Lauren that.

Hayley had exhausted all other options, besides the park, but with November a week away, that wasn't possible. Not if she valued her limbs.

"Okay. Yes. But as soon as I save up enough money, I'll look for something else."

Lauren smiled. "Is the prospect of living with me that horrible?" She grabbed her plate and mug and placed them in the sink.

"I don't know. What kind of roommate are you?"

Lauren leaned back against the counter. "Let's see. The good: I'm clean, quiet." She began counting on her fingers. "I always remember to put the toilet seat down. In fact, there's even a lock on it. I don't watch obnoxious TV, smoke, drink excessively, or hoard my own hair. The bad." She picked up Jerkface and cradled his pudgy, hairy form. "How do you feel about cats? He sadly happens to be the most high-maintenance cat on the planet."

Hayley laughed. She hated cats, but the look on Lauren's face as she said it almost made up for the fur ball in her arms.

"Now you," she said as Jerkface scrambled from her arms.

"Me?" Hayley looked to the ceiling, thinking about all the complaints she'd heard over the years. "Well, the good: I don't have any annoying hobbies, I don't shed, and I'm quiet."

"And the bad?"

Hayley shrugged. "There is no bad. I've been told on multiple occasions that I'm awesome."

"Well, on that note, I'm not scheduled to work until this afternoon. Do you need help moving your stuff over? Do you have a lot of stuff?" Lauren looked around her apartment. While not tiny, it wouldn't accommodate too much more. Again, Hayley was first inclined to say no. But it would probably take her two trips without the help, so she had to weigh her default reaction against her better judgment. "I'm going to infer by that pause, you're saying, 'Yes, Lauren, please help me.'"

Hayley scrunched her face up. "Thanks."

❖

Lauren had passed by the Palace Arms so many times it had become background noise. But now, confronted with the peeling paint, she could see it for what it was, a dump. Her heart broke a little to think that Hayley had been staying here. The idea that she had nowhere else to go but this horrible excuse for affordable housing was a punch to the gut. That's what was wrong with this city. You had to be rich to live here, except most of the rich people preferred to live in the suburbs, where they could lay their wealth out like expensive carpets.

When they entered, a man in a Hawaiian shirt came out from behind the sealed front desk. "You owe me three hundred dollars."

"I know, you kicked me out of my room, remember? I'm just here for my stuff."

The man, who was doing a good impression of Christian Bale from *American Hustle* minus the moustache, folded his arms and blocked the stairway. "Not until you pay what you owe."

"Ask Alan where your money is."

"Alan paid his rent."

"Of course he did, Ed, with my money. Can you get Dunne for me?"

Ed shooed her away. "I'm not the butler here."

Hayley huffed. She looked ready to curse Ed out, which probably wouldn't help their situation. "You said she owed three hundred?" Lauren stepped in front of Hayley, redirecting his fire.

Ed looked her over, as if he'd just noticed her. "Yeah. Two weeks' rent."

"What if I pay it?"

Hayley grabbed her arm. "No, forget it. He can't hold my stuff ransom."

"Hayley, you can't go around in what you have on until you get paid. You can owe me the money instead, okay?" Lauren didn't care how much money she had to shell out. If it got Hayley out of this hellhole, all the better.

Hayley looked almost offended that Lauren thought she wouldn't pay her back.

In the end Lauren considered the money well spent. They wheeled Hayley's suitcases down the sidewalk in single file. The weather was decent enough for this time of year, overcast but mild. In a few weeks all the leaves would be gone from the trees, and the city would look drab and grey. Lauren hated winter. It really felt like the city died for six months of the year, especially when you lived across from the park.

Hayley had her face to the sky, her blue hair cascading down her back. She was wearing the same thing she'd been wearing for the last two days, dark-grey skinny jeans and a blue hoodie under an old leather jacket. And for the hundredth time that day Lauren asked herself why she was going to so much trouble to help Hayley. The employees at the diner were pretty tight-knit, and she'd like to think she'd offer her spare bedroom to anyone who found themselves homeless, although Luna might try her patience after a couple of hours. But she wouldn't have offered to go get their stuff with them or pay their lapsed rent. Yet she wasn't sorry she'd done it.

"Don't you just love fall?" Hayley asked from up ahead.

"Fall's okay." Lauren brushed a pile of red leaves aside. "It's what comes after that I dislike."

She breathed in deep. "I don't know what it is about decomposing leaves, but the smell is comforting."

Maybe Lauren didn't mind helping Hayley out because she always had such an upbeat attitude about everything.

CHAPTER FOURTEEN

Hayley scraped the griddle before turning it off. It had been a long day, but a good one. Theo had shown her a few more items on the menu so that she had it pretty much covered. She'd yet to actually man the kitchen alone though, but she was confident she could cook most of the breakfast and lunch items. The cooking part wasn't hard; it was memorizing the stupid names of everything.

Lauren had just shut the door for the night and flipped the sign. She looked more tired than usual. They'd had a busy dinner rush. In fact, Ramiro had stayed longer to help them through it, but Lauren was on her own for most of it.

Hayley wiped her hands and came out of the kitchen. "Have you eaten anything lately?" she asked.

Lauren plopped down on one of the stools and rested her head on her hand. "I was just going to make myself some toast when I got home." She pulled her hair elastic out and massaged her scalp. "I'm too tired for anything more serious than that."

Hayley spread her hands instead of saying, Duh, you're in a restaurant. "Let me cook you something—anything you want." She went over and took a seat on the stool next to Lauren. "It's the least I can do for what you did for me today. And by your rules, when you're working, you can eat meals here, so it's not like we'd be stealing food."

Lauren untied her apron and folded it in her lap. "That's…" She looked up at Hayley. "That would be amazing. Thanks."

Hayley stood, her energy still at seventy-five percent. "What do you feel like?"

"Surprise me."

"Mind if I turn up the music a bit?" Hayley called from the kitchen.

"Go for it."

Hayley plugged her phone into the stereo system and scrolled down until she found the playlist she was looking for. She hit shuffle, and Dinosaur Jr.'s cover of "Just Like Heaven" came over the speakers. With the soundtrack set, she pulled open the fridge and surveyed her options. She wanted something fast and easy but with enough of a wow factor to impress Lauren. And definitely nothing from the menu. She was sure Lauren had tried everything a million times.

She spotted a container of panko on the shelf next to the fridge and had the best idea ever. She pulled a bowl of eggs out of the fridge and got to work.

By the time she set two plates down in one of the booths, Sure Sure was covering "This Must Be the Place."

"God, that smells good." Lauren stopped filling the ketchup containers and rounded the corner. "What is this?" she asked, taking a seat across from Hayley.

"It's eggs benny with a twist. I coated the eggs in panko and deep-fried them after I poached them."

Lauren cut into her egg and watched as the yolk spread over the tomato and English muffin underneath. She dunked it in hollandaise sauce before taking a bite. Her eyes closed and her head dipped up. "Holy crap, that is next level. Where did you learn to cook like that?"

Hayley sat back and watched the show. She loved how much Lauren was enjoying it. "My mom and nana are big on cooking, and I love playing around with flavours. I had an ex who was into experimenting quite a bit, and she kinda got me hooked."

Lauren only nodded, her mouth full. Hayley hadn't tried this in a while, and she was really happy how it had turned out.

"So what job did you come here for?" Off Hayley's confused look. "You said you had a job lined up but got laid off. What was it?"

"Oh." Hayley shook her head, sending blue hair over her shoulder. "Nothing special. It wasn't so much the job, more the...escape?"

Lauren speared a home fry and dipped it in hollandaise. "That sounds so ominous."

Hayley's laugh echoed through the diner, mingling with the happy, upbeat music coming from the kitchen. "Not even. My life is so boring. At least it was until I came here." She looked around the diner, contemplating whether she would share this tidbit with Lauren, figured why not, and continued. "I got dumped in a small town and was tired of seeing my ex parading around with her new man. Small towns suck for that sort of thing."

"Oh, shit. I'm sorry. What a bitch." Lauren popped her hand over her mouth. "I'm so sorry. I didn't mean that, unless she was—in which case, I did."

Hayley was heartened that Lauren would take her side. "No worries. She is." Hayley grinned and swirled the last of her egg in ketchup before popping it in her mouth.

The last chords of the Talking Heads' "Once in a Lifetime" finished playing, leaving the diner in silence. Beyond the locked door the sounds of traffic and streetcars filtered in. A woman was yelling about pizza toppings from across the street. When Lauren peeked around the booth, she saw the woman standing next to a tree yelling into one of its large knots, as if she'd mistaken the tree for a take-out window.

Lauren pushed her plate forward and leaned back. The lukewarm coffee sitting in front of her was her sixth cup of the day, and she was reluctant to finish it. Comfortable sitting here across from Hayley, she wasn't sure if the good food, or the quiet diner, or the company had affected her this way. Whatever it was, she shouldn't overthink it like she usually did.

Hayley yawned, stretching her arms in a move very reminiscent of a cat. Lauren's gaze drifted to her chest, which stretched a circular yin yang across her breasts.

Hayley looked down too. "You like it? Found it in Kensington Market."

Lauren's cheeks burned, but she focused on the design. "What is it?"

"You're kidding. This is a Boo and Bullet Bill from Mario wrapped in a yin yang. Oh, right. You mentioned you never played video games as a kid, which, by the way, I think is a serious violation."

Lauren shook her head. "My mom was big on school and academic clubs, which didn't leave a lot of time for sports or games."

"That's a shame. I grew up on Mario Kart. It's why I'm such a good driver now."

Lauren raised her eyebrows. "Is that a racing game?"

Hayley's hand went to her heart. "You're killing me here. How do you not know Mario Kart?"

Lauren shrugged. She couldn't understand why it was such a big deal. Pete used to make fun of her all the time when she couldn't name what movie they were talking about or missed a pop-culture reference. It was different when she was younger. Not knowing what the kids were talking about had made her feel like an outsider.

"Video games weren't a big part of growing up for me. My parents thought it was better that I focus on school instead." Her mom had been relentless about homework and after-school programs. By the time she started university she was so tired of school she wanted nothing to do with it. "And it's a good thing too." She smiled and raised her hands to encompass her surroundings. "Because if I hadn't been so diligent, I might not be in charge of this fine establishment."

"Hey, don't play down what you do. Running a business isn't easy, especially when it deals with entitled customers."

Lauren laughed out loud. They'd had a customer in earlier who threatened to have them shut down because they'd run out of dark rye bread. "True."

In the few weeks since Hayley started at the diner, she'd quickly become one of Lauren's best cooks. She wasn't slow like Theo and didn't complain about everything like Ezra. And she liked working with Hayley because she didn't have to worry about her. Hayley was like a female version of Pete. Lauren sat back and almost dropped her coffee at the thought.

Hayley looked up. "You okay?"

Lauren shook herself. "Yeah. I'm just tired." She sat back, kind of stunned by the revelation. She never thought she'd be able to replace Pete. But sitting across from her was someone who'd fit into her life almost seamlessly.

Hayley stood and grabbed Lauren's plate.

"No. Let me do the cleaning. You cooked." Before Hayley could object, she added, "I insist." Lauren grabbed the plates and stacked them as she headed toward the kitchen, Hayley close behind.

The kitchen was a bit of a mess. Lauren was learning that cleaning as she cooked was not one of Hayley's skills. "My nana always told me I leave a kitchen like the Tasmanian Devil tore through it looking for lunch." Hayley ducked her head in embarrassment.

And that's exactly what this kitchen looked like. Murphy, the guy who loaded the dishwasher, hadn't shown up, and the rush had them all scrambling so that a towering pile of dishes stood next to the dishwasher. Cups lined every available surface.

She'd dropped the panko container, scattering little bits everywhere across the centre island and a good foot around her workstation. Dirty knives and kitchen utensils covered the counter, and a mouldy tomato she'd found in the back of the fridge sat in the middle of the island on top of the panko container.

Hayley stepped over to the stereo and pressed play.

"This is…." Lauren stood frozen in the doorway as Springbok's "Too Late for Goodbyes" began playing. "You were only in here ten minutes. How did you manage to get it so messy?"

Hayley gave a sheepish shrug. "It's a gift."

Lauren blew a breath out, and the air ruffled her bangs. "Okay. I'll load the dishwasher, and you clean the rest."

They worked to the sounds of Hayley's eighties covers playlist. As Hayley scrubbed the counter, Lauren loaded the dishwasher. Her actions were quick and efficient, almost like a graceful dance she'd memorized and was performing for Hayley alone. She'd pulled her hair into a lazy bun, leaving her neck bare. She couldn't be sure, but when she looked up to check on Hayley, her cook's gaze flicked back to her task.

"So what did you want to be when you were busy being the perfect student? I'm guessing it wasn't an academic."

Lauren pulled a stack of plates from the top of the dishwasher and stacked them beside her. "It's silly."

"Ballerina?"

Lauren laughed. "I definitely don't have the feet to be a dancer."

"Circus clown?"

"Nothing so exciting. I wanted to design cakes. The multi-tiered monstrosities that look too good to eat."

"That's not silly. That's amazing." Hayley held the trash can up to the ledge of the counter and scooped the spilled panko into it. "Is that why Ramiro calls you sweetums?"

"Ugh. I hate that name. Mostly it's because I have the biggest sweet tooth. He's watched me eat almost an entire red-velvet birthday cake. In one sitting." Lauren held her hand up. "It's not something I'm proud of, but that cake was so good, the stomachache afterward was worth it."

"I don't think I could eat that much sweets in one sitting. I like cream-filled liquorice, but that's the extent of my sweet craving."

Lauren scrunched her face up. "That sounds kind of disgusting."

"7-Eleven sells them for ten cents apiece. They're so good, especially when you're tucked into bed with a good book."

Lauren stopped loading the dishwasher and turned around. "You're a bit of an odd duck, aren't you?" She smiled softly to ease the statement.

"I'm not the one who ate a whole birthday cake in one sitting."

"Fair enough."

After the dishes were loaded and the kitchen sparkled, Lauren set the alarm and held the door open for Hayley. "Thank you for dinner. It was amazing and delicious and definitely fattening in a good way."

Hayley turned back in the doorway. "And thank you for getting my stuff out of hock. I will pay you back."

Lauren squeezed her arm. "I'm not worried."

❖

"Dad, you never told me they had lawn bowling across the street," Lauren said.

His eyebrows shot up his forehead.

She handed him the brochure. "You didn't know there was lawn bowling across the street?"

"I'm not surprised. What makes you think I'd care?"

"You used to love bowling."

"Lauren, honey, those are two very different sports. One is played by men—" Off her look he amended his remark. "I mean, able-bodied adults. Lawn bowling is for old farts who eat dinner at three and go to bed at five."

Lauren opened his hall closet and searched through the hangers to find a jacket that would fit the weather. "Which you are rapidly becoming if you don't start exercising better." She pulled out a burgundy linen jacket with minimal padding.

"What's that for?"

"We have an appointment today." She held out his jacket to him, wiggling it like her mom used to. Sometimes she felt like she was the parent. She supposed that's how the cycle went.

"I don't remember having an appointment on Monday." He still hadn't budged from his recliner in the living room.

"It's not Monday. I switched my day off with Vic so I could come with you."

"Make sure I go, you mean."

"You've missed the last three appointments, so yes. I had to switch my one day off a week to make sure you go to your own doctor appointment."

He had the good grace to look embarrassed. Lauren spent almost every day off she had looking after him, and all he did was grumble about it. He pushed himself up from the chair and grabbed the jacket she offered.

"What's wrong with your legs?"

"Nothing's wrong with my legs. They just give me problems sometimes."

"What kind of problems?"

"Lauren, I'm fine."

The doctor's clinic was packed with screaming kids and crying babies. Her father fidgeted next to her while she tried to read a magazine, but it was hard to concentrate with the noise level.

"Max Hames?" a nurse called from the door. Lauren's father jerked but didn't make it out of his chair as fast as he'd hoped. Lauren offered him her hand, but he waved it off and heaved himself up without any help.

The nurse put her hand up when she saw Lauren approaching. "Only patients allowed beyond here, I'm afraid."

"I'm his caregiver. Dr. Chan's expecting both of us."

"Let me check, one second." She disappeared into the back for a moment before returning. "Okay. Follow me." She steered them into the rear exam area with doors on both sides of the hall. "Just have a seat in number six."

"I don't need you to come with me. I can look after myself just fine," Max grumbled.

"If that were true you wouldn't have missed your last three appointments."

"It's because I didn't need to come. Everyone's just overreacting."

Lauren directed her dad to sit in the chair while she leaned against the wall and read a poster about vaccinations. After five minutes of silence, Max grumbled. "Why do they always do this? They have us come and sit in here and wait. What's the difference from waiting outside in the other room?"

"Just be glad you're not sitting out there with all the diseased people."

"Where do you think the diseased people come after there? In here. They've probably touched every surface."

"At least it's quiet. We don't have any screaming kids to deal with."

The door opened, and a small Chinese woman entered. Her long hair was pulled into a ponytail, and she wore a green dragon pin on her white lab coat. "Hi, Max." She smiled. "How are you doing today?"

"Fine," he said.

"Good." She smiled at Lauren as she sat at the desk and pulled up Max's file on her computer. "Why don't we talk about your last test results first? We can go over any questions or concerns, and then we'll take a look at how you're doing." Her face was open and friendly. It said, as far as she was concerned Max and Lauren were the only two people in the office that day. That's why Lauren liked her. She never rushed them out like so many other doctors she'd had over the years.

They talked for a few minutes about what they'd found. Max didn't have any questions, so Lauren asked for him since she'd be the one taking care of him.

"My biggest concern, Max, is your diet," Dr. Chan said. "You've mentioned you feel tired, and one reason is that your body isn't producing as much energy as it should. We need to get you eating foods that will help your body process glucose better. It's that, or we'll have to put you on medication."

Lauren slumped against the wall. Both those options made her want to pull her hair out. He was too impossible to eat healthy, and forget about taking medication on a regular basis. Dr. Chan wrapped up her gentle chiding and opened the floor for any more questions. Max sat there staring at the floor and shaking his head.

"This morning when I went to pick him up, he had trouble getting out of his chair. He said he has problems with his legs sometimes, which means all the time."

"Is this true?" Dr. Chan asked Max. Her voice was soft and coaxing.

"It's not a big deal. They just go numb sometimes."

Lauren and Chan exchanged a look. "Numbness is a very big deal, especially when it's connected with type 2 diabetes. If you're experiencing numbness, it could be an early sign of nerve damage. The longer this goes untreated, the more likely it will cause permanent damage."

Chapter Fifteen

The soft splatter of water running in the shower filtered into Lauren's room. Even through her closed door, she could hear the muted sounds of Hayley humming. A loud crash and a quiet "mother fuddrucker" woke Lauren fully. She rolled over and checked her phone. Still four hours before she had to be at the diner. Another thud and she was up slipping on her robe.

Lauren rapped a knuckle on the door to the washroom. "Are you okay in there?" No answer. "Hayley?" When she didn't get an answer, she poked her head in and stopped in shock. The place was a disaster. Wet towels were strewn on the floor, one draped over the toilet, and the sink had clogged (something it was prone to do) with a sludge of blue water.

It had been only a couple of days since Hayley had taken over the spare bedroom, and taken over was the right way to put it. Hayley had a way of spreading. Lauren didn't think she meant to be messy, but her things just had a way of showing up. Everywhere. The bathroom cupboard, the sides of the tub, the coffee table, coat rack, even the kitchen table. Lauren had made the mistake of peering into the room she was increasingly thinking of as Hayley's, and it was hard to see where Lauren's well-organized storage ended and Hayley's stuff began.

It was too early to deal with all this. Lauren shut the door to escape to the kitchen, which hadn't fared any better.

"I was going to clean it before you got up." Hayley appeared behind Lauren wearing a loose T-shirt and yoga shorts, a towel wrapped around her hair.

"How?" Lauren looked over at the fridge, a large smear of dark muck dripping down the handle. "How do you manage to get it so messy?" She'd been working with cooks for almost half her life now and had never seen anything so extreme. If Lauren had tried to be messy while cooking, she wouldn't be able to reproduce the havoc Hayley managed to create by accident.

"I don't know. It just happens."

"What were you trying to make?"

Hayley brushed past Lauren and grabbed a mug from the cupboard. She smelled like coconut and soap. "Coffee." She poured Lauren a mug and handed it to her.

Lauren stood shocked as she surveyed the damage. "All this because of coffee?"

"I wasn't sure where you kept your beans, so I had to go through some cupboards." It was as if Hayley had transferred the contents of the cupboards to the counters. Hayley had apparently sorted through the piles of stacked dishes and also decided to empty the dishwasher, but had no idea where anything went.

Lauren took her coffee to the kitchen table and sat, pulling the unfinished crossword puzzle from yesterday's paper toward her. Her first sip was heavenly. "This is amazing. Thank you."

Hayley leaned back against the cupboard. "It was no trouble."

Lauren paused and looked up from her crossword puzzle. From where she was sitting, Hayley's idea of "no trouble" wasn't even on Lauren's scale. But she didn't comment. Usually, when she didn't work mornings, she liked to sit with the puzzle and wake up slowly. At the diner she had her routine and the quiet of the morning. Now that Hayley was here, she'd have to think about the schedule. Obviously, both having the morning off wasn't going to give her the peace she was used to.

As she scanned the clues she could hear Hayley in the kitchen shifting things back to their rightful place. At least she didn't talk or try to intrude on Lauren's time, and for that she was grateful.

After a few minutes of quiet, Lauren raised her head, expecting to find the kitchen empty, but instead, Hayley was leaning against the counter, sipping her coffee and watching her.

"What?"

"I was just curious. When's the last time you lived with anyone?"

"Besides a moody cat?"

Hayley smiled. "As much of a pain in the ass I'm sure he is, pets don't count."

Lauren clicked her pen a few times and set it next to the crossword. "I guess Greta was the last person, and that would've been over four years ago. Why?"

"No reason. She owned the diner before Aaron?"

"Yep. Aaron's mom."

Hayley nodded and leaned forward. The towel uncoiled, revealing deep blue beneath. She flipped her head back, the hair slapping against her back. Lauren watched, mesmerized by the motion of Hayley's fingers combing the strands.

"I always wondered how you got it so blue." Lauren pointed at the wet locks draped over Hayley's shoulder. "Why blue?"

Hayley pulled a strand through her fingers, examining the colour. "Blue's my favourite, but it's not always blue. Depends on my mood."

"Have you ever dyed it a normal colour?"

"Normal?" The look on Hayley's face made Lauren wish she could take back the question.

"I only meant not something from the rainbow."

Hayley shrugged. "Normal's boring." She balled up the towel and pushed off from the counter. "I'll go clean up my mess." She breezed by, her expression neutral, and Lauren couldn't be sure if she'd insulted her or not.

"Rats."

❖

"So you're saying you have the hots for your boss, who is now also your roommate." Kalini tsked and continued through the aisle. Every few minutes she'd pick up an item and scan it, then replace it on the shelf.

"That's not what I said at all."

"I was reading the subtext in your story."

"All I said was that she's a bit Felix to my Oscar."

"And by that admission, you're saying you care what she thinks. I've lived with you, remember? You never cared how messy you were before. Does she strut around in the buff?"

"Of course not." Hayley grabbed a vegetable spiralizer out of

Kalini's hand before she could add it to her wedding registry. "You don't need that."

"How do you know?"

"You hate vegetables."

"Maybe I wouldn't hate them so much if they came in spiral form."

They'd been in the depths of the Bay for over an hour, adding things to Kalini's registry—her mother had insisted—and since her parents were helping out with the cost of the wedding, she found it hard to refuse.

"This is pointless. You don't even like half the stuff you've picked. You'll just end up returning it anyway."

"Exactly. Then we'll get cash, which is what we want anyway."

Hayley picked up a bronze statue of a cat licking itself to examine the price. "I don't think that's how it works."

"Doesn't matter." Kalini linked her arm with Hayley's and dragged her to the next aisle. "More important, what are we going to do about your hot lady boss?" She slapped Hayley with the scanner. "I know. Why don't you bring her with you to Jo's show? It's like a date but not a date."

Hayley stopped mid-aisle and stared at Kalini. "I'm not trying to date my boss. That's not what we're brainstorming here...Besides, she's straight."

"Did you check her straight card at the door?"

"Someone said she'd been married to some guy a while back."

Kalini chucked a small moustache pillow back onto the shelf. "Oh yeah, because no gay woman has ever been married to a dude before."

"I'm not bringing her."

"Fine, but you're still coming, right? It's on the eleventh."

"Of course I'm coming, I've already told Lauren I can't work that day."

"Lauren? That's her name?" Kalini pretended to swoon.

"Get off it. What're you, twelve?"

"It's one of many things Jo loves about me. Okay." Kalini waved her hands in front of her. "I'm done with this whole 'being a good daughter' thing. Let's go get something to eat. I'm starving."

Twenty minutes later and they were hopping off the streetcar in front of Greta's. "Why'd you bring me home? I thought we were grabbing something to eat."

"And does this fine establishment not offer food?" As Kalini crossed the street, she dodged a guy riding his bike with a pug strapped to the front basket.

When they entered, the place was almost dead. It was half past one, so the lunch rush had just ended. Kalini snagged the back booth and slid in, grabbing a menu from the holder as she did. "I need to see what we're working with." She peered around her menu, eyeing the servers. "Which one is she?"

"No. You're not bringing crazytown to my place of work."

"Oh, good. They're wearing name tags. I don't need you for this."

Hayley covered her face with her hands. It was too much to hope that Lauren wasn't working this shift, but Hayley knew Lauren's schedule by heart, much to her embarrassment.

"Hi, Hayley. Who's your friend?" Hayley looked up through her hands. Lauren was carrying a carafe of coffee, a huge grin on her face.

Kalini held her hand out. "It's so nice to meet you, Lauren. I'm Kalini. Hayley and I used to be roommates. I hear you now have that honour."

Lauren shook hands, her smile faltering. "You're the one who kicked her out?"

"What?" Kalini shifted gears, turning to stare at Hayley. "Is that what you told her?"

"No. That's not what I said. That's not what happened."

Lauren hitched her free hand on her hip. "She's rooming with me because she didn't have a place to live." Lauren lowered her voice. "I found her sleeping in the diner."

"What?" Kalini's face fell. "Hale, you told me you'd found a good place."

"I would hardly call the Palace Arms a 'good place.'" Lauren turned, probably to make sure no one was listening.

Kalini whupped Hayley on the head with her menu. "I told you to check out the youth hostel on Spadina. What the fuck were you doing at the Palace Arms?"

"It was the only place I could afford. Jason didn't want me staying on the couch..." Hayley shrugged. "So I got a place."

"Fuck Jason. We would've made it work. The Palace Arms is an absolute shithole. Only addicts use that place. God." Kalini slumped back, folding her arms.

Lauren took a step back. "I'm going to give you two a few more minutes. Let me know when you're ready to order."

Kalini stared up at the ceiling, silent, shaking her head every few seconds. Hayley reached across the table. "I'm sorry I didn't tell you. Things just spiralled really fast."

Kalini shrugged and shook her head again. "I'm upset you didn't think you could come to us. You thought we would be okay with you being homeless?"

"I hadn't known you guys that long, and Jason was really bitchy about everything. I didn't want to impose."

"Hale, you're family now. If we'd known, Jo and I would've figured something out."

Hayley didn't know what to say. She hadn't even considered asking them for help, thinking since they had their own lives and problems. Her whole life she'd grown up with the belief that cities were cold and unfeeling, but so far she'd only been welcomed and folded into the fabric of life here.

Before Hayley could say anything, Kalini waved her off. "I hate all this sappy bullshit." She picked up her menu. "What's good here?"

"Everything."

Kalini lowered her menu. "Well, the good news is, she is definitely into you."

"She thinks I'm weird looking."

Kalini just smiled. "Even if she doesn't know it, she likes you."

❖

Hayley pulled the Post-it from the fridge door and read it. "You've got to be shitting me. There's a chart?" She scrunched up the note and tossed it on the counter. Jerkface pounced on the Post-it from the shelf he'd been lounging on and batted the ball back and forth between his paws a few times before slapping it toward Hayley. She resisted the urge to knock him off the counter.

He'd recently found a new hobby: peeing on her things. She couldn't leave anything lying around, even for a few seconds, or it would be marked with the telltale musk that Hayley had come to loathe. Two days ago she'd thrown her coat on the couch to run back to her room to grab something, and by the time she came back it had a wet patch on the left sleeve. She hadn't even seen Jerkface creep from his hiding spot.

Growing up she'd had dogs, a chocolate Lab named Almond, and then later, Dirk, a pit-bull/husky mix she'd rescued when he was a puppy. She was dog people. Dogs were easy to deal with. They loved you unconditionally, were great walking companions and bed warmers.

Jerkface was the complete opposite. He had this weird quirk where he would sit in a room and meow until you brought him water. Once the water was set in front of him, he would take two sips, then saunter off. It was Lauren's fault for catering to the asshole, but Hayley had also heard how loud Jerkface could vocalize. It was like having an angry toddler scream at you. Sometimes it was just easier to give in.

Hayley opened the fridge and nudged the milk slightly out of line with the Brita water behind it, closed the fridge, and left to get out of her work clothes. She felt better until the front door opened and Lauren swept in.

"I don't want to hear the word 'substitution' for at least a week." She collapsed on the couch with a loud groan. "My feet are done. They hate me."

Hayley shoved her head through her comfiest hoodie and strolled into the living room, where Lauren was resting with her head back and eyes closed. Even after a full day on her feet dealing with customers, she still looked fresh. And beautiful. Hayley tried not to think about that part, but she did. It wasn't even a subjective thing.

Hayley walked into the kitchen and moved the milk back into place. "Why don't we order a pizza and binge-watch *British Bake Off*?" Hayley took a seat a cushion away.

Lauren turned her head on the back headrest to face Hayley. "Can it have red peppers on it?"

"Yep."

"And Italian sausage?"

"Sure."

"And anchovies?"

"Um?"

Lauren reached over and squeezed Hayley's knee. "I'm kidding. I hate Italian sausage." Hayley's brain was still trying to put out the explosion of sensation happening somewhere around her knee when Lauren burst into laughter. "You should see your face, Hale." She pushed herself up from the couch. "Priceless."

Hayley could hear Lauren unzip her uniform as she entered her room. It was one of those cotton-blend dresses designed to look like something from a diner in the fifties. Luna and Vic complained about them constantly. Hayley's imagination at that moment was located somewhere between Lauren's breasts, and while her body was thoroughly enjoying the experience, her mind was not. She looked up at the ceiling and whispered, "This is so not fair."

Chapter Sixteen

Hayley dried her hair on a towel, the shittiest towel she could find, and surveyed the results. In the span of several hours her hair had gone from deep ocean blue to platinum blond. It was closer in colour to her natural blond, although hers was darker. She'd been dying her hair since she turned fifteen and hadn't seen her real colour in a decade.

Surrounding her were the results of her labour. The discarded dye box, an empty mixing bottle, her tint brush, scrapped plastic gloves, and several hair clips. She'd been careful not to let the bleach drop on anything that could stain. Hayley circled the bathroom once more to make sure. She had a feeling Lauren would flip. They'd been living together for only a couple of weeks, meaning they were in that honeymoon phase when you still hid the worst parts of yourself. After the coffee incident Hayley was being vigilant. It was proving harder than she'd thought. Growing up with Hannah, Hayley was used to the OCD nature of her sister. She was more organized than a library, and almost rebelling, Hayley had become the opposite. She didn't go out of her way to be messy, but she preferred the convenience of leaving things where they were instead of selecting a place for them to live. She liked the idea of chaos. For some reason it helped her be more productive.

As soon as she began making a conscious effort to tidy up after herself, it was like her natural tendency to spread had intensified. She couldn't help it.

Her mom might even go so far as to call her a slob, though it would be a gross exaggeration. Hayley just organized things differently than most people did. So far she was having fun messing with Lauren. This morning she'd moved the eggs a few inches out of place just to see if Lauren wrote her another note. Tomorrow she had big plans for the toaster.

She pulled out her hairdryer, unwrapped the cord by letting the dryer spin to the ground, and plugged it in. In the background, Huey Lewis and the News was crooning about the power of love. Hayley loved this song, it always reminded her of her childhood, so she let it play out before turning on the dryer.

She had the day off, her first in a while, and tonight she was joining Kalini at Jo's art opening. Jo would likely be busy schmoozing most of the night. Hayley was happy to fill in as her companion.

Since she'd moved here, she hadn't done much more besides look for an apartment or work, so this would be a welcome change to her routine. And in honour of that she was getting a new look. As she sculpted her hair into a soft wave, she told herself it had nothing to do with the fact that Lauren thought she had Smurf hair. Nothing at all.

❖

Lauren pulled open the fridge. It had been another long day, and all she wanted to do was eat ice cream, drink wine, and binge on Netflix. Maybe Hayley would join her. She hadn't seen her yet today. Because of her double, she'd been up and out of the apartment before Hayley was out of bed. She knew she was home because faint eighties music drifted from the back bedroom.

She was about to go knock when she noticed the eggs. She sighed and nudged the carton a few inches to the right. She knew she was being anal but couldn't help it. She liked things a certain way.

The door at the end of the hall opened, and the music shut off. "Hey," Lauren called. "Do you want to binge-watch—" But her voice stopped the second she saw Hayley emerge from her room. All coherent thought left her, and at that moment if you'd asked her what time it was, she'd have said "Thursday."

Hayley was wearing a little black dress that scooped low in the front, the fabric hugging her breasts and tied around her neck. And her legs. Lauren had never noticed women's legs before, but maybe she should start, because Hayley had fantastic legs. The dress clung tight until mid-thigh, and then nothing but skin showed until three-inch heels. The effect was expansive, smooth legs. Hayley took a couple steps forward, and Lauren watched her calf muscles flex.

And at that moment Lauren's libido, which had been dormant for years, sat up and slapped her in the face. Ideas of what it would feel like to skim those thighs with her fingers inching that dress up trailed through her mind.

"Too much?" Hayley asked. "A friend lent me the dress, but…" She looked down, surveying her cleavage. "It draws a little too much attention to the girls." It was obvious Hayley was uncomfortable showing off that much skin.

"You look…" To be honest, there was nothing too much about that dress. Lauren was practically drooling on the carpet. "So different."

Hayley scrunched her face up. "Different bad?"

"God, no." Lauren reeled herself in a bit. "It's good. You look good." She couldn't get over the transformation, because that's exactly what it was. Hayley's now-platinum-blond hair was styled into soft waves that tickled her shoulders, bouncing ever so slightly with her breasts as she walked. Lauren tore her eyes away. God, she'd never gotten so wet from just looking at a human before. "Where are you off to tonight?"

"My friend Kalini's fiancée has a gallery opening tonight. I'm sort of her stand-in date since Jo'll be busy most of the night."

Hayley walked past trailing lavender and shoved her lipstick, debit card, ID, and phone into her leather-jacket pocket. "Um, are you going to be up later? Or…" She shrugged her jacket on, killing the effect somewhat.

"What are you doing?"

Hayley looked down at herself. "What do you mean?"

"You can't wear that jacket. For one thing, you'll freeze to death, and it just ruins the whole aesthetic you have going on."

Lauren pulled a knee-length, dark-blue coat off the coat rack and opened it for Hayley to slip into.

"But the leather jacket is cool."

"It may be cool, but you're going for sexy."

"I am?"

Lauren shook the coat a little. "You most definitely are."

Hayley slipped out of her jacket and turned to accept the dark-blue wrap. Lauren fixed the collar from behind, then smoothed her hands down Hayley's back. It was an entirely intimate gesture that she hadn't meant to do but couldn't help herself.

Hayley turned and they locked eyes. "Better?"

"Much." But Lauren hadn't bothered to look because she was still staring into Hayley's deep-azure eyes. The platinum hair added a whole different hue that was mesmerizing. Lauren blinked quickly and turned away. "My night is Netflix and chill…the solo version. So I might be up."

Hayley's mouth quirked. "Cool." She sounded cocky and confident and sexy as hell. She opened the front door and took one look at the fire-escape stairs leading down to the back alley. "Crap. Forgot about the stairs." She slipped off her heels and descended in bare feet. "Bye," she called halfway down. And just like that, the real Hayley poked through the exterior.

Lauren slowly closed the door, letting it latch before leaning against it. "What the fuck was that?"

❖

The gallery was packed when Kalini and Hayley entered. She spotted Jo in the back surrounded by several people. She had a glass of red wine in hand and was using it to point out something in the painting on the wall. She was in her element. Usually a pretty laid-back dresser, she'd gone all out tonight, wearing a bright-pink blazer over a silver button-up shirt and skinny white tie. Her pants were also white and so tight Hayley could see the outline of her boxers. She had no doubt Kalini had dressed her. This was a girl who lived in hoodies and jeans.

They stepped farther in, and each took a glass of wine from the bar off to the side. The gallery tonight was showcasing three different artists, all of them mixed media. Jo's was the boldest. She used found garbage from the streets and painted them into beautiful landscape scenes as if they belonged.

Hayley needed this—time away from the diner and the guys. As much as she enjoyed working with them, there was just something about being stuck in the role of cool chick. She spent a little too much time ignoring Ezra's view on women, which he didn't mind sharing with her even though she was female. He had a phone full of women based on body parts. It was offensive to have to listen to him talk about them as a challenge, as if the only thing they offered existed between their legs. The thing about Ezra, though, was that he viewed himself the same way. He felt the only things he had to offer the opposite sex were his muscles and abs.

It was also good to get out of the apartment. Hayley was finding it hard to keep her feelings about Lauren from blooming into so much more. It was almost impossible to avoid her. Everywhere she looked she bumped into reminders of her presence in the apartment. Her smell of vanilla was on everything. Taking a shower had become a dangerous thing. She'd started having fantasies of Lauren in the shower, and that was no good. This was someone she could not have a relationship with. Her mind was aware of this fact; she just wished she could get the memo to her body.

"What's that look for?" Kalini asked. They'd slowly begun their circle of the gallery.

"What look?"

"If I didn't know you better, I'd think you wanted to make out with that guy over there." She pointed to where Hayley had been staring off into space, lost in thought. "Are you thinking lusty thoughts about your roommate slash boss? Please say yes."

Hayley blushed. "No, I was actually thinking lusty thoughts about that guy over there."

"Mmm-hmm. I still think you should've brought her. What better way to see if she's into you than a no-pressure, pretentious-as-fuck art exhibit?"

"She's straight."

"You don't know that. Is that the only reason you're not willing to put yourself out there? Because you think she's straight?"

"No. It's because she's my boss. And we live together. This cannot happen."

"Why not? Are you planning to make a career out of this job?"

"No, but if things go bad, then we still live together. It'll be awkward."

Kalini shrugged her slender shoulders. "So? Move. You've seen how fluid your living situation can get in this city. Why not embrace it? Especially if she's hot."

"What are you? Some sort of matchmaker?"

Kalini laughed and finished the last of her wine. "I'm your fairy godmother granting you permission to give in to your impulses."

Hayley sipped her wine, contemplating that last bit. She'd never seriously considered giving in to her urges. In her mind, Lauren was simply off limits, but what if she wasn't?

❖

The clock above the stove read one fifteen when Hayley slipped in the front door. The place was dark except for the occasional flicker from the TV in the living room.

Hayley set her heels on the front table and slipped out of her coat before heading to see if Lauren was still up.

She'd had the best time. Better than she thought she would. The exhibit was a mix of boring, exciting new work and pretentious fucks, but Kalini said that was normal for those gatherings. She'd gotten tons of attention, unfortunately not from the right gender. But that was the risk of dressing too femme. Hayley had always sat on the fence. Not exactly femme, her usually exotically coloured hair put her in the category of alternative but not necessarily gay. Her hair was long and she wore makeup, but she also rarely wore dresses and tended toward jeans and ironic T-shirts. Yet she found it fun to sometimes slip into a more feminine persona, like tonight.

But more fun than anything had been Lauren's reaction. Hayley would be lying if she said she hadn't dressed with Lauren in mind, but she never thought in a million years it would get a jaw-drop. And she'd seen lust in Lauren's eyes as plain as if Lauren had said it out loud.

Hayley tiptoed into the living room, trying not to bump into anything. She'd had a few glasses of wine. Nothing to get her drunk, but enough to impair her ability to be stealthy. And it had certainly affected her inhibitions. She'd talked so much on the way back, her Lyft driver had dropped her off a block away, mumbling that his engine light was on.

Lauren was curled up on the couch, her black hair sprawled on the armrest behind her. She'd changed out of her uniform into a black tank and yoga pants that stopped mid-calf.

Notting Hill was playing on screen. They were at the scene where Hugh Grant and his friends chase through London to get to Anna's press conference in time. Hayley took a seat on the edge of the couch to watch the ending. It wasn't her favourite romance, but it was pretty good. Her all-time favourite was *Career Opportunities*. She'd had a mad crush on Jennifer Connelly growing up.

Lauren stirred, turning onto her side. Should she wake her or leave her on the couch? It was probably better to wake her. She'd worked a double today and had another shift tomorrow, so the last thing she'd want in that situation was to sleep on some shitty couch.

Hayley reached for the remote, still clutched in Lauren's hand. But Lauren snuggled it close between her breasts, and Hayley decided not to press her luck. Kalini's words came back to her at that moment. The words "why not" mixed with the success of the evening and the allure of Lauren asleep on the couch. She brushed the back of her fingers along Lauren's cheek. Her skin was soft and warm.

Lauren jerked awake, apparently confused for a moment about where she was. She looked over at the movie and then up at Hayley, hovering over her.

"Sorry," Hayley said. "Did you want to sleep on the couch?"

Lauren sat up, bringing the warmth of slumber with her, close enough they were sharing the same air. Her eyes drifted down to Hayley's lips and stayed there.

Before Hayley could conjure the sensible adult she knew was lurking behind those three glasses of wine, Lauren reached up and cupped her face, pulling Hayley's lips to hers. Lauren parted her lips, inviting Hayley in.

And in that second Hayley understood what they meant when everything disappeared. It was like the world stopped to watch that kiss. But not only the world, the planets and the stars. Hayley lost all sense of self as she melted deeper into Lauren.

Hands reached up and circled her neck, bringing her in closer, and it still wasn't enough. Her mind soared with Lauren, the heat radiating from her body, the faint smell of cucumber from her shampoo, the soft moan escaping and floating up between them.

Lauren sucked Hayley's bottom lip into her mouth, and she felt it like a jolt. Wetness soaked her thong. Energy was building. Tiny tendrils of pleasure threaded through every inch of her. She couldn't get enough of Lauren's taste, smell, every tiny thing that made Lauren Lauren.

When Lauren's hand began sliding Hayley's dress up her thigh, Hayley pulled back. The look of surprise and regret on Lauren's face pulled her back even farther.

"I…"

Lauren sat up, her chest heaving. "I'm sorry."

Hayley tried so hard not to stare at the cleavage poking above her tank top, she really did, but it was like her eyes were riveted to Lauren's breasts.

Lauren stood, and Hayley's eyes followed. "I'm…going to go to bed." And with that, she rushed out of the room.

Hayley leaned her head back against the couch. "What the fuck was that?"

CHAPTER SEVENTEEN

Lauren woke to the sound of Hayley in the shower. She lay listening to the water running, imagined it cascading down Hayley's skin. She pulled a pillow over her face and groaned, wondering how she could so easily picture Hayley naked and surprised by how great that image made her feel.

"What does this mean?" she mumbled into her pillow. She shook that thought off. "Why does it need to mean anything?" She was definitely attracted to Hayley. Like, throw down her gloves, rip her clothes off, shove her onto the bed attracted.

Ramiro had been teasing her about it for a week now, but she'd never actually considered the possibility. Had he seen something she'd failed to spot? Obviously, or he wouldn't have been teasing her.

She'd only ever been with Ben. They'd met in grade ten and started dating. When she got pregnant the summer after she started university, they'd gotten married. Even after she miscarried, they stayed married. For ten years. After the first two, it was obvious they weren't going to make it. They shouldn't have gotten married in the first place. But she'd been young and stupid and hadn't realized that she'd mistaken fondness for love. Ben was funny, classically handsome, and kind.

When she heard her friends talk about how bad sex was, she just assumed that's what sex was like for women. It wasn't until she was older, and those friends had moved on from one-night stands to real relationships, that the story changed. She'd never experienced what Vic and Neal had. The way Vic talked about Neal, you'd think the two could keep an entire block powered.

The water stopped and the curtain opened, and Lauren felt a tingle all the way down to her toes. That kiss had opened the floodgates to something Lauren hadn't realized she'd been missing her whole life. Lust. Her body had a very good idea of what it wanted to do at that moment. It wanted to throw back the covers, rip open the bathroom door, and push—hopefully still naked—Hayley against the bathroom wall and finish what they'd started on the couch last night.

Her mind had other ideas. Her mind was always the sensible one, and for the last thirty-five years it had been doing the driving. Maybe it was time to switch drivers.

❖

Lauren dropped onto a bench beside Pete with an air of expectation. She hadn't seen him since he quit over two months ago. It felt like an amputation of sorts. She'd been with him every day for at least eight years, and then he didn't exist in her life anymore.

"Being a man of leisure suits you," she said. "Haven't seen you this glowy since that time you had a threesome with those twins."

Pete preened, patting his cheeks. "Well, thanks for the reminder of good times." His expression turned appraising. "Thankless servitude doesn't agree with you."

"Aren't you the flatterer."

"How many doubles have you worked this week?"

Lauren held up five fingers like a badge of honour. "Vic's kids had the flu this week, and Neal's boss won't give him time off."

"You're such a pushover."

Lauren looked out at Nathan Phillips Square. The crowd was minimal this time of year. City workers stood in galoshes scraping leaves from the drained fountain. In a couple weeks they would fill it back up with water, which would freeze and become a skating rink flanked by the sixties kitsch of New City Hall and the Romanesque beauty of Old City Hall. Lauren hated the touristy feel of the place. She preferred the Bentway, a rink that ran like a frozen river underneath the Gardiner Expressway. But this was Pete's favourite place to get street meat.

"I can't understand why you love this place so much."

Pete handed her a chicken sausage with mustard and ketchup. "It's a good place to people-watch." He picked up his Italian sausage with sauerkraut and pickles and took a huge bite. "Plus, the food is top-notch." A portion of pickle dropped to the ground. Two pigeons dived for it. The one half-dead covered in a strip of gravy came away with the prize.

Lauren eyed the growing crowd of sky rats, as her dad liked to call them. A semicircle of pigeons were prancing and pecking in front of their bench, vying for any scraps like stray dogs with wings. The cooing filling the gaps of conversation.

"I'm not even going to ask what's new with you because I know what you're going to say: nothing."

"Not true. I've been up to lots of things."

"Sign up for Bake or Die this year?"

Ever since trying one of her miniature gin-and-tonic cakes, shaped like a cocktail glass, he'd been urging her to sign up for one of the most hard-core baking contests in the country. It lasted three days, two rounds each day, and tested bakers with the most extreme challenges. One year, the contestants had to create a four-tiered cake that couldn't touch the table or ground. The prize was bragging rights and a hundred grand. The catch? The entry fee was a thousand dollars. That was a lot of money to waste on a whim.

"I kissed someone." She hadn't meant to blurt it out, but it was the only thing she could think of to distract Pete. Up until she'd sat down, she wasn't even sure if she was going to mention it. But she needed to talk to someone about it, and Pete was the best person.

Pete threw his hands up. "What is this, the sixth grade? I mean, I know it's been a while…but give me something better than that."

"It was a woman. I kissed a woman."

Pete's teeth took over his face in the biggest grin Lauren had ever seen him make. "Well, that is a horse of a different colour. You've been holding out on a brother." Pete folded his hands under his chin and batted his eyelashes at her. "Soooo, what's her name?"

"Hayley."

"The Smurf who replaced me? Damn. Didn't see that coming." Off Lauren's stunned look he said, "I still talk to Theo and Ramiro. They keep me up to date. Isn't she also living with you now?"

"Only temporarily, until she finds a place."

"Wow, I leave for two months, and suddenly it's like *Days of our Lives*."

"My life is hardly like *Days of our Lives*."

"Maybe not the twenty-first century *Days of our Lives*. Probably more like the 1950s version, but still. This is a whole new world for you." He picked up a plastic knife and began crooning the Disney song, soft at first, but two girls on an adjacent bench turned around to watch, and he ramped it up. Lauren buried her face in her hands. She'd forgotten what a showboat Pete could be. He jumped up on the bench, his sausage forgotten for the time being, and really began belting, his voice echoing throughout the square.

There was only a smattering of applause when he finished. This was probably one of the least strange things most people would see that day.

"So, are you going to kiss her again?" He picked up his sausage from the end of the bench just as a brave pigeon hopped onto the edge, eyeing the meat.

She was saved from answering by a round of applause for a skateboarder who'd misjudged and landed in the dregs of the leaf-infested fountain. One of the city workers pointed to the sign next to the man, which warned that wading was prohibited.

Pete stuffed the last of his lunch into his mouth. "You didn't answer my question."

"No. I'm not going to kiss her again. It was a one-time thing." Although she'd like to kiss her again, it wasn't practical. "We work together, and at least for the time being, we're roommates."

Pete wiped his mouth. "The air must be getting kind of stale in that bubble of yours."

"What does that mean?"

He grabbed both Lauren's arms and shook her a little. "Aren't you tired of watching other people live their lives? All you do is work. As far as I know, I'm the only person you hang out with, besides Vic occasionally, and we haven't seen each other in over two months."

A couple months ago, she would've thought Pete was being ridiculous. Her life was great. She had her dad, a job she liked enough, and good people she worked with. Her life was almost stress free. What else did she need? But since Hayley had started working at the diner, things had started to change. She hadn't even noticed it at first, but looking back, she envied the lives of her coworkers, and it had started with Hayley.

Lauren had overheard Hayley and Theo discussing their weekend plans, and for the first time the idea of going out sounded fun.

"I'm not even going to ask the last time you got laid, because I don't want to know. But I want you to think about it."

"Not everyone's life is about getting laid."

"True, but most people's lives include a little fun, and getting laid is fun." He waved Lauren's next comment away. "That's all I'm going to say about it. Think about rejoining the real world."

Later that night, Lauren sat on the roof people-watching. She was wrapped in a colourful quilt Greta had left behind, trying to recall when exactly she'd stopped living her life. It was as if at some point she'd climbed into that glass ball Pete had mentioned and become an observer instead of a participant. But she couldn't figure out when. Perhaps it had been a slow transition. She'd stopped dating after Ben. The payout wasn't worth the gut-wrenching pain she'd gone through. She'd stopped going out as much when she became manager. But was that an excuse she could use? After Greta died she'd pretty much given up on going out at all. It was easier to stay curled up on her roof looking down at other people enjoying their lives.

When had easy become the goal?

❖

Almost twenty-four hours had passed since their kiss. Hayley found herself reliving it throughout moments of the day. She hadn't been scheduled to work today, but Theo had called and asked that she take his evening shift. It had done a good job of keeping her thoughts off her mind-blowing kiss with Lauren. Almost. She'd burned some guy's burger because she was trying to recall how high Lauren's hand had travelled up her thigh before she'd stopped her. The rest of the day she dwelled on why she had.

Hayley hadn't seen Lauren all day, and the longer she went without seeing her, the more nervous she got. Would it be awkward? Hayley sighed. Of course it would be awkward. She wasn't surprised to see Lauren out when she got off work. She was probably avoiding her.

And this was why Hayley had stopped Lauren. Even if Lauren wasn't straight, the complications of why it would never work were mounting.

The door swung open, banging against the wall as a burst of air followed Lauren into the apartment. She had a colourful quilt wrapped around her shoulders and ratty slippers on her feet.

She pointed to the ceiling. "I've been on the roof...It's a good place to think."

Hayley stood rooted, letting her gaze rove over Lauren like she hadn't seen her in weeks. All the daydreams she'd had that day couldn't compare to the real thing. Even with her windblown hair, lack of makeup, and general dishevelment, Lauren was beautiful. Hayley's decision to distance herself was warring with the sight of Lauren.

Lauren focused on Hayley's hair, which she'd shoved into a quick ponytail. "I still can't get over your hair."

Hayley skimmed her hairline with her hand. "The blue was starting to fade. I thought it was time for a change." She stopped herself short of asking if it looked okay. That sounded too needy. Part of her really did want to know if Lauren liked it, but she'd never lived her life caring what people thought of her, and she wasn't about to start now.

"Mission accomplished." Lauren took a step forward. "It looks..." She was about to twirl a strand between her fingers, but Hayley took a step back, panicking.

Hayley hated that things were now awkward between them. "I..." She stood frozen, undecided whether she should mention the kiss. Lauren's light-brown eyes searched her face, mirroring the indecision Hayley felt.

"It's okay," said Lauren. "We don't have to talk about it. I mean, unless you want to."

"I don't." A whole chunk of Hayley's past was fighting with her common sense. After Violet, she'd vowed never to date straight girls again. She didn't need to be someone's experiment; the fallout was too harsh. Violet was just the last in a long line of bad ideas. Hayley liked Lauren, and for that reason she wanted to keep things friendly.

Lauren's whole demeanour sagged, and Hayley rushed to reassure her. "It's not that I didn't like it. I did. It's just..."

"You don't want it to be awkward."

"Right."

"Because we work together."

"And live together—temporarily, of course."

Lauren touched Hayley's arm. "It's already awkward."

Hayley sighed. She was much better at hiding the mess in the closet. Lauren's attempt to bring everything out in the open to show how unorganized life and relationships could get wasn't something she could deal with. "It doesn't have to be awkward." She shrugged and took a step back. "It happened. No big deal. We're friends, right?" Hayley stuck her hand out, holding it toward Lauren until she took it and smiled.

"Sure, we're friends."

Hayley let go of the warm hand and took another step back. "I'm… I'm going to go read for a bit." She turned and fled to her bedroom and threw herself on her bed. What a disaster. Could this day get any worse?

She heard a chime and checked her phone. A text from her sister Hannah: *Roll out the red carpet and get the Doritos ready. I'm coming for a visit.*

Shit. And the day just got so much worse.

CHAPTER EIGHTEEN

Hannah's voice carried through the kitchen window without much effort. Her sister had always been a loud talker. She wasn't even addressing Hayley, she was ordering herbal tea, but Hayley couldn't miss it. She finished prepping the tomatoes and wiped her hands on a towel.

"Is it okay if I take a few minutes, Ramiro? My sister's here for a visit."

He shooed her away with the flick of his hand. "We're not busy." He poked his head up and looked through the window. "She the one that looks like she's having a litter?"

Hayley grinned. "The one ordering tea at the top of her lungs? Yeah. That's her."

"She's cute." He moved his spatula in the general direction of Hayley. "What happened?"

"Very funny."

As soon as Hayley poked her head out, Hannah squealed. It was also the same moment Lauren entered the diner. Hayley's attention was immediately engaged, and she stumbled coming around the corner of the counter. Her face heated. Why couldn't she react like a normal human being for once? Scratch that. Why did she have to react like a teenager? Why couldn't she pull her shit together like an adult? Like Hannah, who had gotten her shit together the second she turned ten.

Hannah pushed herself up off her stool and practically crashed into Hayley. "Your hair is a fairly normal colour. My God, how long has it been since you've had hair that wasn't the colour you'd find in a box of Froot Loops?" Hayley's face heated, because, of course, the whole diner had heard that remark. "It looks really good." Hannah pulled Hayley's black beanie off her head to inspect it further. "Fuck, it's good to see you." She pulled Hayley in for another hug and whispered in her ear. "The hair change wouldn't happen to have anything to do with the woman standing behind me, would it?"

Hayley groaned, but Hannah just laughed and poked her flaming cheek. She'd always been able to embarrass her.

"How many kids are you having, anyway?" Hayley prodded her sister's enormous belly, all the while keeping one eye on Lauren. She checked the clock. Lauren was fifteen minutes early for her shift. What exactly did that mean?

Hannah nudged Hayley. "Hello? Where am I staying? Your text didn't give your address."

Hayley froze. She hadn't even thought of that. Hannah would have to stay with them. The last thing she wanted to do right now was ask Lauren for a favour. But no way would she let her pregnant sister, who she hadn't seen in months, stay in a hotel. Not that either of them could afford it anyway.

"Um…" Hayley steered her sister back to her stool where a hot mug of lemon tea waited for her. "Have a seat, drink your tea, and let me confirm something."

Hannah allowed herself to be corralled but eyed Hayley with suspicion all the same. Hayley didn't think she'd be getting out of this without some sort of lecture. She'd left out vital information, and her sister, who took that sort of thing very seriously, was about to find out how hard a time she'd been having. Hayley was prepared to defend her choice to stay in the city, but she'd rather not have to.

Hayley caught up with Lauren in the basement storage room. Her hair was up in a ponytail, as usual, but today Hayley noticed the way the strays curled under, brushing her neck. Lauren reached up and brushed them away, then returned her attention to her clipboard. The act felt intimate, and Hayley rapped her hand on the doorjamb, not wanting to intrude further.

"Hey," Hayley said from the doorway. "How do you feel about guests?"

Lauren pulled her attention from her inventory list. "In general?

Or is there a specific guest we're talking about?" She pointed up. "I'm assuming the pregnant lady belongs to you?"

"My sister." Hayley shrugged. What could she do? Family sometimes sucked. "She sprung this visit on me."

"Does she know—"

"No. And I don't want her to." Hayley stepped into the storage room and lowered her voice, even though no one upstairs could possibly hear them. "I'm not asking you to lie or anything, but can we not mention how long I've been living above the diner?"

"Okaaay. And how long is she staying?"

"Just until Sunday, if that. She has to be back at work Monday. She'll sleep in my bed."

Lauren took a step closer. "And where will you sleep?" And with that one sentence it was as if a furnace was heating the room.

Hayley swallowed. It had been an innocent enough question, but her mind went so many places at that moment. And without meaning to, almost like her eyes had betrayed her thoughts, they dipped to Lauren's lips. How easy would it be to reach out and wrap her hand around the back of Lauren's neck? To pull her close and end the distance? Her lips would be soft like the other night, and she wanted to know what Lauren's lip gloss tasted like. She was seriously contemplating it when she heard her name. She physically shook her head and scrambled backward out of the storage room.

Hannah was standing at the top of the stairs. "Hayley?"

Hayley took a deep breath and tried to clear her head still stuck in a haze of lust.

The second Hayley and her sister left the diner, Lauren couldn't think of anything else. Would Hayley tell her what had happened between them? Should Lauren care? After talking to Pete, Lauren was sure she knew what she was going to do. But now, with Hayley being so awkward about the whole thing, she was having second thoughts.

These thoughts followed her throughout the day. They hammered at her as the diner filled up, first with the lunch rush, which bled into the dinner rush. They were heavy thoughts that weighed her down. The day became longer than usual, her shift harder because of it. Everything seemed to be going wrong.

So when Luna showed up ten minutes late for her shift, Lauren wasn't even mad, only relieved that something had finally worked out. Those ten minutes had her worried that Luna wouldn't show up at all. The relief lasted forty-five minutes before Luna sliced her hand open with a broken plate and had to leave to get stitches.

That's when things took a downward spiral. Ezra and Theo were working the kitchen, and Lauren was the only server working the floor. And they couldn't do anything to keep up.

By eight the place was still crammed, which wasn't unusual for a Saturday, but this was Friday, and they rarely had this many people. That's when they discovered there'd been a Halloween concert in the park across the street. Booze must have been involved, or perhaps people had snuck their own in travel mugs, because the evening crowd had brought the concert with them.

An hour before the diner closed, Lauren was taking an order from the kitchen, a bowl of cream-of-broccoli soup and burger to the last booth, when one of the concert-goers waltzed—and that was really the only way to put it—into the diner and twirled into Lauren, upending the soup all down the front of her uniform.

The man in the blue London Fog coat turned around in horror. "Oh shit, my bad," he said, and with a sympathetic expression, he twirled back out of the diner. Lauren stood there, her arms outstretched, drenched in the thick, light-green sludge, ready to cry. It felt like minutes, but it was probably only a few seconds before Theo came out of the kitchen and bent down to help clean up the mess on the floor.

Lauren grabbed a cloth from the back and wiped the soup off her uniform as best she could, but she didn't have time to go up and change. They still had too many orders to take and get out before they tried to shove everyone out of the diner so she could close.

❖

"So, are we going to talk about your new apartment?" Hannah checked her watch. "I think three hours is my personal best." She was propped up on the couch, a pillow from Hayley's bed squeezed between her knees, watching her sister make her gunk, a recipe their nana used to cook for them. It looked gross, and whenever Hayley listed the ingredients it also sounded disgusting, but it was the best kind of comfort food.

Hannah had demanded Hayley make it the moment they entered her apartment. She'd been craving it for a week now, and she could never get the biscuits right. Not the way their nana or even Hayley made them, where they fell apart in buttery, flaky goodness.

Like the rest of her nana's recipes, Hayley suspected this one came off the box of some 1950s product. Hayley removed the pot of hard-boiled eggs from the stove and ran them under cold water. "What about my new apartment?"

"Last time I checked in, you had three roommates, and none of them were named Lauren. And you mentioned you were living in Kensington Market, not Queen Street West."

Hayley searched through the drawers for the can opener. It was in the second drawer, hidden under a hodge-podge of cooking utensils.

Hayley didn't know what to tell Hannah. She hated lying to her, but she didn't want to worry her. She hadn't said anything in the first place because Hannah would've raced in to rescue her, and she wanted to show everyone, including herself, that she didn't need that. She paused in mid-thought, the can opener suspended over the unopened can of salmon. Had Lauren rescued her? She would pay half of Lauren's rent, because no way was she taking charity.

"Hello?" Hannah waved from the couch. "Are you and Lauren… together?"

"No." Hayley shook her head, perhaps a little too vigorously. "No, no. She only offered me a place that was cheaper and closer to work."

Hannah heaved off the couch, using the coffee table to pull herself forward. "Hmm. I'm getting a certain vibe here."

Hayley turned her back to her sister as she stalked into the kitchen. "No vibe here." She broke the salmon into chunks, dropping them into a pot, and added milk, stirring rapidly.

"Uh-huh." Hannah leaned her hip against the counter and watched as Hayley peeled the eggs, throwing the shells into the compost bin. "You're such a bad liar."

Hayley cut the hard-boiled eggs into quarters and dropped them in the pot. She'd be able to hold her sister off for only so long. Hannah would badger her until she gave in and told. It had always been like that, even when they were kids. She'd never been able to keep a secret from her sister for long.

The first time she'd ever kissed a girl, Hayley had managed to hold on to that moment for two whole days before breaking down and telling Hannah everything. She'd been fourteen and terrified her parents would find out, terrified of what it meant about her, terrified by how much she'd liked it. But Hannah had been kind and understanding and encouraged her to go talk to Mom about it because she'd feel better if she did. And she had. She found something cathartic about giving away her secrets.

"Okay. We kissed. The other night." Hayley pulled a bag of frozen peas out of the freezer and dumped a bunch in a glass container.

"She kissed you? Or you kissed her?"

Hayley stood for a moment thinking about the way she'd melted into Lauren, how Lauren had opened to her, her hand slipping up her thigh to the edge of Hayley's dress.

"So I'm guessing it was a mutual thing?"

Hayley scrubbed her hands in the air. "It doesn't matter. She's my boss and roommate. She's forbidden fruit."

"Then why'd you kiss her?"

"Ugh. I don't know. It makes everything more complicated." The oven timer beeped. Hayley grabbed the oven mitts off the counter and pulled out a tray of freshly baked biscuits. The smell of flaky buttered pastry exploded into the kitchen.

Hannah reached for one, but Hayley shooed her away. "You'll spoil your dinner."

Hannah spread her hands over her belly. "No amount of food will satiate this little monster. I eat like I'm training for a food-eating competition."

"That explains why you're as big as a house."

Hannah picked up one of the discarded oven mitts and swatted Hayley with it. "Hey. Don't be cruel."

"You know I'm kidding. You look amazing and glowy."

"And starving. Let me have just one."

Hayley tossed the peas into the microwave. "It's almost ready. Can't you wait five minutes? Go set the table." When Hannah didn't move, Hayley picked up a biscuit and waved it at her. "You can have this if you set the table for me."

"If I'd known I'd be forced to work for my room, I might have chosen a better place to stay."

The front door creaked open, and there stood Lauren, her uniform covered in some sort of creamy liquid that had since dried into a stiff mess. It was also smeared into her hair, coating it in chunky globs.

Chapter Nineteen

Holy shit." Hayley took a step forward when she saw Lauren. "Is that the clam chowder?"

"Cream of broccoli." Lauren looked close to tears. "Luna cut herself and had to leave." She held her hands out in front of her, inspecting the mess down her front. "I had to work the last hour of my shift like this." She pulled the fabric away from her chest.

Hayley came out of the kitchen, wiping her hands on a towel. "Why didn't you come up and change?"

"It was packed tonight, and I was the only server. I couldn't leave."

"You should've called. I would've covered for you while you changed."

Lauren stood frozen. She hadn't even thought of calling Hayley, even if her sister hadn't been visiting.

Hannah spoke up. "Why don't you join us? Hayley made enough for a small army."

Lauren hesitated. She didn't want to impose or insert herself in a family reunion. But it smelled heavenly, and she hadn't eaten since before her shift.

Hayley pushed her toward her room. "Go shower and definitely change. It'll be ready by the time you're done."

When Lauren had disappeared into her room, Hayley turned to Hannah. "Do not embarrass me," she whispered. "Or you and your unborn child will be sleeping on the street." She pulled three plates down from the cupboard and motioned for Hannah to continue setting the table.

"Could you be any more obvious?" Off Hayley's shrug, she added, "Your eyes were glued to her breasts."

"They were not." But they had been. "I was looking at the spilled soup."

"Oh, please. Besides, why shouldn't you? She's cute."

"Shut up."

While the sound of the shower filtered into the kitchen, Hayley cracked the biscuits in half and laid four on each plate, ladling gunk onto the steaming centres. Hannah finished setting the table, and by the time they had the table full of food, Lauren had emerged from the shower, towelling off her hair.

"It smells amazing. What is it?"

"Don't ask." Hannah handed her a glass of red wine before she even reached the table.

Lauren sat and stared at the mess filling her plate. A light-grey chunky sauce covered it. The only colour was the stray pea dotting the slop.

"It's best to try it first. You'll like it. I promise."

Both Hannah and Hayley cut into a biscuit and scooped as much of the sauce as their forks would hold. Hannah ate with an urgency only pregnant women and dieters could muster.

"The biscuits are amazing. You're getting better than Nana at them."

Hayley smiled but didn't say anything. She watched Lauren push the gunk around her plate before spearing a piece of hard-boiled egg and tasting it. Her eyes went wide, and she looked over at Hayley.

"Wow."

"Not what you were expecting?"

"Not at all. What's it called?" She took a bigger bite, this time with some of the biscuit.

"Gunk," Hannah and Hayley said together.

"It's a family recipe."

"It's really amazing." Lauren took a large sip of wine, then another. The gunk didn't really go with red wine, but after the day she'd had, she needed it. It was hard to believe how much her emotions had flip-flopped in one day. First had been that awkward exchange with Hayley. She'd spent the last half of the morning psyching herself up for a conversation with her that never happened and then the absolute hell of a day.

At least Hayley seemed to be back to her normal self, although that probably had more to do with her sister being there than anything. Hayley hadn't even mentioned she had a sister, but then, they really hadn't gotten into personal details yet. It always took her longer to get to know a roommate than someone she was dating. She felt on guard with a new one because so much was at stake. If you didn't like who you were dating, you could just break up, but if you didn't like your roommate, they were harder to get rid of.

With Hayley it had been different. She hadn't felt as hesitant to hide behind that barrier of politeness—maybe because they worked together, or maybe it was Hayley.

She watched Hannah scrape her fork through the gunk, getting the last bits of it off her plate and into her mouth. She didn't look a thing like Hayley. She had light-brown hair swept back into a ponytail. Her eyes were brown, almost the colour of dark chocolate, and where Hayley was pale, Hannah had more of an olive complexion.

Their personalities didn't align either, but she'd known so many siblings who were nothing alike, so this didn't surprise her. Immediately she could tell Hannah was the older of the two. When she spoke to Hayley, her voice had a teasing quality, something that seemed to have been cultivated over the years. But Hayley didn't seem to mind.

"So where do you live?" Lauren asked Hannah.

"In Casper Falls. My husband and I moved back after we finished school."

"And are now going to subject my future niece or nephew to the hell that is small-town life." Hayley pointed her fork at Hannah, an affectionate smile on her lips.

"You're not a fan?" Lauren pushed her clean plate away and rested her elbows on the table.

"Of Casper Falls? No one's a fan. It has one stop light, which becomes a four-way stop after nine."

"It's not that bad. There's never any traffic, you can always find parking, the housing is affordable, and everyone's really friendly." Hannah grabbed both Lauren and Hayley's plates and stacked them on top of hers.

"There's nothing to do, no jobs unless you like administration or restaurant work, they play the same one movie for an entire month, and nobody can mind their own damn business."

Hannah waved away Lauren's offer to help and cleared the dishes off the table. "If you can't tell, my sister's a bit bitter about being the only lesbian in town."

Hayley went three different shades of red, each one darker than the last. "I wasn't the only lesbian. And I'm not bitter. I just think people should find more important things to do than talk about other people's business."

"You remember about the one-movie-a-month thing, right?" Hannah turned to Lauren. "You heard her say that, right?"

Lauren was enjoying the dynamic between the two sisters. She'd never seen Hayley so relaxed. Not that she was uptight, but there was always an edge to her, some part of her that stayed below the surface hidden. This Hayley seemed more open and approachable.

"Are you sure you don't want any help? I didn't even help cook." Lauren grabbed the bottle of wine off the counter and offered to refill Hayley's glass, but she shook her head.

"You worked all day, and Hannah didn't do anything. She may be pregnant, but as she's pointed out a million times, she's not an invalid."

Lauren refilled her wine glass. "When are you due?"

Hannah stacked the dishes next to the sink and began filling it with soapy water. "Not until January."

"January's better than December," said Hayley. "You don't want it born around Christmas. Those birthdays are the worst."

"Oh." Lauren stood up so fast she almost knocked her chair over. "I just remembered. I have dessert." She went to the fridge and pulled down a small opaque container and set it on the kitchen table. "I made these this morning." She lifted the lid to reveal three circles of chocolates decorated like Halloween characters. The inner circle was filled with white mummies, the middle circle was little green Frankensteins, and the outer circle was witches with black, pointy hats.

Hayley stared in obvious awe. "You made these this morning? Like, out of stuff you had in the kitchen?" She turned the container, looking at each chocolate. "When you said you liked to decorate cakes, I thought...I don't know what I thought actually, but these are awesome."

"Is this like a side hustle you have? Making specialized baked goods for people?"

"Side hustle? No." Lauren rarely made any money off her baking. She'd planned to take these to the diner for everyone tomorrow. But beyond making some cupcakes for her dad or the odd birthday cake for a friend, her desserts were mostly something she shared with friends and family.

"You really should think about it. At least post some pictures on Pinterest. People will go apeshit when they see them. They almost look too good to eat."

A ball of warmth settled in Lauren's chest. She loved baking and sharing what she made with her close friends and family, but she'd never considered it good enough to actually sell. Maybe she should think more about what Pete had said. The deadline for the Bake or Die contest was still a couple of weeks away.

"There is this contest that happens every year that my friend Pete's been trying to get me to sign up for a couple years now."

"You're crazy not to." Hannah took the last bite of her chocolate, finishing off the witch's head and closing her eyes as she chewed.

"The fee is a thousand dollars."

"Holy shit!" Hayley grabbed a ghost and twirled it around. "Why so much?"

"The prize is a hundred grand." Both Hayley and Hannah stopped eating. Lauren shrugged. "Hundreds of people sign up, and there's only one winner. That's a lot of money to give up."

"But this Pete guy thinks you're good enough."

"And your creations are amazing, so what's the problem?" Hayley grabbed a witch and popped it into her mouth. "Your flavours are amazing. Although…"

"Although what?"

"If you added cinnamon extract to this, it would give it a French-toast taste. Like if you could make them look like little pieces of French toast, that would be cool."

Lauren stared into the beady little eyes of one of the ghost chocolates. The problem? She didn't have a thousand dollars to give up, but more important? She didn't have the confidence to think she could win.

❖

Hayley turned over as quietly as she could, but it was hard to manoeuvre around Hannah's belly. Yesterday the double had felt huge, before she'd had a seven-months-pregnant woman hogging two-thirds of it. Maybe she should go sleep on the couch after all, although then she'd have to deal with Jerkface.

He'd stayed hidden in Lauren's bedroom while they'd had dinner, but Lauren kicked him out before going to bed. Otherwise he'd drive her crazy. No, here was better. It might be cramped, and any second Hannah would start snoring, but it was better than having a fat cat use your back as a scratching post in the middle of the night.

Hayley turned onto her back and tried to find a comfortable place for her left arm. Finally she settled for her stomach and began drumming her fingers. Hannah reached out and placed her hand on Hayley's.

"Stop that."

"Sorry."

Hannah groaned and flipped onto her back, then immediately turned back to her original position on her side facing Hayley. "Ugh. I miss Benjamin."

"Who the fuck is Benjamin?" Hayley turned on her side facing Hannah.

"My body pillow."

"You named your body pillow?"

"You're surprised?" Hannah named everything—her cars, her appliances, even her computers had names.

"No. I guess not. What does Derek think of Benjamin?"

"Probably not a fan. Benjamin replaced him in bed three weeks ago."

"Ouch."

Hannah yawned. "We all make sacrifices. I'm making his progeny in my body, so he can sleep on the couch for a couple months."

"Why's he on the couch? What about the spare bedroom?"

Hannah opened her eyes and stared at her sister. "It disappeared a month after we found out about this thing growing inside me." She pointed to her belly.

"Oh. Right." Hayley studied Hannah. She looked exhausted and irritable. "Are you doing okay?" Hayley hadn't even thought to ask what had prompted her visit.

"Besides feeling like I'm running a 10k in ninety percent humidity every day? Yeah. I actually came to check up on you."

"Me?"

"Yeah, the one who came here with a job and an apartment and then all of a sudden has a different job and a different apartment. You. The one who always lets everyone think she's okay so as not to rock the boat. You always put everyone else first, and I'm worried about you."

"I don't put everyone else first."

"You stayed in Casper Falls working with Mom and Dad because you were afraid they wouldn't be able to handle the place without you. You put off school, and you put off moving here even though it was so obvious you weren't happy back home." Hannah placed a hand on Hayley's cheek. "We get it. We all do. You belong here. Casper Falls was never going to hold you forever. Are you happy?"

Hayley nodded. She didn't even have to think about it. Even though things hadn't gone the way she'd planned, there was something vital about being in the city. And it wasn't that she thought she was meant to be here, destiny and all that crap. She felt more alive here than she ever had in Casper Falls. And even if she'd managed to find a job she liked back home, she still wouldn't be as happy as working as a short-order cook here.

❖

Lauren stopped, her hand poised on the fridge, when she saw movement out of the corner of her eye. At first she thought it might be Jerkface, but he was nuzzled in his favourite place, right over the floor vent in the living room, blocking the heat from getting to everyone else, naturally.

Hayley sat up on the couch, pushing her hair off her face. "Everything okay?"

"I was going to ask you the same thing." Lauren motioned toward Hayley and her new position on the couch. She had one of the throw blankets and a quilt tucked around her.

"Hannah finally fell asleep, and she snores like a razorback pig."

Lauren laughed softly, coming to sit on the coffee table. "And what exactly does a razorback pig sound like when it snores?"

"Like something that needs to be slaughtered and gutted if you have to sleep next to it."

"Wow. Okay. That took a sharp turn."

Hayley shrugged, the neck of her sweater slipping down, revealing a bare shoulder that glowed blue in the light from the street.

Lauren was reminded of their positions the other day, only this time reversed. Since the kiss she'd felt a tension that hadn't been there before. She would give anything to unravel it, not that it would take much. A tug here, a pull there, lips meeting, skin touching. Then almost as if on cue, a loud sawing noise shattered the silence.

Hayley grinned. "The razorback speaks."

The invitation was a breath away. Lauren could hear herself asking if Hayley wanted to share her bed. However, she didn't. She knew what the answer would be. Hayley had made her choice. She wanted to be just friends, and even if Lauren was only offering a bed and nothing more, Hayley might not know that, and the rejection would be crippling.

"Would you like one of my pillows?" Lauren asked instead.

"Thank you. Mine was stolen."

"You have to be careful who you let into your bed."

They both paused, contemplating that sentence. "Hmm," Hayley finally said. "A lesson I wished I'd learned earlier."

Lauren wanted to ask but didn't. She retrieved a pillow from her bed, still warm, and handed it to Hayley. She couldn't be certain, but it looked as if Hayley had brought the pillow to her nose before sinking into it on the couch.

CHAPTER TWENTY

I know a bribe when I see one."

"A bribe? Dad, I shouldn't have to bribe you with junk food to get you out of the house. You're retired, not dead. All you do is sit and read and watch shows. All day. Every day. Don't you want a little variety?" Lauren settled into the booth at the family diner around the corner from his apartment.

"I want to be left to do the things that make me happy."

And sadly, one of the things that made her father happy was eating food that exacerbated his diabetes. He hadn't been out of the house since his last doctor's appointment, over three weeks ago. She was afraid to stop doing things for him, like bringing groceries, because he'd just order delivery. She'd barely been able to coax him out for this.

Max flipped open a menu to the burger section and scrolled down until he found the banquet burger. "I don't need the life of a young person. I'm not young anymore. The goal isn't to make life harder. It's to simplify it."

Lauren rolled her eyes. "There's nothing simple about kidney failure and heart disease."

Max motioned for the server. "You sound like your mother. She was constantly on my case about my diet." The sentence hung heavy in the air, the implications clear. Lauren's mom, who had lived her whole life by the rules—eating right, getting plenty of fresh air, never drinking, nor indulging in sweets—had died ten years previously of cancer. Lauren often wondered if Max felt it was unfair that he was still alive. And if her mom had lived, would her dad be such a recluse now?

They ordered and sat staring out the window as rush-hour traffic passed. The nights were growing longer, so even at six in the evening it was fully dark, which made the world feel colder. Lauren preferred to be home by now, curled up on her couch with a glass of wine, covered by her favourite throw.

Max arranged the silverware on his paper placemat. "So are you going to tell me why you asked me out for dinner?"

"Why do I need a reason? I thought it would be nice to see the inside of other walls besides your apartment."

Max waved her off, then grinned as their server set down his banquet burger—all three levels—in front of him. "Now this is a burger. Can I get some vinegar?" Their server nodded.

Lauren poked one of the rubbery eggs on her plate. She'd never let an order go out looking like this. The eggs were overcooked, the hash browns were undercooked, and the bacon was crisp enough to use as a shiv.

Max put down his burger and stared at Lauren. "What's really bothering you? I know this has nothing to do with getting me out of my apartment."

Their server set a glass bottle of vinegar on the table. Lauren smiled up at her. It didn't matter. The woman wasn't even looking; her focus on a new group of five that had entered. Lauren recognized the haggard expression of someone who'd been on their feet all day and probably had several more hours to go. Her hair was pulled tight into a functional ponytail, no amount of makeup could hide the dark circles under her eyes, and what little foundation she'd applied earlier had since melted.

She looked down at her eggs. Why had she dragged them out to this diner? After thinking about it, she realized she had wanted to get herself out, not her dad. Hayley had plans tonight, and the thought of staying in by herself was unbearable.

Lauren shrugged as she looked up at the kind eyes of her father. "I think I just wanted some company." But it wasn't just that. She'd wanted to have plans. More specifically, plans with Hayley.

Max smiled and squeezed her hand. "Your company is always welcome. Next time, though, let's order in."

❖

Hayley lay sprawled on her bed, facedown, softly snoring. One foot poked out the right side of the bed, while her hand dangled over the edge on the left. Lauren guessed she was reclaiming her territory after having shared with her sister for two days.

Hayley shifted, pulling part of the cover down and exposing a bare leg and the skin on her back above the waistband of her boxers. Lauren stared at the skin just below the edge of her boxers, remembering how soft it had been. How much she'd wanted to explore it.

Lauren stopped inching toward the bed. Perhaps she should've knocked. If Hayley were to wake up and see her standing there, it would look creepy.

Before Lauren had a chance to back out of the room, Jerkface jumped up on the bed and began pawing at Hayley's back.

"G'off." Hayley swatted blindly, and Jerkface took that as a game and began taking swipes at her hand. "You stupid cat." She bolted up to shove him off her bed but stopped before she got the chance, stunned that Lauren was standing at the foot of her bed. Her hair was mussed in the most adorable way, pulled and tangled on one side.

Lauren covered her stomach, hoping that might help the dip and flip it seemed to be doing at that moment. "I'm sorry to wake you so early. Ezra called in sick, and I can't get ahold of anyone else." Lauren's eyes dipped to the duvet cover, realizing what an invasion this was. She was, after all, Hayley's boss, and instead of knocking or even texting, she'd felt she had the right to just barge in on her. "I should've knocked."

Jerkface was still on the bed kneading Hayley's thighs with his claws. Lauren reached over and scooped him off the bed, chucking him to the floor. When she looked back up, Hayley quickly averted her eyes from Lauren's cleavage, on full display in her housecoat. She resisted the urge to tie it tighter.

Silence filled the room, thick and charged. Lauren had lost the thread of conversation, and clearly so had Hayley. She slumped back on the bed and grabbed her phone to check the time. It was ten to five.

"Oh, God." Hayley pulled the covers up over her head.

"Is that a yes?"

"Fine. But I want one of Ezra's afternoon shifts as a thank-you." Hayley's voice was muffled under the blankets.

"Thank you." Lauren backed out of the room.

❖

Staring at Hayley that morning in bed, Lauren had made up her mind to ask her out on a date. Actually, she'd come up with the idea the other night when she'd had dinner with her dad. He'd said something about having earned his solitude. Like Pete had said, she'd stuffed herself inside a bubble, able to watch the world around her but not participate. Well, she was tired of being an observer in her own life. It was time she did something to shake things up, and the scariest, shakiest thing she could think of was to ask Hayley out on a date.

She'd solidified that thought this morning, but now, as Hayley worked in the kitchen and Lauren set up the front, her nerve had disappeared. Any minute their first customer would come in, and the chance would be gone.

Lauren found Hayley in the back pantry pacing in the dark, shaking her arms as if getting ready for a marathon. "What's going on? You okay?"

Hayley nodded. "What's up?"

Lauren bit her top lip. It was now or never. "I wanted to revisit this friends thing." She motioned between the two of them. "Would you like to go have coffee with me sometime? Maybe after work?"

Hayley's eyes widened. "Are you asking me out on a date?"

"Yes."

"No…Absolutely not."

Lauren opened her mouth but was interrupted by the chime on the front door and Kaleed's voice calling, "Hey, Lauren. Where do you want these pies?"

She paused a minute, studying Hayley's face, mortified to have been rejected so thoroughly. "On the counter, please. I'll be there in a second." Lauren reached for the cloth in her apron pocket and wiped her hands, wishing she could wipe away her memory of this moment. "Okay, then. Forget I asked." Without saying anything else she fled to the front.

❖

"It was the right decision," Hayley whispered to herself. It had become her mantra. She'd been saying it every few minutes out loud and had it on a constant loop in her head.

Ramiro stopped behind Hayley, peering over her shoulder. "I have to disagree, Pollyanna. Sprinkling panko on a chicken burger like that is most definitely the wrong decision."

Hayley looked down at the plate in front of her and groaned. Her day was a mess. And it had nothing to do with starting a rush on her own and everything to do with Lauren asking her out for coffee. Where had that come from? But as soon as the diner had opened, she'd been fucking up large. Luna had come in and screamed at her four times because she couldn't get one of her orders right.

"If they tip bad it's your fault," she spit out, then left with the new, hopefully correct, order.

Lauren wasn't any better. She hadn't said anything with words, but she didn't need to. Her face said it all. She'd given Hayley at least three what-the-fuck looks. And each time Hayley just got worse. She'd been behind all day, even with Ramiro's help. He'd only just gotten his cast off a few days ago, which meant he was still awkward on his feet, so they'd agreed he'd do prep and Hayley would take lead, a first for her.

She knew the menu, and thanks to the cheat sheet on the wall, the lingo was finally starting to sink in. It was her speed. She wasn't used to making several things at once or doing it quickly. Hayley could cook, no question about that, but she was used to doing it for friends and family, where she had no time limit.

Finally, at ten to nine, Lauren stepped into the kitchen. "What is going on, Hayley?" She looked around at the gargantuan mess surrounding Hayley. About a half-dozen broken eggs littered the floor, flour and oats were strewn on every surface, and pancake and waffle mix covered half the counter. In one spot it had run to the edge and was dripping onto the floor. Ramiro had left an hour ago, and Hayley had finished her regular shift, making this the second double she'd worked that week. Usually she wouldn't mind, she could always use the money, but with Lauren also working a double, the mood in the diner had gotten cold.

Hayley wiped her hands on her apron and repeated the words to herself. *I made the right decision.*

"This is the job, Hayley. This is what you were hired to do."

"I know. I'm sorry." The last thing she wanted to do was show weakness. She was better than this. She wasn't okay with doing the bare minimum, or even being decent at her job. She wanted to excel. This mess was the opposite of that.

"Cowboy with Spurs." Luna rang the bell and slipped the chit into the roundabout.

Hayley reached for it, and as she did, she placed her hand on the grill, burning her index and middle finger. "Fuck." She pulled her hand away and looked at the red welts forming on them.

"Let me see." Lauren grabbed for Hayley's hand, but she pulled away.

"I'm fine. Just go. It's only a little burn." She waved Lauren out of her kitchen and went back to the mess surrounding her. This day couldn't end soon enough.

❖

Lauren sat in her room afraid to venture out, afraid she might bump into Hayley, who hadn't come in yet. She was still closing with Luna, and any second she would come home, and that awkward moment would be between them.

This morning everything had seemed so simple. She'd ask Hayley out, although now she couldn't think for a second why she'd thought Hayley would say yes. She'd been convinced of it, but it was Hayley who had decided they should be friends. Lauren was sure those had only been words. But sitting there, on her bed, dejected, she couldn't figure out why asking Hayley out had been the best solution for getting out of her rut. Hearing Hayley's footsteps on the fire-escape stairs outside, she felt both panic and a thread of excitement and knew the reason.

Hearing a soft rap at the door, Lauren hesitated, not sure if she was ready for this.

"Can I come in?"

Lauren arranged the blankets around her. She'd taken her shoes off and her hair out of its ponytail, but hadn't yet taken her uniform off. "Um, I guess." Her heart lodged in her throat.

Hayley swung the door in and leaned against the jamb. "I'm really sorry about today."

Lauren waved the apology off. "We all have bad days. It's fine."

Hayley stepped into the room, shaking her head. "Not about my performance. I mean, I'm sorry about that too, but about this morning, when you asked me out."

"It's all good. Let's just forget about that."

"I realized today that it probably sounded so mean saying no the way I did. So I wanted to clarify why I said it." Hayley stepped farther into the room. "When it comes to women, I tend to lead with my... heart? Or something. And I like you, Lauren, I really do, and I don't want to screw that up. That's why I said no."

Lauren pulled at the fuzzy throw covering her legs. Hearing it didn't make it hurt any less. Instead it made her feel pathetic. "I shouldn't have asked in the first place. I'm your boss and we live together and it's just..."

"Those are good reasons, sure. But the more I think about it, that's not the reason. I mean, I don't plan on working as a short-order cook forever. And living here is only temporary." Hayley heaved a sigh and sat on the bed without being invited. "Remember the girl I told you about? Violet? Well..." Hayley laughed and looked away. "As Hannah put it, she took me for a ride. We were on-again, off-again for a while, but then we moved in together, and she ended up borrowing a lot of money from me to start a business." Hayley paused for a second to think of how to put it. She hadn't thought of it for weeks now. Moving had been the right choice, but it still hurt to think of how Violet had used her the way she did. "I made some decisions about dating after that, and I'm trying to stick to them." One of those decisions had been to stay away from situations where she might get her heart broken, which, as Hannah had pointed out, meant dating in general.

"Can I ask what happened?"

"She'd opened a store for cat paraphernalia and hired Kevin to help with the books."

"And you think he was helping with more than the books."

"I do, but you're focusing on the wrong part of that story. She opened a store for cat shit in a town with a population of about ten thousand. If that wasn't a clue we weren't meant for each other..."

Lauren reached over and took Hayley's hand. "I'm sorry."

"For what?" Hayley gazed down at their hands. Lauren was

smoothing her thumb over the skin, which sent shivers up Hayley's spine. It was getting harder to remember why she'd said no to a date.

"That you were hurt. But she sounds like an idiot. Anyone who would cheat on you with a Kevin is just plain dumb."

"You want to hear dumb? Ask me what the name of the store is." Hayley removed her hand on the pretence of fixing her messy bun.

"What was the name?"

"It was called Caterific. It sold only cat items."

"Good Lord. That's really all you had to say about her."

"What does it say about me? I bankrolled the thing."

Lauren stood. "Would you like a glass of wine? Maybe we could veg and watch a baking show? I think we've both earned it today."

Hayley followed her into the kitchen. "So, listen. If we're going to be friends, I have some requests. Simple favours, really, to make friendship a little easier."

Lauren turned at the fridge, her fingers on the handle, waiting for what came next.

"They're more rules really—for both of us, if you want." Hayley held up her index finger. "One, no showering when the other person is home." She ticked off a finger. "Two, no walking around in revealing housecoats, or boxer shorts, or yoga pants, or tank tops. And no licking the spoon after stirring your coffee. No licking of anything, in fact." Hayley waved her hand through the air. "Licking is off the table. And—"

"Hey." Lauren grabbed Hayley's hand. At first she'd been worried that she'd misread Hayley, that Hayley had said no because she wasn't interested, but the more Hayley talked, the warmer Lauren became. The heat had started in her stomach and soon spread to her whole body, sinking lower until Lauren felt like she was glowing.

Hayley stared back, and the look in her eyes told Lauren it wouldn't take much to change her mind. All she had to do was take a step closer and lean in, and she was sure Hayley would melt against her. Instead, she dropped Hayley's hand and turned to grab a bottle of white out of the fridge.

"No problem. I think I can manage those things."

Chapter Twenty-one

The next few weeks Lauren and Hayley settled into a routine. Halloween came and went, as did the leaves on the trees. Soon the park looked empty and depressing, a sign that the cold half of the year had arrived.

Hayley loved winter. She always found so much more to do. Skating, skiing, snowboarding, and hockey season were in full swing. Hot chocolate tasted better, especially after an afternoon of skating. The air always smelled fresh, and a warm fire could fix anything.

She was learning people in the city didn't feel the same way. Sure, they had tons of activities, but as soon as the cold weather descended like a foul mood on the city, everything became less vibrant.

Lauren called it hibernation season, which was how most people felt about it. Winter was an excuse to stay inside, catch up on Netflix shows, host dinner parties, head south, anything to avoid being out in the cold.

One Sunday in late November Hayley woke to the smell of burned Brussels sprouts. She kicked off the covers and wandered into the kitchen to find Lauren preparing a feast.

"What's the occasion?" Hayley leaned on the counter and yawned.

Lauren stood mourning over her Brussels sprouts. "No occasion. I'm heading over to my dad's, and I usually take him a bunch of preprepared meals so he eats healthier." She groaned and dumped the sprouts in the compost bin on the counter. "He's diabetic."

Hayley lifted a container with chicken seasoned with pepper and something green. "And he eats this?"

Lauren looked up for the first time at Hayley. The question clearly caught her off guard. "Yes." She sighed. "Not usually. I find a lot of empty delivery containers in the garbage. But I hope some of this makes its way into his stomach. I mean," she looked around her kitchen at all the food she was planning to take: two containers of chicken, two more of plain brown rice, and three with fish and roasted vegetables. "What a waste if he doesn't."

"I'm sure he eats some of it." But Hayley wasn't sure of that at all. The food looked like something you'd serve to someone without taste buds. She was sure Lauren could cook. She just didn't. Now that Hayley was living there, she made most of the meals, not that they had a lot of call for that. They both ate at the diner most days. But if they spent a night in, Hayley was in charge.

Hayley slid off the stool in search of coffee. The kitchen was spotless. All the dishes had been loaded in the dishwasher, the cupboards washed, the packaging thrown in the garbage. Hayley couldn't fathom how someone could do all that work without making a little bit of a mess.

"What are you doing tomorrow afternoon?" Lauren asked as she packed her containers into a small cooler.

Hayley poured herself a cup of coffee and yawned again. "I'm opening, so I hadn't planned on doing much. Just hanging out. Why?"

"Forget it. It was silly."

"No, really. What?" Hayley nudged her. She was always careful of how much she let herself touch Lauren. They'd reached a precarious balance in the weeks since their talk, and she didn't want to do anything to spoil that.

"I'm going skating with Vic and her kids on the Bentway. Would you be interested in coming with us? I remember you saying once you loved ice-skating."

Hayley grinned through the steam in her coffee. "I'd love to. Oh, but I don't have my skates with me."

"You can rent them. No one here actually owns skates. Who has space to store them?"

❖

"Are you a fucking moron?"

Hayley dropped her head onto the booth table and groaned. She shouldn't have even mentioned her decision to Hannah.

"The woman you're in love with asked you out on a date, and you said no? How are we related? When someone you like asks you out, you say yes. Got it? *Yes.*"

"I'm not in love with her."

"Okay. But you're too old to use the word 'crush,' and I'm pretty sure one date with Lauren, and you'd be singing dopey love songs to yourself in the shower."

Hayley scooped mayo onto a fry and crunched down on it. They served shoestring French fries at the diner, Hayley's favourite. She was on dinner break and had taken the down time to check up on Hannah, who she hadn't been able to get ahold of lately.

"Well, as it happens, we're going skating tomorrow. It's not a date. Other people will be there. But I just don't want complications right now."

"Hale, Violet was an asshole. Actually, she's still an asshole, and you're well rid of her, believe me. I've met Lauren, and I approve of her. It doesn't mean she has to be your forever person—if there is such a thing—but at least give it a try. Or else you'll end up alone and bitchy like Aunt Beat. Nobody wants that."

Hayley scrunched up her face. Their Aunt Beatrice had divorced her husband back in the eighties and spent the last thirty-some years complaining about everything. Hannah and Hayley were convinced that getting laid would solve most of her personality issues.

"What if it gets awkward? If it doesn't work out?"

"It's only a date, for fuck's sake. She didn't ask you to commit to raising her awful cat with her. And besides, you've already rejected her once. Isn't that as awkward as it could get? Besides horrible sex, but she seems like the type who'd be good in bed."

"Hey, now."

"Oh, right, like you haven't thought about it."

Hayley rung off after enquiring about the unborn litter Hannah was incubating, an unsettled feeling in her stomach. Hannah made it sound so easy, as if getting over having her heart wrenched out and cut into a million pieces with a fork was an everyday thing. She wasn't in love with Violet, not anymore, but getting back into the buffet line was proving harder than she'd expected.

❖

There was something about the smell of cold air—the way it tickled Hayley's nose as it rushed in. Her lungs were full, her heart hammering as the air whipped by. The Bentway was packed that afternoon with skaters of all skill levels. A group of beginners was taking a lesson off to the side, pushing chairs around to keep them upright.

Zoe, Vic's seven-year-old, zipped past, giggling as her older sister Aubrey chased her through the maze of people. Farther behind was Vic, meandering along. She could skate, but only enough to keep an eye on her girls. Lauren was beside her laughing at their antics. She was a fair skater, but nothing like Hayley.

The Bentway was more like a river of ice running under the highway, which made it bumpier than most rinks, but Hayley had grown up skating on ponds, which were anything but smooth. She sailed past the beginner group with ease and rounded the bend to continue down the path.

She found something magical about watching people pair off into couples. Winter was the best and worst time for that. On the one hand, it was nice to fit into a mould, to belong to someone and to claim ownership of another. Hayley missed that. She missed the connection that came with being a *them*.

They hadn't been there more than an hour when Vic flagged Hayley down. "The girls are getting cold. We're going to grab some hot chocolate. Do you want to come?"

"The girls are cold?" Lauren bumped her arm. "Don't believe her," she said to Hayley. "She uses hot chocolate as a bribe to get the girls to come in."

Vic laughed, and the sound came out big and throaty, echoing under the expressway. "Otherwise they'd stay out here until they were blocks of ice sliding around."

Hayley turned to Lauren, gauging her interest. "What were you thinking?"

"I'm still good if you'd like to stay out longer."

Hayley nodded. As much as she loved the city, she missed parts of Casper Falls, especially this time of year.

They said good-bye to Vic and her girls and continued along at a quieter pace.

"You really love this kind of thing, don't you?" Lauren asked.

"It's the community stuff I miss. By now the main drag of Casper Falls will be an explosion of Christmas decorations—too much if you ask my nana—and Jackpine Lake is iced over. Every year they string up fairy lights around the pond. They make everything glow."

"This doesn't compare?" Lauren pointed out at the Bentway, which, by now, had turned on their own fairy lights. The city sparkled in the background, masking the last dying embers of the sun as it sank behind the cityscape.

Hayley gazed at Lauren, who had flushed cheeks and a red nose, her hat pulled down and framing her face with soft, white knit. It was a beautiful sight. "This view has other perks, believe me." She grabbed Lauren's hand and skated a little faster around the next curve.

Lauren breathed in the fresh night air. This was only her second time skating at the Bentway, but she wasn't much for winter. She preferred all the indoor advantages of the cold weather—snuggling under an electric blanket, hot chocolate with marshmallows, and movie marathons. Lauren managed to keep up, barely. "Whoa. Slow down. I'm not as good as you. I only learned to skate a couple of years ago."

"You didn't go skating as a kid?" Hayley asked. They drifted past a couple who were holding hands, taking sips from a travel mug and passing it between them.

"My mom said skating was not a skill I needed in life." Lauren stumbled, but Hayley pulled her back, steadying her. Hayley slowed their pace so they were ambling, overtaking few people. "I sometimes used to wonder how my parents got together. My dad is this big, burly guy who loved to laugh and tell stories. He used to take me for walks on Sundays when my mom was grocery shopping, and we would have little adventures, just the two of us. My mom believed in order and facts. If it didn't get you something in return, it was pointless." Up ahead, a small group had gathered to watch a young man practicing his triple lutz. "I remember one year for my sixth birthday, my dad got me a bike. It was purple and had tassels, and even though I didn't know how to ride it, I loved it. My mom told him to take it back. She said I didn't need to ride a bike in order to succeed in life and that the money was better put to tutors or piano lessons."

"Well, that's just mean."

"She wasn't trying to be mean. I think she was trying to prepare me for life. And look how that turned out. I'm a university dropout who works in a diner."

"Are you happy?"

Lauren almost tripped, struck by the simplicity of the question. Was she happy. Was she? "Sometimes. I get to work with a bunch of great people. I don't sit in traffic every day for hours, getting angry at the world. Is my life perfect? No. But it's not horrible."

"Wow. That's a goal right there. You sure your standards aren't too high?" Hayley was teasing her.

"My standards might be changing. You mentioned a bad breakup. Mine is less recent than yours, but I think I've been shying away from things too long."

"Is that why you asked me out?" Hayley steered them to the side lines so they could take off their skates. The temperature had dropped, and only the diehards were on the ice.

"I asked you out because I like you."

Hayley hesitated for only a second. "Does the offer still stand?"

Lauren grinned. "It does."

Chapter Twenty-two

L auren pulled Hayley, guiding her through the dark hallway.
"I can't see anything," said Hayley.

"You will." The idea had been Pete's. One of his classmates had helped build part of the structure and had put them in touch so Lauren could see it before it premiered.

Lauren opened the door at the end of the hall, and light bombarded them. It was almost like they were on a stage with spotlights aimed at them. As they adjusted to the brightness, the scene changed. They weren't seeing spotlights but rather several projectors aimed from a balcony above them. Lauren pulled Hayley off the small stage and down a short flight of stairs. The farther away they got, the easier it was to determine what was on the screen. By the time Lauren pulled Hayley up to the balcony, the whole scene fell into place. It was the start screen for Super Mario World. At the railing of the balcony were two controllers nestled on soft cushions.

"What is this?" Hayley asked. They were in a church up in the gallery. Below them the pews had been removed, leaving an empty space where the words *Bow to My Power* were painted in an elaborate gold script. The lights from the projectors bounced off the stained-glass windows, which had been replaced with new images. Some depicted heroes from popular video games such as Mario, Link, and Lara Croft in glory poses. Others pictured battle scenes from various video games.

"It's a commentary on the real first-world gods of the twenty-first century. Generation Z and Alpha, even most Millennials, have never known a world not dominated by video games." A young man, dressed in paint-covered overalls, stepped out from the darkness in the back. "These are our new legends." He pointed to the stained-glass windows. The closest one to them was a scene from Assassins Creed.

"Wow. This is amazing." Hayley turned back to the screen.

The man stepped up to them, laughing. "That's pretty much the only response I've gotten so far: Yes, but can I play it?" He picked up one of the controllers and pressed start and handed it to Hayley. "It's fully functional." He pointed to a bin beside them. "And there are other games. Go nuts."

Hayley looked back at Lauren, her expression pure joy. "Awesome. Which game is your favourite?"

"I've never played."

"Never? Not even as an adult?" Hayley handed her the other controller. "Okay, this game is pretty easy, and fun too." She showed Lauren how to use the four buttons and D-Pad to control her character. "I'll be Mario, so I'll go first, and you can watch what I do. You'll be Luigi." Hayley entered the first level and grabbed the red shell to fling it at a row of turtles. Lauren watched with rapt attention, knowing she was never going to be able to figure this out. But the joy on Hayley's face made her total annihilation worth it.

By the time they'd reached the Donut Plains, Lauren had finally determined that if she held the X button down while using the D-pad, she could run faster.

"Thank you," said Hayley.

"For what?"

"This. You're really good at dates."

"Who knew?" Lauren jumped Luigi onto a vertically moving platform and dodged the first Bullet Bill, but she forgot to duck for the second and promptly died.

"When was the last time you went on a date?" Hayley made it through the level without any problems. She was obviously an expert. Her lives count was quadruple what Lauren's was; in fact, she'd already had to give Lauren some of hers.

"I don't know if I've ever been on a real date."

"What? Oh, come on. You're what? Early thirties?"

Lauren sighed and put down her controller. "The only person I ever dated knocked me up while I was in university, and we got married. After the divorce I decided not to date for a while."

"Okay. Back up." Hayley laid her controller next to Lauren's. "There's a lot to unpack there. You have a child?"

"I miscarried."

"Oh, God. I'm so sorry."

"It's okay. I was so not ready to be a parent. But Ben and I had already gotten married and decided to, I don't know, prove the world wrong, I guess. But by the time we realized how big a mistake we'd both made, eight years had passed. It took another year or two before we called it quits for good. So it's been…" Lauren gazed up at the ceiling, calculating in her head. "Five years since our divorce was final." Five years? Where had the time gone?

"Well, it's a good thing I came along to get you out of this dry spell, huh?" Hayley leaned in and whispered, "Let's go get some hot chocolate. I know a really good place that puts salted caramel liquor in it."

❖

"I told you you'd come back." A great bear of a man with a hipster moustache and bald head greeted them. He was pointing at Hayley as she and Lauren entered a small cafe. The place was tiny, with only three tables, and packed. On the left side was a small stage taken up fully with a large, glowing Christmas tree.

"There was never any doubt, Abe. I said I would be."

"But I can always tell. I know potential regulars when I see them." He placed his giant fists on the counter and leaned over. "What can I get you?"

"Can I get two knocked-up Santas to go, please?"

"You sure can."

Lauren leaned in. "Knocked-up Santa?"

Hayley shook her head. "I don't know where he comes up with these names, but it's fucking good. Just trust me."

With their steaming drinks in hand, Hayley led them to the top of Trinity Bellwoods Park. At this hour there wasn't much activity, the odd dog walker and couple strolling along the paths, but as they followed the north path, snow began to fall, carpeting everything in white dust.

"So your one and only major relationship was with a guy…"

"And you're wondering what exactly that means, right?"

Hayley nodded and sipped her hot chocolate.

"I think part of the problem with Ben and me was that I loved him, but wasn't in love with him. I loved hanging out with him. We made great friends, but that's about it. And honestly, it was kind of gut-wrenching when it ended because, at one point, he was in love with me, and I couldn't be what he needed. So to answer your question more specifically, if there were a guy I could be in love with, it would've been Ben."

"So you like women."

"I like you."

It wasn't exactly the answer Hayley had been hoping for. But as Hannah had pointed out, Lauren was not Violet.

The lampposts dotting the path cast a soft, white glow over everything the light touched. Hayley tilted her head up and let the snow fall over her.

"Have you heard about the white squirrels?" Hayley asked, head still tilted.

"In Trinity? Of course. I've never seen one, which tells you how rare they are because I live across the street from the park."

"My friend Dunne says the one and only time he's seen one was the day he met his wife. They were together fifteen years, and then she died of cancer, which is why he's an alcoholic now, I think. He says they're good-luck love omens."

Lauren cut through some grass leading to one of the prettier paths in the park. "I guess that's why I've never spotted one. As far as I know I haven't met my…I don't want to be cheesy and say soul mate, but I guess it sounds better than person I plan to be with until I die."

"Hmm. My sister calls it your forever person. She's about as down to Earth as I can imagine, so I like to go with that term."

"How is your sister, by the way?"

"And her litter of gargantuan children? She's well. Even though she's about to explode if she doesn't find out what the sex of her baby is."

"When is she due?"

"In January. I was hoping for a Christmas baby so I would only have to make the trip home once. But alas, yet again, she refused to make things easy for me."

"It must be fun, though, having a sibling. I used to wish I had a little brother because it would make dealing with my dad easier." A bell behind them signalled a bike was approaching, and they moved to the right of the path.

"Still not eating your food?"

Lauren lifted the lid of her hot chocolate. "Nope. I went over last week and found four—FOUR—different Popeye's containers in the garbage. Foodora is the worst thing to ever have been invented. He wasn't as bad when pizza was the only thing you could get delivered."

"Have you tried sprucing up the food a bit? Making it less bland?"

"Bland?"

"Some would argue boiled chicken is the worst thing to ever be invented."

"But it's healthy."

"You can still eat good-tasting food and be healthy. My uncle has type 2 diabetes, and my aunt found this great site with all sorts of good recipes on it. If you'd like, I could make a few things for him, see if he likes them?"

"Really? That would be amazing. Thank you."

They'd stopped at a fork in the path. One would sweep back around and take them north, and the other would lead to the south gates and, across the street, home.

Hayley dropped her empty mug into the garbage and looked expectantly at Lauren. "Home, Jeeves? Or once more around the park?"

Hayley leaned in close and lightly brushed her lips against Lauren's. Maybe it was the romantic setting or, more likely, the booze Hayley had consumed, but there was a ball of fire in the pit of her stomach keeping her warm.

"Once more around the park, please."

❖

Lauren couldn't remember the last time they'd all gone out. It was rare to have everyone together, at least almost everyone. Lily and Luna couldn't make it because they'd had other plans, and Ezra never joined them for these types of things. When Pete was around, they'd gone out more, before Lauren became manager. Or maybe they'd stopped inviting her when she got promoted.

The brewpub was jammed with people talking over each other.

Ramiro had snagged a table for the group because he'd gone to school with the brewmaster.

Lauren raised her cinnamon-bun stout to her lips just as their server came by and pointed to the back. Lauren nodded and looked expectantly toward Hayley. It was her birthday today. Lauren had spent the week setting this up. Behind Hayley, a large cake was making its way toward the table. It was a 3D sculpture of Lemmy Koopa. The base was a chocolate-fudge cake, shaped and decorated to look like a rubber ball. The figure of Lemmy Koopa, which was balanced on one foot, was a Madagascar bourbon vanilla, and the tiny purple bomb in his hand was red velvet cake. From afar, it looked as if it were an actual statue; the details were unbelievable. The rubber ball was decorated with tiny stars, Lemmy's mohawk sprang from his head in a rainbow of colours, and the bomb in his hand sported a fuse that was lit.

As the cake weaved its way through the crowd, people stopped to look and point at the marvel passing by.

It had taken several days, mostly because Lauren lived with the person she was surprising. The end result, however, had been spectacular. And the look of surprise and sheer joy on Hayley's face when it was set in front of her made it all worth it.

After a quick and off-key rendition of "Happy Birthday," Hayley turning pinker by the second, and then a quick toast to the birthday girl, Hayley stood up and blew out the flame on the fuse.

"Lauren, this is amazing. How did you even know it was my birthday?"

"Hannah called me. She wanted to make sure you didn't spend it alone."

"Is this thing even edible?" asked Theo. He was poking at some of the fondant on the ball.

"Of course it's edible. What would be the point of making a cake you can't eat?"

Their server handed Lauren a knife, and she began dissecting the cake, a job almost as intricate as baking the cake itself.

"How long did it take you to make this?" Hayley accepted a piece of red velvet from Lauren.

"About four days. The tricky part was getting it to balance properly because it has a lot of weight. The bottom ball cake is made with a really dense sponge so that it would hold. And then I used PVC piping with a base to partially support Lemmy's body. For the top sections I used a really airy sponge, which helped it stay up."

"Well, honey, you outdid yourself this year." Vic pushed her beer out of the way to make room for a slice of the red velvet.

"What's the excuse this year?" asked Ramiro, holding up a slice of the bourbon vanilla.

Hayley scooped a large piece into her mouth. "Excuse for what?"

"Bake or Die. It's a baking competition that happens every year. And every year someone else wins because Lauren refuses to enter."

"Was this the competition you were talking about around Halloween?"

"Oh, so you haven't forgotten it exists?" Ramiro pointed his fork at her.

"The fee is a thousand dollars. I don't have a thousand dollars to throw away on a lesson in humility."

"She's saying she won't win, but I've seen her stuff over the years. You can do as well as any of the winners have."

"I've never baked a gravity-free cake."

"But you could."

"Last year over three hundred people signed up. That means, in order to win a hundred grand, you have to beat out hundreds of people. Do you know what the odds of that are? Every single person who enters is an idiot."

"What does second place get?"

"There is no second-place winner. That's the point."

By now, other patrons had begun to congregate around their table. "You guys sharing?"

Everyone looked to Hayley, whose cake it ultimately was, for a response. "Hell fucking no." She licked the back of her spoon. "This is too good to share."

CHAPTER TWENTY-THREE

Hayley and Lauren walked south on the rail path toward Dundas. They had the trail to themselves at this time of night. Even the trains had stilled. Far off they could hear the hint of traffic, but currently they were cocooned in nature. Their boots squelched in the new snow, braiding a path with their treads.

"I love this." Lauren sniffed the air. "It even smells like nature. Like you could forget we were so close to so many major streets."

"I'm surprised you even like this. I thought all city dwellers were nature haters."

Lauren was carrying the leftover cake in a box with an improvised string handle. The beer and atmosphere from the brewpub had given her a slight buzz and warm feeling. It was good to see Hayley so happy and have everyone come out and celebrate her birthday. "Of course I like nature. I live across from a park."

"That's not nature."

"Then what is it?" Lauren stopped next to Hayley, who almost collided with her. They stood under the soft warm glow of the lamppost. Lauren exhaled, her breath vapour in the cold air. She'd thought about this moment, often enough that the idea of leaning in warmed her better than her mittens or winter jacket ever could.

Hayley guided Lauren backward, pressing her against the streetlight post. It felt cold and sturdy, which was good. Lauren wasn't sure if she'd be able to stand on her own much longer.

The kiss started soft, almost a request, but soon turned urgent, decadent, indecent. Lauren dropped the cake at their feet and reached up, pulling Hayley closer, warming them until they drew apart, out of breath.

"Not here," Lauren panted.

Hayley nodded, picked up the cake, and grabbed Lauren's hand, pulling her down the path toward home.

Once home, Lauren pushed Hayley into her room. But once there, Lauren was uncertain how to move things forward. She had ideas, many ideas, but wasn't sure how to initiate them.

Hayley took a step toward her and pulled her hair out of its ponytail. It fell in soft waves around her shoulders. "I love your hair down like this." Hayley ran her fingers through Lauren's black locks, tugging when she reached the ends.

Lauren closed her eyes. Already she was more aroused than she'd ever been with Ben. She let Hayley undress her, taking in the different sensations. The way the air hit her skin as Hayley pulled her sweater over her head. The featherlight touch of Hayley's fingertips as she peeled the straps of her tank top off her shoulders. The tickle of her breath as Hayley bent to kiss her neck. Lauren's skin tingled as she let her clothes pool at her feet. She was now standing in nothing but her underwear.

More than anything she wanted to touch, to explore, something she'd fantasized about almost nonstop since she saw Hayley in that dress. Tentatively she placed her hands on Hayley's hips and backed her into the bed. She inched up Hayley's T-shirt, running her hands over the warm, smooth skin of her back. Her fingertips danced up Hayley's spine, eliciting a gasp. She felt empowered.

"Take it off," she whispered in Hayley's ear, wondering where this boldness came from.

Hayley held her gaze as she reached down and pulled the hem of her shirt up and over her head. Her breasts practically spilled out of the top of her purple lace bra. Lauren's heart nearly stopped.

"The bra too."

Hayley smirked. "I like you when you're bossy." She reached around and unhooked the clasp, slipping it forward and running it down her arms until it dropped to the floor next to Lauren's sweater.

Lauren had never seen anything so sexy before. She ran her fingertips over the tops, caressing the soft skin underneath. Hayley moaned softly, and that was all the encouragement Lauren needed to take one of Hayley's nipples into her mouth.

"Jesus."

Lauren glanced up at Hayley, who had her eyes closed and her head tilted back slightly, obviously enjoying this. She moved to the next nipple while reaching down to undo Hayley's button on her jeans. She pushed them down Hayley's legs and smiled when she noticed the Wonder Woman underwear.

"If I'd known my day was going to end like this, I would have planned my wardrobe differently," whispered Hayley.

"Why? They're cute."

"I'm not going for cute right now."

"I happen to like cute." Lauren planted a kiss right above the waistband, thrilled by the play of muscles in front of her. She kissed her again, this time lower, running a finger up and down the logo. Wetness greeted this move, and Lauren was dying to pull the panties right off. She couldn't decide if she wanted to prolong this moment or rush ahead.

"I'm not going to be able to stand much longer."

"Then don't." Lauren nudged her onto the bed, climbing up to straddle her. "I like you better in this position anyway."

Hayley weaved her hands into Lauren's hair and drew her in for a kiss. Her hands skimmed down Lauren's back, pushing into the back of her underwear. Lauren's heart hammered as every point in her suddenly focused on what Hayley's hands were doing. The soft stroke of Hayley's fingers between that sensitive dip had Lauren so turned on she was pretty sure she'd come any second now, and Hayley hadn't even touched her yet.

Lauren broke free and pushed her underwear down and off, then settled back on top. Hayley continued to caress softly, teasing, until Lauren's hips pulsed against her, pleading. She was so close now, it wouldn't take much.

Hayley moved her hands to the front, running them through her folds. "Oh God, Lauren."

Lauren leaned forward, bracing her hands on the bed, and began thrusting back onto Hayley. As she was about to come, she captured Hayley's mouth, crying out as she rode out her climax, then collapsed on the bed next to Hayley.

"Holy shit," she said once she'd caught her breath. "That was…"

"The best birthday ever."

Lauren swung a leg over, draping herself onto Hayley. "And it's not even over yet." She kissed the side of Hayley's breast, then the soft skin underneath. Slowly she made her way down to Hayley's hips, nipping at her skin as she went. Each time she did, Hayley twitched and squirmed. She trailed her fingers up the inside of Hayley's thigh and received a gasp. But what she really wanted was a moan. She wanted to hear what Hayley sounded like when she came. It had been an obsession of hers for weeks now.

Lauren kissed the inside of Hayley's thigh, first one side, then the other. "Tell me what you want," she said.

Without hesitation Hayley answered. "You."

"Where?"

"Inside."

Without teasing any further, Lauren pushed two fingers inside, marvelling at how incredibly turned on her boldness made her feel. Part of it was the power, knowing that she could make Hayley this wet, but another part was being connected in this intimate way. She hadn't expected it to be so intense. As she began a steady rhythm, she dipped her head and circled Hayley's clit with her tongue. Her hips bucked, causing Lauren to smile and apply more pressure. Before long, Hayley was gripping the sheets, her hips thrusting forward, and a deep throaty moan escaped her lips. Lauren slowed her tongue and fingers and crawled up Hayley's body.

"Best. Birthday. Ever," Hayley said as she pulled Lauren close.

They lay there for a few moments, coming down from the high, the sound of the street below mingling with their breathing. Lauren's stomach gurgled, making her laugh out loud. She covered her stomach. "Sorry. I guess we worked up an appetite."

"Hold that thought." Hayley jumped off the bed, pulling clothes on as she made her way to the door.

"Where are you going?" But it was too late. The bedroom door had already shut with a loud click. Lauren sank back into bed. That was without a doubt the most intense experience she'd ever had. But what exactly did this mean? The clock on her nightstand read eleven fifty. It was too late for overanalyzing. It was better to leave all this thinking until the morning.

Five minutes later she heard the door creak open, and Hayley entered carrying the rest of her birthday cake. She set it on the bed with two forks and began taking off her clothing.

"Didn't want it to go to waste."

Lauren grabbed one of the forks. "And there's no doubt we've earned this."

And that's how the best birthday of Hayley's life ended, with the two of them sitting cross-legged on Lauren's bed eating birthday cake.

❖

Lauren woke up warm and cozy, snuggled into the crook of Hayley's arm. A hissing sound was coming from the end of the bed, but she ignored it and buried deeper under the covers.

Jerkface made his way up the bed, clawing his way along Hayley until he reached her head and gave it a quick swat.

"Your cat is a menace. I vote we kick him off the island."

Lauren reached up and grabbed Jerkface from Hayley's back, cuddling him to her. "But he's too pathetic to kick out. Look at this face." Lauren turned him so he was facing Hayley.

"He's got you brainwashed. He's just waiting for you to keel over so he can eat you. Why do you think he kneads your back like that? He's preparing you for future consumption."

"That is so not true. Jerkface would never eat me, would you?" But the scowl Jerkface gave her left it up to debate.

Hayley snaked a hand over Lauren's stomach, caressing her hip. "At least kick him out of the bedroom. I'm not baring skin until his claws are sheathed."

Lauren huffed, but it was just an act. Hayley ducked her head under the covers and ran her tongue around Lauren's nipple, sucking it into her mouth. The hand that had been caressing Lauren's hip inched lower, trailing down her stomach, and Lauren opened her legs, inviting Hayley in.

"Just imagine how much more fun this would be with one less pussy in the room."

Lauren's loud laugh reverberated around the room, but it quickly turned to a moan when Hayley's fingers dipped inside. She spread her legs farther and released the cat to the floor but didn't have the inclination to move. She was too preoccupied with what Hayley was doing to her.

The phone on her nightstand beeped, and she looked over to see that Vic had texted her. Aaron was downstairs waiting for her. Shit. "Hayley, honey. I have to go."

Hayley didn't answer. Instead, she switched to Lauren's other nipple, pulling it deep into her mouth. Lauren sank back, lost in sensation. Maybe it could wait a few minutes. She pulled back the duvet covering Hayley, wanting to watch. There was something so incredibly sexy about watching. And when Hayley turned her azure eyes on her, Lauren's breath caught at the sight, and she was over the top before she knew it, tightening and convulsing as Hayley continued to thrust deep inside of her.

❖

Lauren slid the bolt shut on the diner and flipped the sign. A light sprinkling of snow was dusting the pavement. The flakes fluttered in the orange glow of the streetlamp. For a second their beauty lulled her, until she remembered she'd have to shovel the front walk tomorrow morning.

In the back, Hayley cranked "The Passenger" by Siouxsie and the Banshees, and by the time Lauren had refilled all the sugar dispensers, Hayley had doubled the volume and was dancing around the kitchen with a rag. Lauren stopped to watch at the door, enthralled. When Hayley noticed she had an audience, she danced over to Lauren and pulled her into an embrace, spinning them around the island.

The music changed to The Specials' "Friday Night, Saturday Morning." When the bridge came, Hayley slowed them and pinned Lauren against the counter. She leaned close and kissed her softly on the lips.

"I haven't been able to do that all day." Hayley licked her lips and smiled. "You taste like cinnamon and apples."

"It might have something to do with this thing called work." Lauren circled her arms around Hayley's neck and gazed into those impossibly blue eyes.

"Work? Isn't that something only schlubs do?"

"Nope. It's for everyone now."

A silence sprang up between them as they stared at each other, both full of heavy thoughts. It was a promising silence.

They'd been packed for most of the evening, and usually Hayley loved the quick pace. It meant her shift went a little faster. But today, it meant she hadn't had as much time to watch Lauren, which was quickly becoming her favourite hobby.

Hayley felt the vibrations against her stomach. She reached down and fished Lauren's phone from her apron. "For you, madam." She hiked a thumb toward the kitchen to indicate she was getting back to work.

They hadn't really defined their roles while at work, but Hayley was thinking it was probably best if they didn't work too closely, or alone. Otherwise the frozen buns might get a show they never expected.

"He's where?" Lauren's panic filled the diner.

Hayley stuck her head out from the kitchen. "What's wrong?"

Lauren turned away from Hayley's question, the phone pressed hard to one ear, a hand covering the other. "Okay. I'll come right away…No. I'll be there." When she turned to face Hayley, her face was ashen. "My dad fell. He's in the emergency room. I have to go."

"Of course, go. I'll lock up."

Lauren stared down at her phone, and then, almost like she was shaking herself out of a panic, she shook her head. "Right. I'll leave the keys and the code. The register needs to be emptied and counted. Do you know how to tally till receipts?"

Hayley grabbed Lauren's coat from its hook in the back. "Of course. I grew up working in a grocery store, remember?"

"Right." Lauren slipped into her winter pea-coat. "Oh, and the cash needs to be night-dropped at the TD down the block."

"I've got it. Go. Take care of your dad."

Lauren nodded, evidently in shock. She rushed out the door, then back in and pecked Hayley on the lips. "Thank you," she whispered.

Chapter Twenty-four

T hat's ridiculous."

"It's not, Dad. You need help getting around. The doctor said it would take several weeks to recover, and you can't do it on your own."

Max was propped up in his hospital bed, a tray of hospital food untouched to the side. "Why can't you come stay with me until I'm well?"

"Because with the hours I work, it's impractical. You'd still be on your own most of the time." He was in a room with an older woman whose family was having an almost identical conversation. Max's bed was next to a giant window overlooking Dundas Square. It was bright, but a definite chill was coming through the double pane.

"I'm not moving into any old folks' home."

"It's an active living community."

"They can call it whatever they want now, but it's still where you stick people you don't want to deal with anymore." He was still attached to an IV, the tube sneaking up under his arm to a mobile pole next to the bed. The doctors were encouraging him to move around with help. It surprised Lauren to hear that he should be up and walking so soon.

Besides her, the only people who came to visit him were his physiotherapy team once a day to help him use a walker to get around. This situation was wearing on her dad, apparently making him feel old and useless.

Lauren sighed and took a seat on the bed. Until a few months ago her dad hadn't looked old, but when she watched him try to maneuver in his hospital gown to the bathroom, he seemed like a totally different person. She'd been there all morning arguing with him. He'd fallen down the stairs at the back of his building. They hadn't salted that entrance to the building because so few people used it, and he'd slipped on the ice and broken his hip. It had been three days since he'd had surgery to replace it, and they were planning to release him in a few more. No way was she letting him go home alone to his own apartment. She'd found him temporary space in a short-term-care facility, but trying to convince him to sell his apartment and move to an assisted-living space was proving harder than convincing him to let her borrow his car when she was seventeen.

"Dad, what are you going to do if you fall again?" Not only the fear of him falling had her pushing for this. These communities all had restaurants that catered to the tenants, and she could guarantee that he was eating much healthier. In fact, his doctor had mentioned that one possible cause of his break was lack of a good diet.

"I'm healthy and strong. The doctor said there was no reason I wouldn't be able to recover from this."

"Yes, with help."

Max lay down and looked out his window, his eyes glazed. Lauren was about to give up the fight for another day when she heard a soft knock on the wall behind them. Hayley stood there holding a small container.

"Hi." She waved. "I hope it's okay that I stopped by to visit." She held up her package. "I thought your dad might want to eat something that isn't hospital food."

Max perked up at the mention of food. The hospital's idea of good food was a toasted multigrain bagel with sugar-free jam and a hard-boiled egg. He'd announced that he'd rather starve than eat that crap. He pulled himself up to more of a sitting position with the help of the railing.

Lauren waved her in. "Dad, this is my friend Hayley. And this is my dad, Max."

"Hi, Max. I made you some chicken."

His face fell a little when Hayley mentioned she'd made it.

"Hayley is one of the line cooks at work. She's really good."

Hayley set the box down on the table in front of him, pushing the tray of food and a tall pile of books out of the way. She opened the box to reveal lemon chicken in a bed of brown rice seasoned with cilantro. The smell that filled the room was enough to entice the pickiest eater.

Max grabbed the utensils from his breakfast tray and cut into the chicken. "I seem to recall something about a new roommate named Hayley."

Lauren took a seat on the side of the bed. "Yep. She moved into the spare bedroom two months ago."

Max nodded but didn't respond, his mouth full. He pointed his fork at the food, still chewing. "This is delicious. You said you're a line cook?"

Hayley sat in the chair across from his bed. "For now, yes."

"You're wasting your talents. This is really something."

Hayley's cheeks pinked. "I'm glad you like it."

"So is that the end of your ambitions? Line cook in a diner?"

"Dad," Lauren warned him. "This isn't an interrogation."

"What? I'm curious." He cut another slice and rammed it into his mouth. You'd think he'd never eaten the way he was shovelling it in.

Hayley shrugged. "I'm not sure. It's all right for now. I hadn't really thought about the future."

"Did you go to culinary school?"

"Not even close. I learned at the heels of my nana and my mom. They're the real cooks in my family." Hayley leaned forward to check out the selection of books next to him. "Mysteries, huh? My nana is a huge fan of Dorothy L. Sayers. I used to read her books when I was in high school."

"I've read some of her stuff, but I prefer P.D. James."

"I started *Death Comes to Pemberley* but couldn't get into it. I did like her Cordelia Gray novels though."

Max grunted and continued to devour Hayley's lemon chicken. They chatted for a few more minutes before Hayley looked at the clock on the wall and excused herself for a shift she didn't want to be late for.

Max waited a whole five minutes before saying, "You know, you don't need to hide behind a roommate. If you two are dating, you can tell me."

Lauren stilled. She hadn't meant to bring it up until she'd had more time to digest what was happening. "What makes you say she's more than a roommate?"

"If she were just a roommate, she wouldn't have brought me food.

That's something you do for someone you care about." That thought followed Lauren for the rest of the day, warming her against the frigid weather.

❖

Lauren heard the loud clang before she even turned off the faucet in the shower. "What was that?"

"Nothing," Hayley called.

Lauren grabbed her towel off the rack, afraid to leave Hayley alone in her kitchen. Lauren had a system. She hated explaining it because people tended to stare blankly when she pointed out her fridge chart. She saw nothing wrong with being organized. But since Hayley had moved in, her clean, orderly house had become less ordered, less clean.

When she entered the kitchen, Lauren wished she'd stayed in the shower. Jerkface was lounging on one of the shelves above the sink watching the mayhem below with mild anticipation.

Every surface was filled with either dirty dishes or spilled food, sometimes both at the same time. It was as if Hayley had decided to make breakfast by throwing everything into the air and hoping it would land together in edible form.

"You weren't supposed to see it like this." Hayley began stacking dishes in the sink, trying to consolidate the mess.

Jerkface rose, stretched each leg in succession, then hopped onto the counter, picking his way through the mess until he reached Lauren. He slinked past, rubbing up against her, fluttered his tail, looked back at Hayley as if to say, *You're in so much shit*, then jumped off the counter and disappeared.

Hayley turned, sheep-faced. "It was supposed to be breakfast in bed."

"You didn't have to." And Lauren meant it. As sweet as the gesture was, the cleanup was enough to give her anxiety for weeks. "What's the occasion?"

Hayley turned back to the counter and began arranging two plates. "We don't need to have an occasion, do we?" But her tells were showing. Living together was a crash course in getting to know someone, even if you weren't dating. In the few months since they'd known each other, Lauren had learned Hayley was failingly honest. Not that she couldn't lie, but when she did, it was obvious. She'd do anything to avoid eye contact, and with the softest nudge, she'd spill everything. So Lauren decided to give her a nudge.

Lauren slipped up behind Hayley. "So you just thought I'd like," she leaned over Hayley's shoulder to see fluffy blueberry pancakes in the shape of hearts, "some pancakes for breakfast?"

Hayley turned and grabbed some napkins and utensils on her way to the table, sliding past Lauren. "Yep. Don't you like pancakes? That's a silly question. Everyone loves pancakes."

Undeterred, Lauren sauntered over to Hayley and placed her chin on Hayley's shoulder. "As far as I know, the only reason you'd make me breakfast is for my birthday, but that isn't until March." Lauren planted a kiss on Hayley's neck. "Are you buttering me up for something?"

Hayley let her head fall back. "If you keep doing that, I might just submit to anything."

"Okay, spill." She pulled away despite Hayley's protests. "You're up to something. You're not quitting, are you?" That thought filled Lauren with dread. Hayley had quickly become one of her best line cooks. She was reliable, had a great attitude, and didn't give Lauren any crap. She could work on her speed, but that would come with time. The sad fact was, Lauren knew Hayley wouldn't be there as long as Pete had. Her dad had spotted what Lauren and Ramiro both knew— Hayley was better than this, and if she put even a little bit of effort into formalizing her culinary skills, she could do great things. Lauren loved Pete, he was family, but his worth had been in who he was, not so much in his cooking skills. Losing Hayley would mean searching for another decent line cook, and she wasn't up for that right before the holidays.

"Why don't we sit for this?" Hayley grabbed two plates of pancakes. She set one down at Lauren's place and took a seat opposite.

"You're not quitting, are you?"

"I'm not quitting. No." Hayley poured syrup on her pancakes, slathering the mound with the light-brown gloop. "I..." She hesitated, her fork poised to cut into the first pancake. "You know what?" She set her fork down and reached toward the counter for her phone. Hayley scrolled through until she'd pulled up an email and handed the phone to Lauren.

Beyond confused now, Lauren accepted it and began reading. It took a second for understanding to dawn.

"I didn't know your email, so I used mine." Hayley worried her top lip.

Lauren looked up at Hayley, shocked. "You entered me in Bake or Die? I…"

"You keep saying you don't have the skills to win, but how are you going to know unless you try? Besides, winning isn't always the goal. Sometimes it's important just to compete."

Lauren was speechless. She would never have signed herself up, and it wasn't the thousand-dollar entrance fee. It was the fear of failing. Again.

"How did you pay for the entrance fee?"

"Don't worry about that. You just worry about baking like the fucking queen you are."

Before Lauren could press the matter, someone started pounding at the door. Hayley answered, to find Theo, sopping wet from the waist down, eyes wide in panic.

Lauren was out of her chair in an instant. "What happened?"

"A pipe burst. There's water everywhere."

"Okay. Give me five minutes to get dressed."

When she came back out, only half dressed, Theo was peering into the kitchen. "Holy shit. Did you let a hurricane cook you breakfast?"

"It's not that bad." Hayley shooed him out of the apartment.

Lauren swept past Hayley.

"Do you need any help?"

"Probably best if you stay here. Too many cooks and all that."

❖

"Jesus fucking Christ."

The entire kitchen paused to look at Lauren, none of whom had ever heard her swear. Theo looked almost panicked.

The kitchen floor was covered in several inches of brown water, and it was sweeping toward the counter and main dining area.

"It's just streaming water. I don't know how to stop it." Theo pointed to a spot under the sink where a waterfall was gushing onto the floor.

Lauren took a moment to assess the situation. They'd be fine if they could redirect the water that was already there so it didn't make it to the diners. "Ezra, we need to shut off the water. There should be a valve behind the pipes in the sink."

Ezra held out the handle to a valve. "You mean this? Yeah. It broke off."

Lauren groaned and scrubbed her hand over her face. "Okay. See if you guys can pop the drain lid in the floor by the freezer and redirect the water. Do we have anything that can cover the broken part of the pipe to keep it from coming out so fast?"

Ezra turned to run out of the kitchen. "I'll check the basement."

"In the meantime, I'll call a plumber and see if we can get someone over here as soon as possible."

Lily and Vic were up front, keeping an eye on the situation in back, but trying not to let on there was any problem. The last thing they needed was to shut down and lose business. Aaron would flip out.

In the end they had to turn off the water for the entire building to stop the flow. Theo was able to stockpile several buckets of water beforehand, so they were able to wash dishes and make food. Lauren called Hayley in to help with the cleanup, and once the plumber arrived and patched the pipe, things improved. Lauren considered the disaster averted since she hadn't had to close for the day, and as far as she knew, none of their customers was aware of any problems.

It wasn't until much later, after she'd locked up for the day and was cozied under her favourite throw with a glass of wine, that she stopped to think about the Bake or Die contest. The idea of it filled her with dread but also excitement.

Chapter Twenty-five

A week ago Hayley would've assumed the only person who could make such a mess in the kitchen was her. But here they were. The kitchen was a disaster, and she'd had no part in it.

Lauren popped up from behind the counter. "Good. You're home. I need to you to taste this." Her hair was pulled back in something resembling a ponytail, her blue-and-purple-plaid shirt had more flour on it than a three-tier wedding cake, and chocolate was smudged across her cheek. At least in this she matched her kitchen.

An explosion of some sort of white goo was dripping off the counter onto the floor. Jerkface approached, sniffing the substance before deciding it was not up to his standards of consumption.

Lauren handed Hayley a small pastry ball, which she popped into her mouth without asking any further questions. "God, yes." Hayley closed her eyes to savour the taste. "What's it filled with?"

"Crème patisserie flavoured with salted-caramel liqueur. I got the idea from those knocked-up Santas we had."

Still chewing, Hayley nodded her approval. If that wasn't enough of a thumbs-up, the noises she was making would've been a good indication.

For the past week Lauren had been experimenting with various recipes in preparation for the contest coming up this weekend. The closer they got to the event, the more elaborate Lauren's concoctions became. They knew the categories ahead of time, but there was always a catch.

Hayley plopped herself down on a stool on the other side of the breakfast bar, still chewing. "So why so much prep? Haven't you been baking your whole life?"

"The trick is to prepare a couple of different selections in each category. Saturday morning we're doing pastry, but that's all we know. When we get there, they could say we're not allowed to use flour or it has to include pomegranates or some equally absurd ingredient. The more prepared I am, the better I'll do."

"You're going to do fine."

Lauren looked around at the chaos in her kitchen. "Everyone else in the building is convinced of the same thing."

"So come Saturday, show 'em who's boss." Hayley hopped off the stool and leaned over to give Lauren a peck on the nose, dusting off the small amount of flour on it first. "Is there anything I can do to help?"

"Actually, could you pop over to Kensington and grab me a few sticks of vanilla?"

"Wow. Going fancy."

"There's no comparison in flavour. If you can't find the beans, then I'll take the paste. It's cheaper anyway."

"How much are we talking?"

"Silk Road usually has them at sixteen bucks for a bag of three."

"Holy shit, Lauren. That's insane. How much paste do you get out of one bean?"

"You asked me what I needed. I don't need the commentary." Lauren stuck her tongue out.

"Actually, I think what you need more than ridiculously expensive ingredients is a break." Hayley nudged Lauren over to her room. "Go get decent—you look like you fell in a vat of batter—and I'll treat you to lunch. I happen to know a good place."

❖

"Kalini showed me this place. It's kind of lucky we're so close. And Theo said you never eat here." Hayley stopped at Grnds and pulled the door open for Lauren.

At ten fifteen in the morning, the place was still pretty busy. The four out of five tables were full, and only one spot was left at the window bar. Lauren baulked. She never ate here for a reason. As long as Hipster Dan was the owner, she refused. But the look of earnestness on Hayley's face pushed her forward. Maybe he wasn't working.

However, the second they entered, she heard a gloating baritone say, "Why, Lauren Hames. I thought you'd never grace us with your lovely self." Dan scratched his beard in contemplation. "In fact, I think the exact phrase was 'over my dead body.' You look pretty lively to me." He nudged the woman in an apron next to him. "Doesn't she look lively to you?" The woman rolled her eyes and moved away to help the next customer.

Lauren inwardly cringed. She would give almost anything to extract herself from this inevitable confrontation.

"I see you've brought one of your line cooks. Come to show her how real food is made?"

Hayley leaned over toward the counter. "So far I haven't had anything here that isn't dwarfed by what I make down the street." She cringed, as if in apology for suggesting this place.

"Come to poach some ideas for Bake or Die?" Dan asked in his most arrogant tone. "I noticed you'd thrown your name into the hat this year."

Hayley tugged at Lauren's arm. "Come on. Let's go to Abe's place."

❖

Ensconced in one of two overstuffed chairs next to the fire, each with a latte and sandwich, Hayley felt she'd at least gotten Lauren to relax, though going to Grnds had been a fiasco.

"I'm sorry about that. I had no idea you had history there. Theo just said you never ate there, but he never said why."

Lauren took the last bite of her Swiss-and-avocado croissant, scrubbing her fingers of crumbs over the plate. "I'm not sure Theo was working at the diner then. Ramiro knows the whole sordid story, knows why I hate him so much."

Hayley propped her face up on her hands, always eager for a little workplace gossip. "You had me at sordid."

Lauren leaned back with her chai latte, sinking into the cushy chair. "A few years back, Hipster Dan—that's what I call him—won

Bake or Die. He used the money to open Grnds. It's the dream, right? Most of the bakers are hoping for exactly that." Lauren took a sip of her latte. "This isn't the first time I've entered Bake or Die. The one and only time I did was the same year as Hipster Dan. We both made it to the finals, but he was the ultimate winner. The thing is, he used one of my recipes to win. Down to the entire design, it was my idea."

"What an asshole. Couldn't you have said something?"

Abe came over to clear their plates. "Do you two need anything else?"

Both Lauren and Hayley shook their heads. "No, thanks. The croissant was amazing. Do you make them yourself?" Lauren asked.

Abe smiled. "My wife makes them. I could probably eat a whole batch in one sitting."

"I don't doubt that." Hayley passed him her plate.

After Abe had left Hayley asked, "So how did Hipster Dan get your recipe?"

"He used to work as a line cook at Greta's. I'd hired him a few months before the contest and was the reason he found out about Bake or Die. I had no idea he was even interested in entering, so I'd shared some ideas with him. I keep a book with notes and sketches. The morning of the last round, I noticed that the page with the cake I'd planned to do had been ripped out of the book. I decided, for whatever reason, it was a bad omen and to make my second choice. When Dan placed his final cake on the counter, I knew exactly what had happened. But I couldn't prove what he had done. He had the proof."

Hayley slumped back. "Jesus. I want to punch him in his fucking hairy face. And he's entered in the contest this year?"

"Yep," said Lauren. "He enters every year, although the only time he's won was that first one."

"With your idea. What happened after?" asked Hayley.

"I didn't even get the satisfaction of firing him. He never showed up to work again, not even to collect his last paycheque. A year later, Grnds opened down the street, and he came in with flyers to pass out to all our customers."

"The nerve." Hayley wished at that moment she could go back in time and stop herself from ever enjoying anything that man had ever made. She'd have to tell Kalini and Jo. Maybe they could pass on the info, and he'd lose a little business. It was the only consolation—that and Lauren kicking his ass this year in the contest.

Hayley reached across and took Lauren's hand. "You know you're a million times better than that douchebag, right? You can beat him because you've had a few more years to hone your skills and he doesn't have access to your mind anymore."

Lauren smiled. "I'm not worried about Hipster Dan. It's everyone else I'm up against."

Hayley stood. "Well, let's go get a leg up on the competition. You said you wanted to get vanilla beans?" She offered her hand to Lauren. "I think there's a food market with our name on it."

❖

They entered Kensington Market from Dundas and followed Kensington Avenue past the vintage-clothing shops to Baldwin, where the heart of the food shops lay. Any special type of food you wanted, Kensington had it. The market featured cheese shops you would enter optimistic and leave poor, with a bag full of cheese that could easily cost a hundred dollars a pound. They even offered a Bitto Storico, aged ten years, which would set you back forty dollars for three hundred grams. Lauren stayed away from those places because they were dangerous. If you weren't careful you could spend an entire paycheque just on sample sizes. The market had coffee-bean, nut, and produce shops, but Lauren was after the spice shops today.

The World of Spices was one of Lauren's favourites. Its thin aisles were packed high with some of the hardest-to-find spices. They ranged from random, like cucumber powder, to the more trendy, like charcoal. Lauren was looking for vanilla beans and Aleppo chile flakes. The Aleppo flakes were for the game pie she had in mind for the second challenge. They were milder than most chiles but had a sweet yet sharp taste and would add a unique kick to her variation on a spicy cheese bread.

They weaved in and around aisles, with Lauren grabbing items as they went. They chatted about recipes and which were a favourite to make. Lauren tended to bake sweet things, while Hayley preferred savoury recipes.

"All this food prep is making me hungry. Can I share something with you?"

Hayley turned, her azure eyes bright, a hint of a smile at the corners of her lips. "Anything."

Lauren took Hayley's hand and led her out of the spice store and into the crowds. "Come with me."

She pulled Hayley past bakeries and cafes, tattoo shops and pubs to a little stairwell leading to a basement with the most amazing smells wafting from it. Several people were crowding the doorway, waiting to enter.

"These only show up around Christmas for a few weeks, and then they're gone." A group of well-bundled people stepped out of the shop carrying what looked like wontons but were tiny triangular, pinched Tourtieres. "Every year the recipes are new, but even if that weren't true, they're worth lining up for."

They joined the queue, huddling into the side of the building to avoid the wind. They were still holding hands, and Hayley couldn't help but feel warmed by that fact. It had been a great day, and they hadn't done much of anything except hang out together. "Happy endings always involve food," she said.

Lauren laughed. "Happy endings are for Disney movies and rub-and-tug parlours."

Hayley held her hand to her heart. "Oh my God, don't you believe in happy endings?"

"Happy endings are for fairy tales. I mean, they're nice for movies, but once the credits roll, life goes on, and life rarely has happy endings."

"I don't know about that," Hayley said. "I think the world is full of happy endings. You just have to know where to look." By now they'd made it to the front of the line, and each placed her order. Hayley moved to the side and let the next people go.

"Says the woman from the picturesque small town whose parents are still together." Off the look of mild horror on Hayley's face, Lauren added, "I'm sorry that sounded so cynical, but honestly, if my mom hadn't died, I don't think my parents would still be together. They were so dissimilar." Lauren shrugged. "Nothing lasts forever."

"You're assuming a happy ending has to be about happily ever after, but what if it's just a happy ending to the chapter? Yes, I grew up in a small town, and so my expectations are different, but if you look hard enough, you can see little happy endings here. They're small gestures, like sharing a mug on a river of ice under the expressway, or watching for white squirrels in the park, a Good Samaritan stopping to help a woman picking up her spilled cans."

"Those aren't happy endings. They're nice gestures. And I wouldn't live in the city if I didn't love it for all its good and its bad."

Hayley took a bite of her Tourtieres, closing her eyes as she did. "Good Lord, that's delicious."

"Which one did you get?"

"The Christmas one, but it has some sort of roasted-chestnut flavouring that really pulls the whole thing together. Want to taste?" Hayley offered the small pie, and Lauren leaned in and took a bite.

"It's delicious. That one must be new."

"What about us? You don't think we'll get a happy ending?"

The question threw Lauren. She hadn't thought that far ahead. This was her first time in a relationship with a woman, if they were even in one. They hadn't discussed that possibility yet. She hadn't thought about where she wanted it to go. She knew only that Hayley made her want to believe in happy endings.

CHAPTER TWENTY-SIX

The expression of mild horror on the judge's face as she swept past Lauren's row bled panic into her heart. It was ten fifteen on Saturday morning. Earlier they'd all walked in full of equal mixtures of hope, optimism, and dread.

The first year of the Bake or Die contest was held in a catering kitchen in the west end. Only ten people had competed that year. As word got out and the prize money grew, they'd had to move to larger venues. This year the contest was being held at George Brown's culinary school, where they had enough cooking stations to accommodate three rounds per event. Lauren was in the first group, which meant she'd started at five a.m., and if she made it to the next round, she'd be back again at five p.m.

Three hundred participants had entered the competition, but only fifty made it to the next round. After the third round, just fifteen continued, and in the last, there were five.

This first round was pastry. Lauren was creating a croquembouche, which consisted of dozens of choux pastry puffs arranged in a cone shape and held together with threads of caramel. Their instructions had been to make it boozy, and since Lauren had already prepared to add salted-caramel-wine liquor to the pastry cream filling, she hadn't had to change her recipe at all.

As far as directives went, this was one of the simpler ones. One year, contestants had to miniaturize their pastries to fit on the palm of a hand. For those making pies, it had been easy to shrink their confections, but something like croquembouche would be hard to construct properly at that size.

Besides being difficult, Lauren's choice would also test her for time. They had only four hours to complete their entry, and every time she'd made it, she'd come in just at four hours, which was dangerous. You wanted extra time on the day of. She couldn't account for so many things. At home she knew that her oven ran about ten degrees hotter than the dial and that the back right was much cooler than the rest of the oven. Every item in her kitchen had a place, and she was certain where that was—unless Hayley had been in there recently. She could work fast because she knew her space. Here nothing was certain. She'd never used the ovens, and besides the specialty items she'd brought with her, she had no way of knowing where everything was.

These issues caused stress that Lauren didn't need when she was already tight on time. She would have to rely on her years in the service industry, keep her cool under pressure, and hope she'd practiced enough. That was all she could do. But as she watched, the guy next to her making a mille-feuille had not adopted this policy. Never in a million years would she have decided to make a dish where so much relied on the thickness and flakiness of her pastry in an oven she was unfamiliar with.

He pulled out the second sheet of puff pastry, only to see that the pastry hadn't risen. It was as if he'd baked dark shortbread, which was no good. After all, mille-feuille literally meant, thousands of sheets. If you didn't have those flakes, there was no point. The dish was ruined. Lauren knew it, the man next to her knew it, and the judge passing by at that moment knew it as well.

Lauren returned her focus to her own station and continued to fill her pastry puffs with her crème patissiere. She still had to construct the damn thing and string it with tiny caramel ribbon.

The judge passed by Lauren with no expression, which Lauren took as a good sign. The last thing she wanted to see on the judge's face was pity. It was worse than disgust.

As the minutes ticked by, Lauren filled her workstation with tiny puff balls. From afar, she imagined she looked focused on her task, but inside, nothing could be further from the truth. After making a few puff balls, an image would flash in her mind. Hayley's lips wrapped around Lauren's finger licking off a sample of crème patissiere. The crumpled, sleepy smile Hayley gave her this morning when she slipped out of bed at four a.m. Turquoise eyes staring down at her with such love and lust. They all made her feel something different.

It was that night in Kensington Market sharing the Tourtieres when she knew she'd fallen in love with Hayley. The feeling had been subtle and fast and amazing, and now she couldn't stop thinking about her. Hayley was a distraction but also the reason she was even here. For the first time in her life she felt like she had someone backing her, someone who believed she could do anything. Growing up, her mom had always made it clear that Lauren's idea of what she wanted to do with her life was frivolous. Hayley didn't make her dreams feel frivolous. It was the opposite, in fact. She made Lauren feel relevant, like she was doing what she needed to do, and that was everything to Lauren.

Before entering the building this morning, Lauren had decided that, even if she didn't win this weekend, it didn't matter. She would take steps to make her dreams a reality. No more hiding or waiting for life to happen to her. She intended to make life happen for her. It might have started with Pete quitting, but Hayley had shown her that you needed to take charge of your life, and that's what Lauren planned to do.

❖

Hayley's dishcloth landed short of the sink and slipped onto the ground. "Shit." She trudged over and swiped it off the floor and chucked it in the bucket of bleach next to the sink. She'd been working since the morning shift. She'd rather be watching Lauren kick some ass, but Ramiro needed her. Theo was sick, and Ezra hadn't wanted to take her shift.

They'd been in a lull since noon, which was unusual for a Saturday, but then, so was the blizzard raging outside. Vic and Lily were at a booth folding cutlery into napkins.

"So, Pollyanna, have you thought about what you're going to do after this?" Ramiro propped his bulk against the counter, tucking his hands into his apron pockets.

"I'm going to try to get over to George Brown to see the second half of the contest today."

He chuckled. "I didn't mean today. I meant, what are you going to do when you leave here?"

"Greta's? Why would I want to leave? I love working here." It was true. She hadn't thought she'd like cooking as much as she did, but once she'd gotten over the initial fears and picked up the lingo, she really did love it—the pace, the camaraderie, the skill, even the hours. She loved everything about being a line cook, but most of all because she was good at it.

"The money's shit, the hours are horrible, and there's absolutely no glory in it." He held up his hands to stop her from talking. "Hayley, you're great at this, so I'm not saying you have to stop cooking. But you could be really something if you put your mind to it." He shook his head, almost to himself. "I can't believe I'm about to do this." Ramiro pulled a business card out of his apron. "I love having you around, but I know talent when I see it, and so does my friend Rob." He handed her the card. "He's always looking for people he can train from scratch. Even better if you haven't been ruined by culinary school. You'd be starting from the bottom, even lower than here, but you'd be learning from the best. A couple years with Rob, and you could go anywhere."

Hayley took the card. She'd never seen Ramiro so serious. He'd even used her name, which she couldn't remember him ever doing, not since her job interview. "You want to get rid of me?"

"Are you kidding me? Fuck, no. I want a million of you working here. But it's unfair to you. You've been here what? Two months? And already you're better than Theo and Ezra combined. You need to think about the future."

"Have you told Lauren about this?"

"Lauren would have a heart attack if she knew I was encouraging you to leave. She loves you."

Without meaning to, Hayley blushed. She knew he hadn't meant it that way, but her mind went there anyway. She ducked her head, reading the card, hoping Ramiro couldn't see how red her cheeks must be. The card belonged to the executive chef of Brava, one of the most expensive restaurants in the city. She'd never eaten there. Hell, she couldn't even afford the appetizers. Only millionaires and wannabes could pay twenty-six dollars for five pieces of calamari, though it was probably the best calamari she would ever taste. This offer tempted her, but it would mean leaving Greta's, which had come to mean safety for her. And she couldn't do that to Lauren.

Every day for the past two weeks Hayley had woken up in the warmth of Lauren, and that heat followed her all day, mostly because she got to see Lauren throughout the day. As she plated, through the service window, as Lauren shouted her orders, grabbed plates. The glimpses she got were like appetizers, a peek at what was to come later, and she wasn't sure she was ready to give that up yet. Not until she could be sure Lauren felt the same way she did about them.

They'd been hiding it from everyone, which made Hayley insecure about what they were. She hadn't wanted to bring it up so close to the contest, in case it caused Lauren stress, which she didn't need at that moment.

Hayley's phone buzzed, and she picked it up. It was hard to tell what the message said with all the exclamation marks. "Lauren made it to the next round," Hayley shouted so Vic and Lily could hear.

"Of course she did. There's another woman wasting her talent here." Ramiro slapped a hand against the counter and waved Hayley off. "Go. I've got this. Lauren will need the support for the next round. Now the real challenge begins."

Hayley grinned. Taking off her apron and beanie, she dashed out of the diner before realizing she'd forgotten her jacket.

❖

"Lucky me."

Lauren froze. She'd been arranging several moulds next to her station for the next round, but the deep baritone of Hipster Dan stopped her cold.

"I get to bake next to the most beautiful woman in this competition."

Lauren stood and faced Dan.

"Hope I don't get distracted." He wiggled his eyebrows at her.

"You grease some palms to get this station? Unfortunately, you don't have my notebook to steal your ideas from, so you figure watching how it's done will help?"

"Says the waitress."

"Well, this waitress is going to serve you your ass on a platter."

Dan slapped his knee in mock amusement. "Hope you don't count on your humour to bring in the tips."

"You know what, Dan? Kiss my fucking ass."

"Such language. My goodness. Where'd you pick up that potty mouth? Wouldn't happen to be from that blonde you came in with the other day?" He wiggled his eyebrows again. "Oh, and look at that. How sweet. She's come to be your own cheerleading squad." He pointed to the galley, where Hayley had squeezed in front to watch. Lauren's mood soared even as Dan was trying to bring her down. It didn't matter what he said or thought. Hayley was here to cheer her on, and that was the important thing.

She shrugged and turned away from Dan, dismissing him as she should have done from the start. He was nothing to her, and now she knew it. He didn't have her skills, never had. All he had was his bravado, which would only get him so far. Lauren turned her attention to her station and the task at hand.

They had only two hours for this round. The number of contestants had been dramatically reduced, but these were the people to beat. Bake or Die offered no second chances or push-throughs. If you didn't have it in the first round, you didn't make it to the second. It didn't matter why you failed, for this was Bake or Die. If you didn't have it, you were gone.

For the chocolate round she'd decided to do a take on the chocolates she'd made for Halloween. Hayley had suggested she tweak the filling, adding cinnamon extract, which worked out perfectly because the directive for this round had been breakfast, so contestants had been tasked with making a box of twelve chocolates, three different kinds, and they had to have a breakfast theme. Lauren had decided to do a brunch theme. The first was an espresso, mocha-flavoured, white-chocolate bite, the next was French toast, and the third was a maple-bacon flavour. With only fifteen minutes left, Lauren was scrambling to add the caramelized bacon bits to the top of her maple-bacon truffle.

She'd ignored everyone and everything around her for the past two hours, allowing only two quick glances up at Hayley, who was watching with close attention from the galley. She'd done well to ignore Dan beside her. That was until he began tapping her arm.

"Leave me alone, Dan."

"Well then, at least silence the goddamned vibrations on your phone. It's been going off for the last ten minutes, and that's all anyone in this row can hear."

Lauren groaned and glanced down at her phone sitting on the counter next to her discarded moulds. She had fifteen missed calls from Aaron on her display. "What the hell?" Had something happened to the diner? The phone rang again, and she picked up this time.

"Where the hell have you been?"

"I'm not on call, Aaron. I do enjoy a day off here and there."

"My bank just informed me that we're short. Do you know anything about that?" Aaron's voice was tight and low. She'd worked with him long enough to know he was pissed. Greta was the same way. Where other people might yell, she would get quiet, and that's when you knew you were in trouble.

"How much are we short?"

"A thousand exactly."

Realization hit Lauren immediately. Her eyes were drawn to Hayley, standing in the crowd, excitement and expectation on her face. She now knew where Hayley had gotten the money to enter Lauren in the contest. She'd stolen it from the diner.

Chapter Twenty-seven

W hat were you thinking, Hayley?"
"I was only borrowing it. When you won we would've paid it back." Hayley's face was redder than Lauren had ever seen it, and she wasn't sure if it was from embarrassment at being caught or anger that Lauren might quit the competition.

Lauren slid her hands down her apron, rubbing off some of the dried chocolate. "That's all ruined now. I can't continue like this."

"You're going to let it go to waste? You don't get the money back if you drop out. You have to compete. You have to win."

Lauren paced back and forth. They were in a back room at George Brown. The judges were making their decisions about who would continue to the next round. Lauren had barely managed to finish her chocolates. But she had no idea that, if she did make it to the next round, she would continue. She'd been entered with stolen money. At the same time, Hayley was right. If she walked away now, they'd be out the thousand dollars. Now that she was here, she didn't want to give up so easily.

She'd told Aaron she'd look into it and get back to him. That would appease him for about a day, but then he'd want his money, and Lauren didn't have a thousand dollars to give him. And Hayley certainly didn't, or else she wouldn't have stolen in the first place.

Lauren sat down on a milk crate and let her head fall to her hands. All the fight had drained from her. She wasn't sure she could continue, knowing what it would cost if she did. But mostly, she wanted out of this argument.

On the loudspeaker, they were announcing the fifteen who would make it into the third round, which would start tomorrow and focus on savoury pies. Lauren stood and walked to the door to listen. When they called Lauren Hames she walked out and gathered up her things at her station and left before Hayley could catch up. She needed to be alone and think.

Three hours ago she'd been so sure of how things were going, and now she wasn't even certain where she wanted to go. She tramped down Adelaide, ignoring the Christmas lights and holiday cheer screaming from every storefront. The blizzard had let up, leaving everything fluffy and white. Lauren couldn't remember the last time they'd had this much snow before Christmas, and usually that would've thrilled her.

She turned north on Yonge and headed toward Dundas Square, the most Christmas place in the entire city. She didn't care. Last-minute shoppers streamed by, chatting, laughing.

Almost on autopilot, Lauren turned right on Queen and found herself going through the roundabout at St. Mike's. She took the elevator to the eight floor and followed the red line to her dad's room.

He was propped up in bed with an Elizabeth George paperback folded over. Only the side lamp was on, his roommate snoring in the bed beside him. Max set his glasses down and smiled warmly. "Hi, honey. This is a pleasant surprise." He took a look at her and set his book down on the roll-up table next to his hospital bed. "The competition didn't go well, I take it."

Lauren shook her head, then burst into tears, something she hadn't done since she'd left Ben. "I made it to round three."

Max patted the bed next to him. "That's great news. What the hell are you crying for?"

"Hayley stole the money from the till and now I have to win in order to pay Aaron back or I'll probably be fired because it was me who left Hayley with the money in the first place but who thought she'd steal and now I don't know if I love her anymore." It all came out in one blubbering sentence, and by the time she was done, she was sobbing on Max's shoulder.

"Okay. Give me a sec. That's a lot to unpack. Some money was stolen?"

Bit by bit, Lauren recounted everything that had occurred, ending with the phone call from Aaron and explaining exactly what had happened to that money.

"And you think you've stopped loving her because she made a mistake?"

"Dad, she stole money. She could go to jail for that."

"I doubt they'd put her in jail. But let's look at why she did it. She wanted to give you a chance to do what you love. It was a nudge to get you off the ledge. What's so bad about that?"

"She stole." The grunt from the next bed signalled how loud Lauren had become in the past minute. She lowered her voice. "She took money that wasn't hers. It doesn't matter why she did it."

"Honey, you have to stop seeing the world in black-and-white. Not everything fits into a box you can zip up neatly."

"Ugh." Lauren leaned her head back. "You don't get it. If I don't get the money back, I could be fired. I need that job."

Her dad patted her back. "I do get it. I do. And while I think it would be horrible to get fired, it might not be such a bad thing. Life can get stagnant."

Lauren gave him a withering look. He was one to talk. "Better stagnant than unemployed."

"Do you remember when you stopped believing in Santa?"

Lauren leaned back, sceptical this had anything to do with what they were talking about. "Honestly, I don't really remember ever believing in Santa." That probably had a lot to do with her mom. She vaguely remembered her father trying to explain that if he used magic, Santa could deliver toys to every child in the world, and she had responded that magic didn't exist because she couldn't see it. Mostly she remembered the fight between her parents that night. She'd snuck out of her room and crept toward the living room, sitting behind their giant money tree to listen unobserved. Max had blamed Susan for putting, as he said, "that crap in her head." While he was busy trying to create a world of wonder, her mother had been right behind dumping cold water on her dreams. At the time Lauren truly believed her mother had had her best interests in mind.

"Too young. Sometimes you just have to believe."

"Believe in what?"

Max shrugged his sagging shoulders. "In a world that wants better for you. If Hayley is willing to risk jail time to get you to dive into the deep end, then that's someone I want in your life."

He didn't say anything more. Instead he pulled her in for a hug. "Thanks for coming to see me. I'm really glad you're here. I'm getting tired of Inspector Lynley, and Havers gets to me after a while."

Lauren picked up the book and turned it over to read the back. "British Inspector novels. I don't even know how you can like these." She settled in against her dad to listen to him, yet again, explain why they were the best of the best. It was comforting to hear the same things over and over. She was glad she'd come. Even if her mind wasn't made up, she wasn't so upset anymore.

❖

Hayley was awake. She'd been awake for the past five hours staring at the ceiling and waiting for Lauren to come home. It was the first night since her birthday that she'd slept in her own bed, and it felt big and cold and lonely. She'd even left the door open in case Jerkface decided to hop up and join her. He hadn't, which was just as well. She deserved all the loneliness in the world.

Hayley had played it over in her head a billion times. The thought process, the inner argument, all the back-and-forth as she stood there holding the deposit bag in her hand. Granted, it had been reckless, and maybe even a little stupid, but she'd been sure Lauren would win. So sure. The only thing that made her uncertain now was the turmoil she'd seen in Lauren. Hayley hadn't seriously thought she'd get caught before the contest was over, thereby solving the problem before it became a problem.

She'd worked it all out. She'd wait until the flush of victory coloured Lauren's cheeks and let her know how she'd afforded her entry. What was a thousand dollars out of a hundred grand? That was like one pebble on a beach full of them. Lauren would've been mad for about a second until she remembered that she'd won the most cutthroat baking contest in the city, possibly the country. Hayley now realized that's what she'd been counting on. She'd never even let herself think about what would happen if Lauren lost. Because if she did, then it would just be stealing. Hayley would pay it back though. Of course she would. It wasn't her money. It's not like she'd taken the money for herself.

She flipped over onto her side, and that's when she noticed Jerkface staring at her from the edge of the bed. She hadn't even felt him jump up. The light from outside was enough to illuminate his eyes, the vertical pupils contracting to sharp slits. Judgment. But instead of swatting at her like he usually did, he curled up into a fat, furry ball and laid his head on his paws, and went to sleep.

Perhaps it was better to be a cat. They did shitty things all day long and had no problem curling up and sleeping at the end of the day, their conscience clean. Hayley didn't have that luxury. If Lauren got fired over this, she'd never forgive herself.

At half past six she heard the front door snick closed. Hayley sat up, stirring Jerkface, who jumped off the bed.

"Oh, hey, cat," Lauren whispered.

Hayley crawled out of bed. She was still dressed in the same clothes from yesterday, unable to even pretend she'd be getting some sleep.

Lauren looked rumpled, but not too bad for having spent the night out.

"Where'd you sleep?" Hayley asked.

"Didn't do much of that."

Hayley nodded. She hadn't rehearsed what she wanted to say word for word, but she'd come up with a rough outline. Now, her mind was blank. For some reason, when she'd thought to take the money for Lauren, it hadn't seemed that serious. "I didn't mean for any of this to happen."

Lauren shrugged off her coat and hung it on the hook near the door. Her shoulders hunched, she didn't turn around to face Hayley as she said, "You're fired."

"I figured that much. What happened with you?"

"Well, Aaron still doesn't have the money, does he?"

Hayley's heart seized. She turned Lauren around. "Did he fire you? He can't fire you. I was the one who took the money. You didn't know anything about it."

"You know that. And I know that, but I'm in charge of everyone. I left you alone with the money, and this is what happened."

Hayley felt like she was back home on Brewer's Hill trying to race up after an ice storm. Every few feet she'd slide back down to the bottom, never reaching the top. "That's not fair. You know I didn't steal the money for me—"

"Don't say you did this for me, because I was just fine. I don't need this stress. I didn't need to compete."

Hayley nodded defeat. She wouldn't get anywhere. Lauren had made up her mind, and she'd never see it Hayley's way.

"I'm going to go take a shower. I might not have gotten much sleep, but at least I can be clean for today's bake."

At the click of the bathroom door, Hayley ripped her jacket off the hook and shrugged it on as she scrambled out of the apartment. She needed to be out in the fresh air. She ran down the fire escape and bounded into Trinity across the street.

The park was quiet and misty. A slight pink tinged the morning sky, chasing away the midnight blue enveloping the west. Hayley crunched through the thick snow. The city hadn't yet plowed the park paths. After a storm like that, they wouldn't get to it for a while, too busy clearing the major streets.

Since she was a little girl, Hayley had dreamed about leaving Casper Falls. Life as an adult would be on her own terms. She wouldn't have to rely on her parents for a job or be compared to Hannah—the whole town knew she was perfect. All Hayley had ever wanted was something that was hers, a life she could be proud of. This past month she thought she'd discovered it at Greta's. She'd never expected to find something that she loved doing so much and something she was so good at.

She pulled out the business card Ramiro had given her yesterday. He was never going to give her a reference now. She'd stolen money from the till. Would Aaron charge her? Could she go to jail? "Fuck." Hayley rounded the corner before the hill that led down to the dog park. Two owners were out early running their dogs around in circles, the steam from their breath floating like clouds in front of their mouths. She walked by, unable to even enjoy the dogs' happy barks.

Then there was Lauren. Hayley had never expected to find love in the city. She'd been so focused on finding a place to live and getting a job that it was a surprise when it happened.

And now she'd lost it all, with one stupid decision. Hayley kicked at a snowbank and plopped down on an icy bench. Only one question was floating around in her head. *What am I going to do now?*

❖

Lauren sailed through the third round. Her water-crust pastry was something she'd made a million times so was easy to do on autopilot. Their directive had been to make a vegetarian game pie. Instead of using meat substitutes, which a lot of her fellow contestants would do, Lauren decided to stick to hearty vegetables. The main filling would be mushrooms, with a layer of portobellos acting as a meat layer. She'd thought of that first morning with Hayley when she'd deep-fried the poached eggs and decided to add a topper of fried poached eggs.

As mad as she was at Hayley, she couldn't keep her off her mind. It had been an incredibly dumb thing to do, although the more she distanced herself from it, the more she could see it for what it was. Hayley had been trying in her own way to help Lauren get out of her nice, safe life.

Lauren had never planned to compete again. If she lost, it would be another blow to her ego she didn't need, but to lose to Dan would be the ultimate insult. Possibly making it into the final round for a second time spoke a lot about her talent, which she was wasting if she could hold her own with the best bakers in the city. Regardless of the outcome, it was time to start working toward a different goal. Time to get her life in order.

Her phone buzzed as they broadcast the bakers who would be moving onto the final round. It was Aaron. She answered just as they called her name, announcing she'd be one of five making it to the finals.

Chapter Twenty-eight

Hayley woke to the smell of gingerbread. She checked her phone—half past six in the morning. Her mom was a morning person. She always said you could get more done before nine if you were up at five. Hayley couldn't fault her logic, but she'd rather be well rested to do all her stuff.

She slunk out of bed and grabbed her thermal socks from the floor, where she'd dropped them the night before. Her parents' place was all hardwood floors, and in the winter months your feet were in danger of falling off if you didn't cover them. She pulled her warmest hoodie over her head as she stumbled downstairs.

The only light on was in the kitchen, where her mom had several trays of gingerbread slabs laid out to cool. When she noticed Hayley, she checked the time on the microwave but didn't say anything, too aware of what her daughter was like before coffee.

The kitchen was decorated in warm yellows and soft oranges, with pictures of food interspersed with photos of the family. Stacks of cookbooks were organized along the counter, most of them from the eighties or seventies, with titles like *Only Love Beats Butter*, *Let's Play Hide the Sausage*, and *The Magic of Microwave*. Hayley's favourite was *An Unexpected Cookbook*, a Hobbit-themed culinary experience. And her parents wondered where she inherited her geek from.

Hayley beelined for the coffee, searching for the Grumpy mug. The only time she managed to snag it was when her father was still asleep or too lazy to grab it from the dishwasher. It was the largest mug they owned. When Hannah was there—and not pregnant—they'd all fight over it. She filled it to the top and sat down on a stool next to the island, watching her mom cut the gingerbread into walls for the house she'd make when it cooled and hardened.

"You're up early," Sara said.

"I guess I'm still used to getting up to open at five. Don't miss the hours, that's for sure." Hayley had finally told her parents about the company going bankrupt before she even got a chance to work there.

"I don't know why you didn't come home as soon as it happened. It would've been easier on you to look for a new job without worrying about paying for rent." Her mom meant well, but she was infuriating. Everyone else got to live the life they wanted without question. Why couldn't she?

Hayley grabbed a piece of discarded gingerbread and tossed it into her mouth. "I'm twenty-eight years old. I don't want to live at home and work for my parents. You get that, right?" The gingerbread complemented her coffee perfectly. "I sucked at being a manager anyway. I like doing my own thing." She'd even started looking at applying to some culinary schools since she'd been home.

"We miss you. That's all."

Hayley snagged another piece of gingerbread and dipped it in her coffee. "I know of an easy solution to that. Hannah came to visit. Maybe if you saw how I live in the city, you wouldn't worry so much."

"Honey, I'm going to worry no matter where you live."

Hayley turned her stool back and forth. She'd waited until Lauren had left for the next round of the competition and packed up her stuff and left.

"Hannah mentioned you'd moved from your first place."

"Yes, but it's rat and cockroach-free. And only temporary. I'll find a new place soon."

"And how will you do that without a job?"

"I see why I missed you guys. Where else would I get world-class nagging like this?"

Her mom smiled as she trashed the gingerbread scraps. "I nag because I love."

"I will find a job, and everything will work out. Just have a little patience."

"I'm not sure where you got your optimism, but it wasn't from this family. Now, do you want to help me build a gingerbread house?"

Hayley sipped her coffee from her perch and nodded.

"It used to be our tradition, you know. Every year a week before Christmas you'd start pestering me about the gingerbread house."

Hayley set her coffee down on the island and picked up a bag of gumdrops. "It was fun to see how crazy you'd let me go with the decorating." She wondered if Lauren had ever made a gingerbread house. If she had, it probably looked perfect. Hayley was never very good with perfect. She liked things a little off-kilter.

"Can we stage it like a zombie apocalypse?"

"How about this? You get two zombies as long as we keep Santa traditional."

Hayley grinned and began arranging the candy to make her zombies. "Deal. It can be the very beginning, before too many people have been turned."

Her mom laughed and pulled out the candy canes and passed them to Hayley.

❖

Lauren stood underneath the metal arch of Trinity Bellwoods, across the street from Greta's, staring at the Open sign. Inside she could see Luna and Vic taking orders, clearing tables. For fourteen years it had been part of her life, almost her entire life, and now she'd have to move on. She hadn't told anyone yet that Aaron had fired her. She didn't have any energy left for that. Maybe tomorrow? Or maybe she'd leave that up to Aaron. After all, she wasn't in charge anymore.

She leaned against the pillar and let the cold seep through the wool of her pea-coat. In less than an hour, the last round of the contest would start, but she was finding it hard to motivate herself to go. What did it matter if she lost again? She trudged across the street and down the side alley to the rear fire escape.

She saw the envelope as soon as she opened the door. It was propped against her giant copy of the *Cake Bible*. Lauren turned toward the spare bedroom. From the front door she could see that the bed was made and all of Hayley's stuff was gone. She picked up the envelope, expecting to find a good-bye letter, but the only things inside were ten one-hundred-dollar bills and a Post-it stuck to the top one that read, "Kick some ass."

Lauren flopped onto the couch and began to cry. In that instant she realized she wasn't upset about losing the job, or even losing the contest. It was losing Hayley that hurt the most. She hadn't expected that. Was she angry Lauren had fired her? It was on Aaron's orders. If it had been her decision alone, Lauren wouldn't have. Sure, stealing money from the till had been a poor decision, but it would've been paid back in the end. She would've weighed it against other things, like the fact that Hayley was an amazing cook and a reliable employee.

Lauren scrunched up the Post-it and threw it in the direction of the garbage, hoisted herself off the couch, and ran out the door. If she called a Lyft, she'd make it in time for the last round. No way would she let Hayley's bad decision create one of her own. She'd made it to the final round, and she refused to let Hipster Dan one-up her again. She just hoped she had enough time to pick up chestnut paste. After each round, they gave you the directive for the next.

This final round was cakes, and you had to make yours as Christmas as fuck. Lauren had to scrap her original idea and come up with something new. It was a gamble because she'd never made it before, had no idea if the flavours would taste good together, or if she'd even be able to finish in time.

❖

Lauren hadn't allowed herself to glance over at Dan's station the entire round. She was laser-focused on her own cake, which still needed several additions in order to be complete.

"Fifteen minutes left," one of the judges called.

"Shit, fuck, shit," a gruff voice mumbled.

Lauren glanced over at Dan, who had his hand down what was probably meant to be a chimney but looked more like abstract art, and grinned. His face was streaming with sweat, and from what she could see he was nowhere near done.

With renewed confidence, Lauren turned her board around and began piping along the top of her cake. She'd created a giant Christmas ball for the tree. One side looked like glass, and the other was an ornate winter scene she'd carved out of the cake and enhanced with gold leaf and royal icing. The result was pretty impressive. Along the bottom of the cake were meant to be smaller ornaments that, when cracked with a knife, would ooze out a candy-cane ice cream. She still had to assemble those but was making sure the ice cream was as set as possible.

The cake would look good, but she had no idea if it tasted good. She'd gone with Christmas flavours but added some chestnut paste to her buttercream in between each layer, to add that roasted-chestnut flavour. The top and bottom layer were a spice cake, and the smaller sponge cake was a ginger molasses.

With the piping done, she rushed to the freezer to collect her ice cream moulds, hoping they were frozen enough. She let out the breath she'd been holding when the first one plopped out onto a plate, perfectly formed.

A loud scream and crash almost made her drop the first one. At this point she didn't have the time to care what had happened. Lauren worked fast, her movements sure, as she combined the two halves together, creating the balls.

They called time a second after she placed her last ball. Lauren threw her hands up and stepped back from her station, confident that, even if she didn't win, she'd done her best. And after the first judge closed his eyes as he took a bite, she knew she'd done well with the flavours. But was it good enough to win? That she'd have to wait for.

❖

Hayley watched her breath curl into the night air. From her vantage point on the roof of her parents' house, she could see all the stars, whereas on Lauren's roof she was lucky if she could see the North Star on a good night.

Bum-fuck nowhere had its advantages. She took a sip of her Pumpkin Chai tea from David's Tea. Then again, it had its disadvantages too. She was back in the land of boring, where fancy tea meant Earl Grey, and the only latte you'd find was from a Tim Hortons latte machine, which used the word "uncomplicated" in promotional ads.

She'd been here for four days, and if she didn't get out of here soon, she would go insane. Literally insane. When she'd shown up on their doorstep at eight a.m. with no advance warning, the whole horrible story had come tumbling out. They were supportive, of course, because they always were. But after a few hours they began tag-teaming her to move back. They never came out and said it, but they would drop hints. Things like mentioning that her old job at the store was still available, or her dad would ask how much she'd paid for rent.

None of it mattered though. She didn't belong here, and they all knew it. She'd been moping for days. Not only had she lost the girl, but she'd lost her job and apartment all in the same moment.

At first it had been nice to be home and have her mom look after her. But it came with so many strings—like having to listen to her parents' unending campaign to keep her here—she'd been ready to head back a day after she got here. However, she had nowhere to go.

"Fuck." Hannah pulled herself onto the ledge, crawling on all fours to get to the flat part of the roof Hayley was sitting on. "Why do you always have to make everything so goddamned difficult?"

Hayley scrambled up to help her very pregnant sister navigate the roof. "You shouldn't be out here in your condition."

"Don't." Hannah waved her hand in front of Hayley's face. "Don't be like every other person in my life right now. I'm carrying another human being inside me. I didn't suddenly morph into a glass structure."

Hayley hooked her arm around Hannah's waist anyway and guided her to a seated position. "I know that, but if you slip and fall, it's not just your dumb ass that would get hurt."

"Are you saying I'm reckless?"

"You're not not reckless." Hayley didn't add that she felt Hannah had actually started taking more risks since she became pregnant just to prove she could. Her mother had called her frantically a month ago complaining that Hannah had gone with friends to a paintball course. When Hayley asked her about it, she'd said it was her last chance to be a kid. Pretty soon she was going to have to be the parent. Hayley knew, out of everything, that scared her sister the most.

"So what happened? Mom said Lauren kicked you out." Hannah shuffled closer so that her warmth was pressed against Hayley. She put her arm around her. "That doesn't sound like the truth to me. I can't picture Lauren kicking you out."

Hayley bit her lip to start from tearing up. Every time she thought about that night, she broke down. She just wanted to forget about the whole thing, but no one was letting her do that. "She didn't kick me out. I left. But she would've."

"Not out onto the street. What did you do?"

Hayley shrugged and hugged her legs to her chest, resting her chin on her knees. "Lauren and I had a fight, and I left."

"In a huff."

"Pfft. You say that like it's something I do a lot."

"You jump to conclusions. It takes you a while to calm down enough to hear someone's side of the story."

"I borrowed money from the till to enter her in that contest. And before she could win and I could replace it, Aaron found out. She fired me and so I left."

Hannah turned, aghast. "Excuse me? You stole money from the till, and you're surprised this is how it turned out?"

Hayley's chest constricted at the thought. She'd been the reckless one. She'd thought everything would work out. The consequences had been a surprise.

They sat there for a few minutes letting their breath curl up into the air. At this time of year, the neighbourhood was quiet. After dark not many kids were out playing. Occasionally they'd hear a car crunch by. It was quite a contrast to her and Lauren's apartment on Queen Street, which was never quiet. There were always cars, always streetcars, and always drunks yelling in the middle of the night.

"Mom told me she offered you your old job back."

Hayley groaned. "Took her less than two minutes. I think they've been holding off hiring someone to do the work because they knew I'd end up back here."

"And what's so bad about here?"

The scrape of a shovel broke the silence. Casper Falls wasn't very big. From their vantage point on the roof they could see the main strip, which was only two blocks away. The glow from the Christmas lights flickered red and green. It didn't matter how much the world changed. Casper Falls would always stay the same. It didn't matter that everywhere else had moved onto blue-and-white or purple lights. Here they were traditionalists.

Every year they erected a giant tree in the main square and decorated it with angels and holly, probably the same decorations from the fifties. Every Christmas Eve there was the nativity play in front of St. Mary's. Even if it was cold enough to freeze your tits off, they'd still do that damn play. The stores all switched to Christmas music on December first, the same day everyone put up their decorations.

Hayley turned away and watched as Mr. Field, their next-door neighbour, shovelled his driveway with one of those old metal shovels. He was seventy-six, but he refused to let anyone else do it because he'd been doing his own driveway for over fifty years.

That was the problem. Everyone here was okay with how things had always been done, and Hayley wanted new just because it was different. She'd felt that rush the first second she moved in with Kalini, Jo, and Jason. Now here she was, back on the same roof having the same conversation she'd had a million times.

"I don't belong here."

Hannah squeezed her shoulder. "I know that, and deep-down, Mom and Dad do too. But have you ever told them why you don't belong here? I think they keep trying to get you to stay because they honestly can't understand why anyone would want to leave all this." She flicked her hand toward the quaint houses and pines beyond.

Hayley squeezed Hannah's knee. "I'm getting the feeling I leave a lot of things unsaid."

"Hayley." Sara poked her head out the window. "Someone's here to see you."

Chapter Twenty-nine

Hayley entered the living room, her arms folded and her nails digging into her skin, hoping to see Lauren standing there. But it wasn't Lauren. She had no idea where Hayley's parents lived. Yet Violet did.

"I heard you were back."

"Not for long. I'm just home for Christmas."

Violet nodded. Something had changed about her, and Hayley wasn't sure if it was Violet or herself. Hayley had always placed Violet on a pedestal. She was the ideal, with long, silky, golden hair, a rosy complexion, and captivating blue eyes. Today she looked dull, even against the glow of the Christmas lights on the tree.

"Why are you here?"

"I came to apologize. And give you this." Violet handed her an envelope. Violet shrugged, seeming a little self-conscious. She'd unzipped her parka when she'd arrived, and Hayley could see a bump protruding under her sweater.

"You're pregnant. Kevin's?"

"Of course it's Kevin's. We got married last month."

"Wow." Hayley plopped down on the couch but didn't say anything else. Couldn't. She was stunned, sure, but it hurt less than she'd expected. What hurt more is that it seemed everyone else was getting their shit together except her.

"Aren't you going to open it?" Violet took a seat next to her on the couch. "I know I was a gigantic asshole. I just didn't know what I wanted until it sort of landed in my lap. I'm sorry I hurt you in the process."

"You're happy with Kevin?"

"Very. And the store is doing well." Violet turned away, staring at the lights as they cycled through the different colours. Hayley had always thought they would give someone a seizure one day. "That's why I wanted to pay you back. I know nothing will make what I did right. And I can't change the past, but," she motioned to the envelope Hayley was turning over in her hand, "maybe that will help reset some of the wrongs." Violet heaved herself up. "You don't have to open it now."

Hayley followed Violet to the door, locking it after she left.

"What's in the envelope?" Hannah was sitting on the stairs behind Hayley.

"Were you listening in?"

Hannah nodded, a big grin on her face. "Yep. So what did she give you? A long, sappy letter about how much she loves Kevin?"

"Ugh. You're the worst. You know that?"

Hayley ripped open the side of the envelope and peered inside. "Holy shit."

"What?" Hannah pulled herself up using the banister.

"It's a cheque for twenty thousand dollars."

"What?" Hannah grabbed it from Hayley. "She sells cat shit. How is she making that much money? I've only ever seen Mrs. Clarke go in."

"If there's one thing I've learned over the last few months, it's that people buy weird shit."

❖

Lauren settled into a chair across from her dad. "How's the food?"

"Awful."

"Of course you'd say that. It's not takeout." But Lauren knew her dad better than that. He might have grumbled about moving out of his apartment, but it was all bluster. She'd managed to find him an accommodation in an active living community in the west end, so he wouldn't be so far from her. It had helped that she had come into a bit of money lately. It meant they didn't have to wait for his apartment to sell before they could get him a spot.

It still felt surreal. On her way back to George Brown that day, her only wish had been that she'd do better than Dan. The look on his face when she'd been named the winner warmed her heart. The money and prestige were nice too, although it all felt a bit hollow without Hayley there to join in the celebrations. If it hadn't been for her, she wouldn't have entered. As stupid as it was, Hayley's intention had been good.

She'd paid Aaron the money Hayley had given her, but really, Hayley shouldn't have paid for it. Lauren had more than enough to repay her. And she owed her more than money. For the first time in her adult life she didn't have to worry about money. The problem now for Lauren was next steps. She had no idea where to go from here. She still had an apartment that was under market value, and Aaron couldn't kick her out even if she didn't work at the diner anymore. But it was time to move on. Long past time. She'd been thinking about going back to school like Pete, only instead of doing a course she had no interest in, she would study baking and pastry arts.

Vic was made manager, which made sense. Ramiro had hired a replacement for Hayley, who was, in his words, a shit show. Vic said the new hire was fine, but Ramiro missed Hayley. They all did. She hadn't been there very long, but she'd affected them all just the same.

"How are your neighbours?" Max didn't like the loss of independence, which made this place a great fit for him. It wasn't a home for old people, like he'd worried about. He could come and go, but he was surrounded by people his own age, and staff checked in on him daily. Best of all, in Lauren's opinion, was the dining hall. He didn't have to cook for himself, and they weren't making junk food. It was all healthy.

Lauren hadn't realized how stressed she was about her dad being on his own until she'd moved him in here. She didn't have to worry about him the same way. People were looking after him.

"My neighbours? What about them? They're old."

"Dad, you're old. Hate to say it, but it's true." She picked up a pamphlet that had been shoved under his door. "They do euchre nights, and there's a bowling alley. There's tonnes to do, and you don't have to even leave the place. They also have a library right here."

"Okay, okay." He waved his hand at her to stop. "I already live here. You don't have to give me the pitch."

"Just don't sit here all alone, okay? Hey, look. They have trivia tonight in the bar. It would be a good opportunity to see who all the idiots are."

He frowned at her, but the gleam in his eyes told her he thought it might not be a bad idea.

Lauren stood. "Why don't we go grab something for lunch? We can check out all the single ladies."

"Speaking of ladies," he said as they made their way down the hall to the dining room. "Where's the lady who makes all that delicious food?"

Lauren took his arm and continued walking. "Home for Christmas, I imagine."

"She wasn't there to watch you win?"

That had been the one down moment of her win. Pete had shown up to cheer her on, and everyone at the diner was waiting to see how it had gone. But the one person she'd wanted to be there was absent.

"I had to fire her from the diner." They entered the dining hall, which was only half full at one in the afternoon. Lauren imagined most of the residents ate earlier than this.

"I could see how that might put a wrench in things. Did you apologize?"

"Dad, I didn't have a choice. There was good reason to fire her. While I wouldn't have if it was my call, it wasn't. Aaron wanted her fired. I was just doing my job."

"A job you no longer have."

"Someone else would've done it."

Max shrugged and walked past Lauren into the hall. He took a seat at an empty table, and Lauren had a sad premonition of the remaining days of his life, always sitting on the outside looking in. She joined him at the table, vowing she wouldn't let that happen to her.

And the first step in making that happen was to make decisions that made her happy.

❖

Christmas at the Cavellos' was the usual chaos. It was the one time of year Hayley loved being home. She loved the noise as her aunts descended on her mother's kitchen and the inevitable bickering over whose stuffing recipe they were using. She loved the delicious smells that wafted throughout the house, the glow of Christmas lights as her family sat down to play a cutthroat tournament of Uno, and the arguments over whose team was better—the Leafs or the Canadiens. Her Uncle Mitch always won as soon as he brought Stanley Cups into it, citing that half the people in the house hadn't been born during the last win for the Leafs. Her family was everything to her, but it didn't mean she had to live near them to be happy.

Hannah went into labour on Christmas Eve. She hadn't been due until the second of January, but the kid decided to come early. Adalyn Isabel Mathews was born at seven fifteen Christmas morning while three generations of family paced in the waiting room.

When Derek came out to announce that it was a girl, everyone surged, trying to be the first one to see her. They spent the morning and afternoon in shifts. Christmas dinner was moved to Hannah and Derek's place so Hannah wouldn't have to get off the couch to celebrate with everyone.

Hayley sat back, watching the chaos, enjoying her family, though she loved that she could leave. She could have them in small doses. She got to enjoy the great things of a small town—that her family was all together and that it was quaint and picturesque. But she needed a different kind of chaos to be happy.

With the money Violet had given her, she could move back to the city and have a little cushion before she found another job. At least this time, she had a better idea of what she was looking for.

❖

The class was small. Only seven people filled the stations in front of Lauren. She'd chosen one of the smaller private colleges because she liked the intimacy of smaller class sizes. Her breath caught the moment she saw the bright-purple hair in front.

She hadn't talked to Hayley since the night she left. At first, she was giving her space, and then it seemed too much time had passed. Hayley hadn't gotten in touch with her so Lauren assumed she wasn't interested, but a day didn't go by that she didn't think about her— wonder what she was doing, imagine what it would be like to bump into her some time, what she would say. Now that Hayley sat in front of her, she couldn't take her eyes off her, let alone concentrate on what their instructor was saying. It was a good thing it was the first class and they weren't being evaluated on their technique.

After class, Lauren knelt to grab her things from where she'd stuffed them in her station, and when she stood, Hayley was already gone. Swallowing all her anxiety, Lauren rushed out of the room. She saw a flash of purple turn the corner and followed. It didn't matter that she had another class in five minutes. Lauren wasn't letting this opportunity pass her by.

In the three months since she'd won Bake or Die, Lauren had worked hard at putting herself out there. She refused to live on the sidelines anymore.

Hayley crossed Dundas, entering Trinity Bellwoods from the north path. Lauren dodged a Foodora courier and dashed into the park after Hayley. She caught up to her as she knelt petting a bulldog, who was doing his best to lick her face off.

"Aren't you adorable. Oh yes, you are." Hayley tilted her head back to stop the pooch from licking her mouth. "You must smell all the pastry I've been elbow deep in, huh?" And then her head turned to Lauren, who stood off to the side of the path watching her. Her attention diverted, Hayley fell over onto the path. Now with more access, the bulldog climbed up her torso, attacking her face with a new vigour. Hayley laughed. "Enough." She pushed him away as the dog's owner pulled him free.

Lauren helped Hayley up off the ground. She was covered in muddy paw prints and dirt. "Where did you come from?" Hayley asked.

It took Lauren a moment to find her voice. It felt so good to be standing in front of Hayley. "How are you?"

Hayley brushed at the mud, her cheeks pinked. She shrugged. "I'm working at a restaurant downtown. Ramiro knows the chef."

Lauren picked a dead leaf out of Hayley's hair and began ripping it to shreds. "Did Ramiro tell you about this class?"

"The pastry class? Yeah. He said my crusts need work so I should get a little help." Hayley looked behind her. "How did you know I was in a pastry class?"

"I think Ramiro's been playing matchmaker. I'm enrolled in the pastry-arts course."

A smile lit up Hayley's face. "Congrats, by the way. Ramiro told me you'd won. I wish I could've been there to see Hipster Dan's face."

"It was priceless. Something I'll cherish for the rest of my life."

They began walking down the path toward the diner. "Good. The asshole deserved to be handed his ass."

"Well, it was better than that. He's been disqualified from ever entering again because apparently he stole his idea from someone else."

Hayley's surprise was feigned. "No kidding."

"And this time they had proof."

Spring was just starting to make itself known. There were more and more mild days. All the snow had melted, although they probably had one more storm in their future. The end of March and early April usually featured at least one. The overcast sky belied the balmy weather they were having.

Lauren loved this time of year, when everything came back to life. With the hibernation over, the park filled with dogs and squirrels. The birds sang louder, and the sidewalks and streets were free of slush.

They meandered along the path, not sure where they were heading or caring.

"I've been meaning to say something for a long time." Lauren pulled Hayley over to one of the benches off the path. "I should've said it, but I was too scared."

Hayley took a seat on the bench next to Lauren, her azure eyes bright. She pulled out a bag of trail mix and offered some to Lauren, who shook her head. She was too nervous to eat.

"I shouldn't have fired you."

"No. That was exactly what you should've done. I stole money." Hayley picked out a raisin and threw it on the ground. "Is that what you wanted to say?"

Lauren shook her head. "The biggest regret I've had in the last— hell, probably ever—was letting you walk out of my life without saying I love you."

A white squirrel jumped up onto the end of the bench, a raisin between its paws. Hayley stared at it, frozen in shock and warmth and excitement. The squirrel swished its tail a few times, then hopped off the bench in search of more food. Hayley returned her attention to the beautiful woman sitting across from her. If anything, she looked better than Hayley remembered. Her dark bangs hung above her soft brown eyes, catching the light in such a way that they almost appeared golden. Her red lips seemed more so next to her pale skin.

Hayley didn't doubt that she'd made a huge mistake leaving. She'd run from Casper Falls and the whole humiliating mess with Violet, but she was done with that. She leaned into Lauren for the softest of kisses. "My biggest regret is leaving you without telling you how much I love you."

Lauren smiled. "You can't have the same regret."

"No? How about this? My biggest regret will be you not accepting my dinner invitation."

Lauren grasped Hayley's cheeks and pulled her close. "We wouldn't want to make any more regrets, would we?" When they kissed this time, the park and everyone in it fell away. Hayley's grip had loosened, and her bag of trail mix fell to the ground.

The white squirrel, who had been biding its time off to the side, scurried up and began shoving nuts into its mouth as fast as it could. Above, two women sat oblivious to everything in the world except each other.

About the Author

CJ Birch is a Toronto-based video editor and digital artist. When not lost in a good book or working, she can be found writing or drinking serious coffee, or doing both at the same time.

An award-winning poet, CJ holds a certificate in journalism but prefers the world of make-believe. She is the reluctant co-owner of two cats, one of which is bulimic, the other with bladder issues, both evil walking fur shedders.

CJ is the author of the New Horizons series. *Just One Taste* is her fifth book. You can visit CJ on social media @cjbirchwrites or at www.cjbirchwrites.com.

Books Available From Bold Strokes Books

Bet Against Me by Fiona Riley. In the high-stakes luxury real estate market, everything has a price, and as rival Realtors Trina Lee and Kendall Yates find out, that means their hearts and souls, too. (978-1-63555-729-9)

Broken Reign by Sam Ledel. Together on an epic journey in search of a mysterious cure, a princess and a village outcast must overcome life-threatening challenges and their own prejudice if they want to survive. (978-1-63555-739-8)

Just One Taste by CJ Birch. For Lauren, it only took one taste to start trusting in love again. (978-1-63555-772-5)

Lady of Stone by Barbara Ann Wright. Sparks fly as a magical emergency forces a noble embarrassed by her ability to submit to a low-born teacher who resents everything about her. (978-1-63555-607-0)

Last Resort by Angie Williams. Katie and Rhys are about to find out what happens when you meet the girl of your dreams but you aren't looking for a happily ever after. (978-1-63555-774-9)

Longing for You by Jenny Frame. When Debrek housekeeper Katie Brekman is attacked amid a burgeoning vampire-witch war, Alexis Villiers must go against everything her clan believes in to save her. (978-1-63555-658-2)

Money Creek by Anne Laughlin. Clare Lehane is a troubled lawyer from Chicago who tries to make her way in a rural town full of secrets and deceptions. (978-1-63555-795-4)

Passion's Sweet Surrender by Ronica Black. Cam and Blake are unable to deny their passion for each other, but surrendering to love is a whole different matter. (978-1-63555-703-9)

The Holiday Detour by Jane Kolven. It will take everything going wrong to make Dana and Charlie see how right they are for each other. (978-1-63555-720-6)

Too Hot to Ride by Andrews & Austin. World-famous cutting horse champion and industry legend Jane Barrow is knockdown sexy in the way she moves, talks, and rides, and Rae Starr is determined not to get involved with this womanizing gambler. (978-1-63555-776-3)

A Love that Leads to Home by Ronica Black. For Carla Sims and Janice Carpenter, home isn't about location, it's where your heart is. (978-1-63555-675-9)

Blades of Bluegrass by D. Jackson Leigh. A US Army occupational therapist must rehab a bitter veteran who is a ticking political time bomb the military is desperate to disarm. (978-1-63555-637-7)

Hopeless Romantic by Georgia Beers. Can a jaded wedding planner and an optimistic divorce attorney possibly find a future together? (978-1-63555-650-6)

Hopes and Dreams by PJ Trebelhorn. Movie theater manager Riley Warren is forced to face her high school crush and tormentor, wealthy socialite Victoria Thayer, at their twentieth reunion. (978-1-63555-670-4)

In the Cards by Kimberly Cooper Griffin. Daria and Phaedra are about to discover that love finds a way, especially when powers outside their control are at play. (978-1-63555-717-6)

Moon Fever by Ileandra Young. SPEAR agent Danika Karson must clear her werewolf friend of multiple false charges while teaching her vampire girlfriend to resist the blood mania brought on by a full moon. (978-1-63555-603-2)

Serenity by Jesse J. Thoma. For Kit Marsden, there are many things in life she cannot change. Serenity is in the acceptance. (978-1-63555-713-8)

Sylver and Gold by Michelle Larkin. Working feverishly to find a killer before he strikes again, Boston homicide detective Reid Sylver and rookie cop London Gold are blindsided by their chemistry and developing attraction. (978-1-63555-611-7)